Alexander of the Ashanti

Ken Frazier

C.A.I. / Waid Books

York, Pennsylvania

Editing by T.L. Christopher-Waid and Carla Christopher-Waid. Assisted by Elena Bittenger, intern.

cover art by Billy Tackett

www.communityartsink.org

ISBN-10:1535104716
ISBN-13:978-1535104715

DEDICATION

This book is dedicated to my wife Leigh, who endured 6 months alone while I did my small part to go save the world in West Africa. It is also dedicated to the people of rural Ghana, who endure hardship on a daily basis, with frequent power outages, insufficient clean water and the constant threat of malaria, tuberculosis and typhoid, and whose rich history deserves to be shared with the world.

I would especially like to thank T.L. Waid and Elena Bittinger from Waid Books for their help, careful editing and encouragement, those friends and fans who read "Titus of Pompeii" and asked for more, and to Chuck, Krystal, Derek and the two Joes and two Daves, who taught me everything I know about swordplay and historical combat. As with the first novel, I would like to thank Billy Tackett for his incredible cover artwork, to Kevin Stephenson for his skill in making the wonderful map, and to his wife Brenda for review of my grammar. Finally, a word of thanks to the Tropical Laboratory Initiative, GSK and the PULSE team, who allowed me to take some time off from my pathology and toxicology duties to embark on an extended adventure in Africa, and which provided the background for (and some free time to write) this novel.

GUINEA PROPRIA
(MODERN GHANA)
AFRICA, CIRCA 1716

1) ELMINA
2) CAPE COAST
3) ACCRA
4) KUMASI
5) MANSO NKWANTA
6) TONTO KROM
7) AKROKERRI
8) AGOGO
9) DATANO
10) MAMPONG

Alexander of the Ashanti

CONTENTS

Ken Frazier

Prologue: *The Portuguese Man*

I awoke on the floor of a dark, humid room.
There was no light except for the late afternoon sun
peering from a door behind me. I had no idea how long
I'd been unconscious, but my head felt like it was
exploding in cannon fire. I don't ever remember being
hit like that, even in battle. I was caught off guard.
Had I expected trouble immediately in the pub I might
have been able to block the blow. As it was, I had no
chance, as the bludgeon was directed from behind me.
As I stirred, I heard a voice above me.

"What is your name, English, and what is your
purpose here in Akrokerri? Are you working alone or
with a group?"

My eyes were just beginning to see clearly and I
observed the man standing over me. I recognized the
accent and the facial features. There were still many
Portuguese in Guinea Propria.

"Shove it up your Porto arse." I whispered under my
breath as I stood up to face him.

He slapped me hard across the mouth. I guess I
hadn't answered quite discreetly enough.

"No one comes by happenstance to Akrokerri. What
is your purpose?

"I'm not English, I'm a Scotsman, and I came in for directions."

He hit me again, this time with a dueling pistol on the top of my head. He was taller than I, and the wooden butt of the flintlock landed squarely between my ears. It hurt more than it should have, due to the blow I had already received in the pub. I winced.

"I asked you what your name was, English!" "What are you doing here"? Who sent you? Are you a slaver?"

"You aren't listening. I keep telling you, I'm not a damn Englishman!" I replied. "My name is Alexander Fraser and I am a miner, not a slaver."

"Liar! English swine! You're a soldier."

I tasted the pistol on my lips this time. As he hit me, the two large natives holding each arm shook me and threw me to the dirt floor of the room we were standing in. They grabbed each arm and lifted me to my knees facing the inquisitor. The Portuguese man in front of me continued his interrogation as he thrust his flintlock in my face and pressed it to my forehead. He was dressed in tan breeches with a matching tan shirt that was open almost to his navel, exposing dark black chest hair. He had thick brown boots that extended almost to his knees, and a straw hat that obscured part of his face. His dress was unusual even in this part o' the world. I remembered him briefly from the pub a few hours before.

"You aren't listening. I keep telling you, I'm not a damn Englishman!" I replied. "My name is Alexander Fraser and I am a miner, not a slaver."

"Liar!" was all he said again as he slammed the pistol into the left side of my jaw. My face was really hurting but I didn't think any bones were broken. My tongue went o'er my teeth to make sure they were still all there. I tasted blood.

"You're dressed like a native! You are an English spy! You have one last chance to tell me the truth. Who are you and where are you from?"

I spit blood out of my mouth, and replied again. "I am telling you God's own truth sir. My name is Alexander. I was raised in Culbokie, Scotland in the highlands between the Beauly Firth and the northern side o' the Black isle, near to the Muir of Ord and the Crask of Aigas. I fought in the battle of Preston against the crown with his lordship, General Thomas Forster in the Jacobite uprising. We surrendered after the battle and I spent several months in a hellhole called Newgate Prison. I was to be indentured in the colonies. I have no love for the English, nor for any slavers." I rubbed my head, spit some more blood onto the dirt and looked back into the dark brown eyes of my captor. He looked down at the bloody spittle on the floor and then glanced back at me with contempt. His eyes went to my hands and he seemed to notice for the first time the large scars encircling both of my wrists. He motioned to the two African men holding my shoulders, and said something in the local Twi language to them that I did not understand.

"Yaso." They each replied in turn to him and followed with a rapid succession of more words I could barely understand. One word I caught meant "release" and I heard "obroni", which meant "the white man". The two natives to each side let go of my shoulders and I was grateful that they eased up on their rough treatment of my body. The large Portuguese man's

3

stare returned to me. He paused for a few moments before speaking again. His oily black hair hung haphazardly out from under his hat. My head was swimming, and the lack o' focus made the man look a little like a large lion with a dark mane. He had an imposing physique, and I'm sure he was used to intimidating people.

He spoke more deliberately this time, in a lower voice I had to strain to hear and understand, given his thick Mediterranean accent. "How does a poor highlander and former prisoner find himself in the middle of the Ashanti gold coast without being involved in the slave trade? You must think me very stupid, there Scotty. A former prisoner could not afford the 8 pounds sterling for passage it would take to get here by ship from England. You are working for someone! You have no mining equipment. Your hands are not those of one who has been toiling in the soil. You don't even have dirt under your nails. Start telling the truth or I will kill you now. Your highland relatives will never know what happened to you. I need to know how you arrived at this village."

I didn't know what happened to my African companion and I worried for his safety. This was a bad situation but my lot could get worse in a shake of lamb's tail. "Look, I have been in the Ashanti for only a wee bit over a year. I was a miner, but I got sick with Jungle Fever and took some time to recover in a native village in the bush. I am simply trying to get back to my home in the Scottish highlands."

"How? By walking? You have no money. We searched you. How do you expect me to believe a preposterous story like that? You are dressed in the

4

attire of a native, not of a miner or a Highland lord. One would think you are trying to blend in, but you are carrying a fine musket, not a cheap miner's shovel. That is the work of a spy! Even if I thought you were a Scottish insurgent, you wish me to believe half-truths. You have no business in this part of the Ashanti, unless it is slaving. My scouts found the remains of three dead natives along the trail only 8 miles from here. Two of the bodies had been scavenged by lions, but there were no witnesses left about. Manacles, binding chains and several pieces of rope and bamboo were strewn everywhere at the site. My men told me the tracks implied there were originally several slaves in the group, and that the dead were probably Akwamu slavers heading to the coast to sell their captives. Yaw here says the dead slavers were killed by muskets and blades, not lions. Did you ambush the slavers and sell their booty to your English friends? Did you plan to buy the slaves from the Akwamu and the deal went sour? What happened to the rest of the native slaves they were escorting? The captives are worth a barrel of shillings to their owners. How exactly are you tied up in all of this? Tell me all that you know and I may let you live."

He laughed then, and leaned his head in to whisper in my ear. "I do not judge you, Scotty. I don't care about some dead Akwamu. There is no law in the bush. Might makes right, as they say. You might even have done me a favor, killing them, if I can profit from their bounty. I just want to know the truth...and your intentions."

If his scouts had found the slavers' bodies and had time to return and report on it, I must have been unconscious for quite a while. I worried again for my friend and wandered what had happened to him. Had he eluded capture, or were they even aware he traveled with me? I looked around again for Kofi but saw no one but my three captors. His eyes followed mine, and I caught a slight smirk appear. I had to be more careful of my words and actions. He obviously suspected I was not alone. The flintlock pistol again went to my forehead and I saw that the hammer was cocked. This wasn't going well.

I looked again into the Portuguese man's eyes and said simply, "If you are going to kill me without listening, then get it over with. You seem to want to tell me what happened though you were not there. I did not know those Akwamu, though I did play a role in their deaths, and which I assure you they deserved. I have been telling you the truth, but my story is a long one, and begins far from the shores of Africa and this jungle. If you want to hear the tale, then give me a chance to allow it a telling from the beginning. If, at the end of my story, you still don't believe me, I guess my fate is in your hands. Do what you will to me then."

The dark haired man looked at me again intensely and reflected for a minute, before finally pulling the flintlock back from my face. He reached back behind him into a dark corner for a wooden stool. He pulled the hat from his forehead, sat down atop the stool and placed the pistol by his right foot. He said something unintelligible to the two natives and they released their grip completely.

As I sat in front of this arrogant European man, my thoughts drifted back to my first days in the Ashanti region, when I had braved the elements and the dense thick jungle and had faced almost certain death battling the diseases of the wilderness. I had been in West Africa for little more than a year and a half and in the Ashanti region for less than that. Now I had landed here on the floor of a hut in Akrokerri about to sue for my life. I stared again at the tall dark haired man in front of me and decided I had no options but to deliver the tale and see where fate would leave. I had no idea o' the whereabouts of my companion and I needed desperately to stall for time. I not only needed to find Kofi, I had to plan an escape if I could. I wasn't sure this man was a slaver, but I didn't know what his intentions were or why he held me captive. I thought about all that had happened since I arrived on the gold coast of Africa. I quickly reflected on my days working in Accra, my many labors in the mining camps, and my illness and time in the village...

I decided the truth couldn't put me in any greater danger than I already faced. I looked up into the eyes o' my captor, and nodded my head in resignation. "Let me tell you all of my story from the beginning."

"I have some time. Tell me this incredible tale. But I warn you. If at any time I get bored or find you are lying to me to protect yourself, you will enjoy a musket ball to your forehead."

And so I related the story of my life. I decided to fill in every detail and make it last. The longer I talked, the longer I stayed alive, the better chance I had of seeing my friend.

☐

Chapter 1: The Jacobite Rebellion

"I was born in the wee village of Kynmylies, in the Scottish Highlands a half day's ride west of Inverness and a day's ride from Glen Or. I lived most o' my life in the area of Culbokie Ross-Shire. My father was named Hugh Fraser and we were farmers and sometime coopers, and lived simply with my mother and younger sister. We worked the hard ground and raised sheep and even the lone cow, and put together barrels for the local village. A cooper could earn money from those distilling spirits in the whiskey trade, by building good quality casks to age liquor. My kin o' clan Fraser covered the Ross-Shire countryside from Erchless to Killachy along the shores o' the Beauly Firth, all of the way southward to Knockie and Albertarii along the coast of Loch Ness. The Macshimi, our Lords of Lovat, had as their seat, the Castle Dounie, as well as another large manor called "Bunchrew house" in the village of Beauly along the firth.

The region around Beauly is the clan stronghold of the Frasers. There are remains of a priory at the north end o' the village which has been there since the ancient ages, and where many of my ancestors are laid to rest. The hills and trees, laurels and heather are beautiful in my homeland and I often walked the craigs and fished in the plentiful streams."

I paused and thought back on Ross-shire and

realized I had not seen my bonnie Scotland in nigh o'er three years. I was shaken to' by the loud voice of the Portuguese man in front of me.

"Well, Scotty, all of this is interesting, but has nothing to do with your being in Africa. Please get to the point."

I frowned back at him, but needed to explain everything so he got it. "It is quite a long tale and I am just getting started. Please be patient and listen to the whole story for it contains many twists. Your questions will be answered if you can bare your heals and pull on the bit long enough to hear the story."

"We'll see." was all he replied.

"If you know anything of highland or royal politics, you may be familiar at the usurpation of the Scottish and English Crown in 1688 by William of Orange, from his majesty, James the VII, the rightful heir to the throne of Scotland and England. Thomas Fraser, my kin and the tenth Lord Lovat, joined the uprising to help restore the crown to his highness, who was exiled in France. My grandfather and father both fought brilliantly with other Frasers alongside the Camerons and the Viscount of Dundee at the Battle of Killecrankie, but it was to no avail. While the battle was won, William of Orange and his bride Mary retained the throne. Because the Frasers took part in that first uprising against the crown, and many more arose again in the rebellion of 1698, several members of my clan were charged with treason in an English court and some were eventually caught and executed. Most of the Frasers were put to the horn, even those that didn't take part in the rebellion, with their goods and gear forfeited. In the years following, those o' the clan that

didn't get imprisoned or executed were forced to
reconcile with King William or forever remain fugitives.
That was when I was but a wee lad. Even the
chief of the clan fell on hard times. In a conspiracy
engineered to discredit him, Thomas Laird Lovat was
provoked into a situation where he punched, and then
stabbed, a piper who had first challenged him. He was
prosecuted and was forced to flee to Wales. In his stead,
his younger brother, the honorless Simon, took over his
estates. Simon is a haggis-faced liar and cheat, a
traitorous knave who would sell his own mother for a
dram of whisky if it could profit him later. My father
hated him, and refused to recognize him as laird. The
fox, as he has since been known, had the gall to steal
Thomas' house and possessions and took his brother's
wife to bed by force to cement his hold on the lands.
With Simon as the silver tongued emissary, the Frasers
were able to entreat with King William, and in the years
since have finally sought to make peace with the
English royalty. They have retained much of the
baronial ancestral lands that had been foresworn to the
crown. After James VII passed on, when his son James
Edward Stuart took up the Jacobite banner in the
second uprising of '15, almost two years past, the
highlanders were again asked to choose sides and pick a
sovereign. Many Scots again filed behind the Stewart
royal blood and readied for battle once more against the
English Monarchy and their supposed king. Not all,
however. Most of clan Fraser, including Simon the 11th
Laird Lovat, supported the Hanoverian King George I,
instead of the Stewarts. My father, who as I said hated
Simon and mistrusted him, and my uncle, who was
deeply religious and who followed the teachings of the

pope in Rome, remained staunch Jacobite supporters in opposition to many o' the Fraser clan. My cousins convinced my father and me to join the fight on the side of the exiled James, with a horde of other highlanders, including many McDonalds, Murrays, Grahams and McCraes. My father was an acquaintance of the Earl of Mar, a Jacobite commander, and was made a lieutenant in the highland forces when they marshaled in 1715. He and I were both placed in a mixed highland regiment under the direction of Brigadier William McIntosh o' Borlum with about 2000 other highland soldiers. We marched south through the lowlands toward Edinburgh. A contingent of our host was to meet up with a much larger English force under General Thomas Forster of Northumberland to continue the fight in England. We were told that the lowlanders and those in Northern England would welcome us and swell our host, but instead they greeted us with fires and pitchforks as we moved south. Few there were with us in Forster's army, but it should've been enough to face down the royalists, with their Duke of Argyll and his Campbell forces. On November 9 of 1715, we entered the town of Preston, in Lancashire, which was under royal protection. We took control o' the town, and after proclaiming the chevalier of St. George as our king and sovereign, we held the town and remained for several days through some vicious fighting. I was in a group of soldiers holding Ribble Bridge, and we held off several bayonet charges with our broadswords and targes. We could have made a stand there and prevented what ensued. Unfortunately, the royal forces advanced on the town with overpowering numbers, and thanks to the blind cowardice of our English commanders, we were recalled back to the village where our advantage was lessened. Over the next day or two, many were killed in ferocious hand to hand combat in and amongst the houses of the town, and many more cowards fled, especially the English allies and some o' the lowland Scots. The English tried to burn the town to the ground to smoke us out of our entrenched positions, but that failed. My father led a highland charge into their midst and we killed many with our swords before they could get off a second round of musket fire or fix their bayonets to counter our swordplay. When we were surrounded and the English were reinforced, things got desperate. Unfortunately, my father's courage outweighed his sense of danger, and while assisting the southern front and blocking royals crossing the river, he took a musket shot in the back and was killed."

The Portuguese man interrupted me again to ask about the involvement of my clan. "You fought members of your own family clan, other Frasers, at this battle?"

"No." I replied. "There were no Frasers in the opposing force at Preston. We fought some highlanders, but none of my clan, nor of our neighboring McCrae's or Munro's from the highlands of the Black Isle. In fact, Simon Laird Lovat and the clan members who would follow him were engaged elsewhere in the highlands at the time. They had surrounded the garrison at Inverness, fighting for the loyalists, in the same month we marched on Preston. The Frasers there stood their ground with valiant courage against superior numbers, and actually kept the McDonalds from joining the fight at the garrison. The English King was afterward in Laird Lovat's debt, for those efforts and to this day

Simon Laird Lovat is held in high regard by King George. Had my father or I saw any of our kin among those in the street fighting of Preston, we would likely have fled the field. However, our retreat would have been a matter of honor and clan loyalty in that case, rather than from fear or despair."

After revisiting my father's death in my memory, I had to stop my story briefly to wipe a tear from my eye, then continued when the lump left my throat.

The Portuguese man noticed my tears and reflected for a while before speaking again. "I want to hear more of this battle. Give me some details so I know whether to believe you. I have been in a war before. I recognize well the taste of battle and I will know if you are lying."

"As I told you before, our force of Jacobites crossed the English countryside south o' Lancaster without facing much resistance. We took up quarters in the village o' Preston, which is in Lancashire, in the northwest of England. We reached the town in the early morning o' the 9th November. Preston sits on the north side of a bend in the River Ribble, with only two bridges allowing access from the south or west for several miles. The town is basically laid out along two avenues beginning at Church Street, which runs next to St. John's minster cathedral. It divides into Fishergate and Friargate, which branch away from it at the central Market square and form a "Y". The Scots fell under command o' the Laird o' Borlum, Brigadier William McIntosh, a lowland Scot who had courage but lacked tactical knowledge, and two English Earls, Radclyffe and Maxwell. The whole of our Jacobite forces were led by General Thomas Forster, who was responsible for instructing the battle and had brought many o' his own Jacobite English forces from Northumberland. We had two groups of brave highlanders holding each of the bridges on the south, while Laird Borlum's forces took key positions in the town along the two main avenues, and Forster's English Jacobites held the northern plain. I was stationed at the southernmost bridge. By the afternoon o' the ninth, we were met by a large platoon of English Dragoons under the command o' General Wills coming from the south, including cavalry regiments, and a group of loyalist Scottish regiments under the direction o' the Campbell Duke of Argyll. These highlanders were just a tiny portion of the royal forces, but they were courageous and good fighters, and we respected 'em. For the first day or two, we had the upper hand, having owned the entrenched positions and the fortifications o' the town. The royal troops could not breach our defenses along the two bridges. As soon as the lines of soldiers would try to move toward us on the bridge, a hail of musket fire would cut into their ranks. We had blockaded the ends of the bridge with turned over wagons and barrels, and they could not get their horses across. Several o' their infantry charges were countered by hand to hand fighting, and their skill with bayonets were no match for the basket hilts and seasoned swordplay o' the clansmen. The sabres of their officers fared better against our steel than the fixed musket bayonets, but without their mounts, they still failed to break through the bridge defenses, and many o' their rank fell into the water below and drowned with battle injuries. For o'er two days we held those bridges to the south o' Preston. We ate little and drank only what was in our canteens or what we could fill from the river during the breaks in fighting.

Unfortunately, the English Jacobites did not share the highlander's hearts. Thomas Forster's forces on Preston's north met a contingent of mounted dragoons who had forded the river downstream at Ribchester and came upon the town from the northeast. When Forster's lines met the cavalry charge o' the royals, they broke ranks and fled back to town. Forster was used to leading well trained soldiers with discipline and he was dismayed at the behavior of his English recruits. He quickly lost faith in our side's ability to sustain the battle and retreated toward the cover provided by the houses and buildings of Preston, where the more seasoned Scottish highlanders had held their positions. The highlanders under McIntosh watched the disorder evolving among the English Jacobites on the northern plain and came to the rescue of their comrades. They leapt from their positions and took it back to the Royal troops with a series of charges, swords held high and yelling at the top of their lungs. I was told my father led several of those highland charges. We could hear 'em behind us from our position atop the bridge. For o'er a day they fought to a stalemate while we kept the troops on the south from joining the fray. The royalist General Wills sent more and more troops o'er the bridge to the east at Ribchester until there was a matching force of royals to the north of the town. Both sides fought valiantly, and highlander fought highlander, clan against clan, and English Jacobite against English Royal. There were more and more English royal troops joining the other side to the north with every hour. Neither side could claim victory.

At some point, and after another full day o' fighting, General Wills lost patience with progress of his royal forces and ordered dragoons to set the town ablaze. It was a cowardly act, since the town had remained loyal to King George, and he was destroying the property of his own partisans. I was told even the Duke of Argyll protested. Several mounted soldiers rode past the buildings on the outskirts of the village and tossed torches o' fire onto the thatched roofs, which immediately went up in tall flames. There were fires and pillars o' smoke all o'er Preston, and the church was completely ablaze. Women, children and other citizens of Preston cried and wailed and did all they could to put out the fires with buckets from the well in the market square, while the Jacobites and Royal forces clashed in the streets and surrounding fields. Smoke-filled chaos reigned, but the tactic did not work and the royalist forces were eventually repelled. Later that day, General Wills' royal dragoons were reinforced by an additional six squadrons under the command of General Carpenter, who also had forded the river several miles to the east and come upon Preston from the North. At that point, General Forster had lost all courage or will to fight, and it was only the fortitude of the highlanders who kept the town from being overrun. Jacobites held two entrenched positions towards the end of Fishergate and Friargate, and were heavily fortified around Market Square under a group led by my father.

While Carpenter's forces pushed into town from the north, a contingent of Wills' troops that had failed to cross the bridges took to some boats and went across the river in the middle of the two bridges on the south side. I don't know where they pilfered the boats, but they may have gone to a neighboring town to bring 'em back. The River Riddle empties into a bay and there are many boats in fishing villages to our west. Our Scottish regiments were too thin to put up much of a defense at this crossing, and no assistance came from the other Jacobite battalions still holding the town. Hence, soon there were royal troops completely surrounding the town, and now twixt those of us holding the bridge and the Scots within Preston. At that moment, my father came charging out o' the square and into the midst o' the royal troops to the south o' the town. I watched from the bridge as his unit hacked and slashed their way completely through the English troops. They had almost completely annihilated their opposing force and were turned to go back to the town center and fight, when another group o' soldiers with fresh muskets arrived from boats on the river. In a burst of gunfire, they hit the center of the highlander group who were armed now only with their basket hilt swords. My father and several other good clansmen were hit by musket balls in the back. I watched him fall and several of us from the bridge then charged the royals who were still on the ground trying to reload their muskets. With two McDonald highland lads at my side, we jumped the line of English from their left flank. They had no time to fix bayonets and none could get off a shot. Three brave highlanders cut down seven of their rank. I had the satisfaction of running my blade completely through the chest o' three Englishmen who shot at my father, and the McDonalds finished the rest with hacks and slashes across faces, backs and limbs. My father was gravely wounded and was carried back to the village. He bade me farewell in his last minutes and told me he was a proud lad to die in my company and in service to the stone of scone. He died there several minutes later and begat the long sleep underground.

At this point in the battle, one forward thinking highlander had taken a blazing timber and lit all of the boats on fire, so the English could no longer use their wee barges to cross the river. This quelled the advance and the English paused to regroup. I took advantage o' the lull in fighting to briefly grieve at my athair's side. I cried for a few minutes as I had not done in my entire life. I would miss him dearly, but the pressing battle cut short the time for shedding o' tears and lamentation. After a short respite, I returned with the two Scots to the bridge. The southern forces, having no other chance to ford the creeks, tried again to fight their way across the two bridges.

I told you that Forster had by this time lost his will to fight, and was trying to protect the majority of his force. Unwisely, and thinking because there was a battle on the south side of the town that one of the bridge positions had already been breached, he ordered us to retreat from both bridges. He didn't realize that we highlanders would have held 'em to the death as Wallace and our ancestors did in long past. Forster ordered us to come back to join the fight within Preston. This allowed both southern and northern royal forces to join up. Even then, we fought valiantly house to house and building to building, and no clear victory was apparent for either group for the remainder of the day. I sent many an English royal to their gory bed that afternoon with my sword only, and killed one more English knave with my bare hands.

If I had been a smart man instead of a

courageous one, I would have joined the many men who snuck out of the town that night under cover of darkness. I was too despondent over the death of my father and instead sat with other highlanders in our defensive position lamenting how we were going to exact vengeance on the royals the next day.

Unfortunately, after we Scots had fought to the man in the alleys and streets of Preston all day, and waited that night with sick stomachs fearing for the course o' battle the next morn, treachery was afoot amongst our noblemen and officers. The backstabbing and underhanded Forster had by then plotted with the English Earls and had already joined hands with his counterpart from the Royal force. I do not know if Laird Borlum was involved or not, but he was at least aware of the arrangement immediately afterward. Forster surrendered to the English Commanders at 7 o'clock on the following Monday morning, November 14th by selling out the highlanders. He ordered us to drop our arms and assured us we would be treated fairly. We were then drawn up under arms in the center of the village and all taken prisoner. Over 600 Scotsmen were force marched to the nearest English fort to the southeast. It took several days of humiliating walking to reach the fort. We were kept there under harsh conditions and beaten by the royalists until our captors decided upon our fate. I expected to be shot at any time. Eventually we were all transported to one o' four prisons in England. I had the privilege of lodging at Newgate Prison on the northern outskirts of London. Others were sent to Lancaster or some equally ghastly and disgusting place, while Forster, Maxwell and Radcliffe were allowed to live the easy life in some manor in Northumberland. The highlanders paid the highest price for Forster's treachery. We drained our dear veins for naught but servitude."

I spat on the ground at the sound of Forster's name, and I stopped the telling long enough to wipe the blood from my lips and to see if the Portuguese man could see the truth in my tale and understood the mix of passion and regret for which it left me. I could tell by his face and manor that he knew there was no deceit in anything I had just said. My hatred for the English was as true as my Scottish blood.

"Your contempt for the English and your description of the battle are true enough, but there are things about this I don't understand. How did you get into a Jacobite army in the first place? Why would you defy your own people? Why didn't you fight alongside this Lord Lovat at Inverness? Just because your father disliked him?" He seemed incredulous."There are things you are withholding and motives here I don't understand. I sense subterfuge and intrigue that you have not disclosed." He toyed with his pistol as he brewed over the story so far. I did my best to answer his questions.

"After the debacle to the clan following the original uprising twenty five years ago, most of clan Fraser were very weary of becoming again involved in machinations of the crown. Some, like Lovat, wanted to curry favor with William of Orange and hence they fought in the second uprising on the side of the Royals, but I don't think there were any Frasers fighting with the Duke of Argyll and the Royals at Preston. The ones that followed Simon to Inverness did so out of duty to the clan, or perhaps just because my kinsman always did love a good fight. And some probably had a grudge to bear against the McDonalds or other competing clans. We have had our share of outs with the McDonalds, all the way back to the famous Battle of the Shirts along Loch Lochy. They hold much of the ground to the west of the Fraser lands. Each has kinsmen that have massacred kin o' the other in former days."

"But you yourself fought alongside the McDonalds at Preston. That must have been a tense truce and uncomfortable arrangement, if they were your enemies." He glanced at the two natives behind me and said "I would not be at ease fighting aside the Akyem. I would be looking for musket fire from both directions."

"Frasers have fought alongside o' the McDonalds about as often as we have fought against 'em. I know many McDonalds and call most of 'em friends and allies. Clan politics is a complicated game that falls mostly to the chieftains. The heads of the clans are gentry that use perceived slights and historical vendettas often to excuse squabbles over property or money. Often it just comes down to greed. The Macshimi says fight and we fight. But for me, what is past is long past. I harbor no ill against any of the other clans, even the Campbells. However, some of the Frasers will jump at the chance to battle anyone, even if they are not English. It's a matter o' clan pride a Porto gent wouldn't understand."

"Hmmph. So you didn't fight because of politics or clan loyalty. Perhaps you joined the rebellion because of your religion? You don't strike me as a man of the cloth, Scotty."

"My fighting had nothing to do with being a certain type of Christian. I am not very religious and do not have the knowledge of letters. I can't read the good book. Therefore, I can't tell you the difference between the Catholic word and the Presbyterian bible, nor even how these differ from the Church of England. As a young man, I had drifted away from religion in pursuit of other things more akin to the tastes o' a young highlander. I only went to church when they were going to feed us. Others fought for their faith, but I fought for my friends and family and against Simon. I consider "the fox" a traitor to his people and in league with the English; one who does not and should not speak for my clan."

I paused for a long breath, and then added, "I am a highlander, so I also fight because I like it."

"And then you were sent to the English prison." He made some gesture with his hand. "I assume you were paraded and charged in the English courts?" He smiled again with malice as he thought of the pain and humiliation that would have caused.

"Aye. There was a court of sorts. An English judge presiding, but we were never allowed to speak. They, with their nice powdered wigs and shiny black capes, held all o' the power and privilege and treated us as the basest of creatures. The bastards even stripped us of our tartans. We wore only dirty white wraps like common criminals while in their presence. They kept calling us savages as if we were no more cultured than these natives by my side."

"Don't belittle my servants. I doubt you are even a shadow of the worth of these natives, Scotsmen. These two are highly trained warriors and my personal guard." He smiled and said something to the two African men and all three laughed.

"Then we are of the same ilk. I meant no

disrespect." I replied and looked at each native man in turn and nodded my head to each in a sign o' respect.

"What of your time in prison?"

"The horrors and cruelty o' that place are almost beyond comprehension. I can still remember the colossal gate o' brick and stone, with its imposing twin ramparts. I was shackled in irons, covering my wrists and ankles with bracelets o' rusted metal. I still bear those scars today." I held up my wrists in front of him and showed him the areas of dark, thickened flesh just below my hands. He only nodded.

"My cell was a wee pit the size of a hog wallow, with a straw floor and brick walls that smelled o' piss and shat. I remember the huge thick door of wood and iron, which had only a few squares of space to let in the light, and a wide horizontal notch at the height o' my sporran where they would spoon me gruel. I could never tell if twas day or night as there was always only dim candle or torch light along the guard's walkway. I could not see outside into the free light o' London. I was held in constant twilight. It was damp and cool all o' the time, especially cold in winters. I received no letters, no notes, no word from my kin. Even if I couldn't make sense o' the letters, at least it would have been nice to know someone cared where I was. I had no news o' my mother or sister. Days turned to weeks then turned to months. I aged in that hellhole like a swaybacked old nag; on the swag they fed us and the sewage they passed as fresh water. I was sick for days and weeks at a time and I withered to the scrap o' man you see before you. This grey hair belies a lad who has not yet reached his fortieth year. I was once a ballish bloke who had his run of ladies, with more than a few romps in the heather. No more. Worse yet, was constant harassment o' the keepers. Jailors extorted everything they could, in order to line their own pockets. They demanded payments from inmates for everything, including food. Most o' the Scots had little or no money and so retribution by the sheriff's keepers was fierce. We were routinely beaten or starved, and continually threatened. If not for money sent from some highlander's patrons on the outside to support all Scots, things would have been much worse. We had no comforts o' the hearth, and no new clothes to keep us warm. Once a month they would throw a bucket of water on us to bathe some of the stink away. Many twas the night that I wanted to attempt an escape like the famous Jack Sheppard. He was a burglar who made it out of Newgate's walls by stealth and guile just before I was sent there."

"Escape did you? Is that how you got here?"

"Unfortunately, I am not so gifted in those arts as Mr. Sheppard, but I still plotted and schemed, especially as the months wore on."

I decided that telling this man I had a want for escape was probably a mistake, given the circumstances. Better to let him think I was content as a captive. However, once he heard my whole tale, he would realize soon enough that I was hard to cage and had a taste for freedom. Having heard the story of two successful escapes in my life, the matter o' my abilities would be clear to him anyway.

"What of your other kin at the prison? How would you speak with your other prison mates?" he asked.

"The undersheriff kept us separated and in isolation, but we were able to get word betwixt us, cell to cell, by speaking Gaelic in hushed tones. I knew that my cousins accompanied me to the prison, and occasionally we could get word to each other by passing information from others. That was how I found out that after 6 months or so of captivity, Duncan, Hugh and William Fraser, three o' my kinsmen, were going to be shipped to plantations in the Americas. I began to hope above hope that I would also be freed."

"You said some of the Scots had relatives who sent money to the guards. If you needed money to survive within the prison and to pay off the guards, how is it you were able to get food without any money on your part? Did they provide for all?"

"Fortunately for the 6 or so Frasers in Newgate, we had a benefactor who constantly acted on our behalf. I told you about Simon the Fox who took his older brother's position as Laird of Lovat, head o' the clan."

"Surely he would not have supported you, as he was acting on behalf of the crown in the rebellion, not supporting your side of Jacobites. You were in effect, his enemy."

"No. He would not endeavor to help any of us. But you remember I told you that he married his brother's wife, Lady Amelia, who was Baroness Lovat."

"Yes. She was your benefactor?"

"No, actually it was her daughter, the younger Amelia Fraser, who despised her stepfather/uncle for his complicity in her father's downfall and who she knew was responsible for an assault on her mother. I would not have been surprised if she also feared that Simon might actually try to rape and wed her if her mother died. For all o' those reasons and the fact that she knew and loved my mother, she continued to support the imprisoned Frasers and paid a substantial part of her dowry to keep us alive. Her maternal grandfather was John Murray, the Marques of Atholl, and one of the greatest supporters o' the Stewarts. Despite her stepfather's intent, she probably remained a Jacobite like her grandfather's clan. I think she admired those of us who fought at Preston against the wishes and intent o' the fox. She used her position and influence as Simon's daughter to garner favor with the crown and provided the sheriff of Preston and jailors with money on our behalf. It helped pay for all o' my meals during my imprisonment. I did not become aware of her patronage until late in my captivity. Perhaps she also helped me as a favor to my mother or sister, but I don't know for sure. I never knew the woman except for brief encounters at events in Beauly tied to the clan, but my mother called her a friend. The lady Amelia probably saved my life and those o' my five kinsmen. I also believe it was she who achieved a bargain with the king's court, to allow us to be freed from the prison and to serve the remainder of our terms as indentured farm workers in the colonies."

"She sounds like an amazing woman."

"I wish I had known her better. I'm told she had an iron will and a persuasive temperament to accompany her striking looks, especially so for one so young. She was barely out of her teens. Had she not persisted on our behalf, it is very unlikely I would be kneeling here in front of you."

"You still have not answered my question. How is it that you came to be in Africa if you were to be indentured in the Americas? I have never heard of ships sending Scottish slaves to America from England,

and if they had previously shipped through the Slave Coast here in the Ashanti, I would have seen others like you."

"There were a total o' ten ships taking Scotsmen to the colonies over a span of a year or more. None before that I recollect ever sent the Scots abroad, and none that I am aware came through the slave coast of Guinea Propria."

"Your story is beginning to fall apart with my questioning. It is beginning to sound more and more like a ruse to delay your death. You have just admitted as much by saying the slave ships never came to Africa, yet here you are." He again raised the pistol to my forehead and I was afraid he would shoot.

"Wait. Please...I did not say that I came here on one o' those ships. I was simply answering your question. The tale is true, but you must listen to the whole story to understand it."

He again lowered the pistol and placed it on the floor. "Continue then, but I warn you again to get to the point and answer my questions directly."

"I was one o' many highlanders destined to come to the colonies on one o' ten ships. Had fate not intervened, I would be there now. In fact, I was told that over 100 o' the Scots captured at Preston were sent to the American colonies within months after we arrived in Newgate. They were to act as indentured farm workers on the Carolina tobacco plantations. This included my cousins, Hugh and Duncan of Dunain, and their younger brother William. Despite the money and help from our benefactors, the isolation and lack of contact with the outside world meant that we did not know of our situation or future, nor did our kinfolk

know of our destinies. My cousin's father never saw
Hugh or Duncan again after we left for war against the
crown, and he may not even know whether they are
alive to this day and live across the sea. For my part, I
don't either. To my equally great misfortune, I never got
to tell my mother or sister how my father died in battle.
Such is the isolation within the English prisons, and
lack of speech back and forth with the outside. While I
was held in Newgate, I had no way of knowing whether
I was to be freed or not. I didn't even know of Lady
Amelia's efforts to help us until a few weeks before I left
Newgate. I was held in that stone hole for several
months after other Scotsmen left, waiting my turn to
board a ship to the colonies. I almost died in that
rotting den of stench and filth. There were only a few of
us left when I was finally led, still in shackles, out to
Tyburn for 'final sentencing'. I wasn't sure at the time if
I was to be hanged or pardoned. I had heard the rumors
o' slave ships to the Carolinas, of course, but this was
only hearsay and I had no guarantee that the ships to
America were real. They could just as easily have been
a lie by the jailors to engender our cooperation. I was
highly skeptical that the English would let the
highlanders off so easily. Instead, when they walked a
few of us to Tyburn on the day I was finally let out of my
cell, I thought it more likely that the jailors were taking
us to the gallows. I did not think they would so easily
break our servile chains."

The Portugese man interrupted me. "You
continue to evade my question and go into pointless
detail that I find irrelevant. I ask you again! How come
you to Africa? They must have pardoned you and sent
you toward the Americas. But then how is it you have

appeared on a completely different continent?"

"Sir, if you would please indulge me, I will get to that."

"Please concentrate on answering my questions then. I am quickly losing patience."

He was feigning impatience, but I had noticed he was listening intently, and at least he didn't press the flintlock pistol to my forehead again. I was hoping my story had finally piqued his curiosity, and hoped beyond hope that he would want to wait and hear the conclusion o' the tale. I considered my options. I could skip directly to what had happened in the past few months and how I found myself in Akrokerri, but that was more of a side tale and didn't really answer how a Scottish soldier got to Africa. I decided that, rather than following his suggestion to shorten my story, I instead would continue to go into great detail and tell the whole thing. At least, it might prolong the interval until he shot me. Perhaps if I could maintain his interest, he might even sympathize with my plight and would spare my life. Maybe. He wanted to get to the end quickly, but I was determined to extend this tale into an epic poem if I could. I just hoped he would not poach me with his weapon and gut me like a prized hare as his patience wore even thinner.

Chapter 2: An Unexpected Voyage

"You must hear how I left England if you are to know how I came to Africa. I could tell you it was by ship but that is not answering your question. How I ended up on the ship is more important."

"Fine. Let us hear about it then."

"I was explaining about my release from prison. After almost a year had transpired in my cell, one of the jailors knocked on my door and told me to get up. He escorted me out o' the room at gunpoint and down the dark corridor to the interior o' the prison and o'er into the bailey's building of Tyburn, a dismal place with a courtyard notorious for hangings. I was taken before the English magistrate with two other Scotsmen (William Young and another man named Johnathon). I was asked to confess to my crimes of sedition and treason against the crown, and was also told that I would be treated humanely and offered a commuted sentence upon my confession. I had no council to plead my case before the court. In fact, I had no advocate at all, except the Ordinary from the Church of England, a minister who would hear our confessions to God. I saw no other Scotsmen there from the battle of Preston, and none of my kinsman from clan Fraser were present. I believe now that most o' the imprisoned Scots had already been sent to America on earlier ships such as the *Goodspeed* or the *Susannah*.

The man named Johnathon said he had nothing to confess to. He tried to argue that he was only following the orders o' the head of his clan, and was only performing his sworn duty as a soldier under his watch. This did not seem to garner any sympathy or favors with the court. In any case, I was on the opposing side from my own clan chieftain, Simon Laird Lovat, and therefore I could not have used that defense anyway. They asked us to sign a "letter of regret" apologizing for our sins. I really had no choice, so I made my mark on the scroll they presented.

We were paraded, still in iron shackles, out into the courtyard of Tyburn, in full view o' the gallows. I remember being blinded by the brightness o' light and I couldn't see any faces as I had to hold my eyes shut from the pain o' the sun's rays. After several minutes, an undersheriff warden of the court poked, prodded and pinched the three of us to see if we had any infirmities. They opened my mouth and checked my teeth and looked at my hands and feet to see if the damp prison air had rotted off any fingers or toes during my months in the cell. He scribbled his findings onto a parchment and then proceeded to do the same to the man named William next to me. A few other prisoners were brought in with us, and I think they were thieves and murderers from London. They were also inspected briefly, but remained separated and were all sent to go talk to the Ordinary and I suppose to get last rites and give confession before they were hanged or beheaded. I did not see any that were later put on the ship for the colonies. For we three highlanders who remained, they went to each of us in turn. A smiling man with a

parchment and a pen came up to me and began
speaking. I was offered the chance to board the *Anne*, a
slave ship bound from Liverpool to the new world. I was
to be indentured for 7 years on tobacco plantations in
Carolina, after which time I would be given an
opportunity to pay for my freedom and remain as a loyal
colonist, perhaps to work my own land. It sounded a
little too good to be true, but the alternative would have
meant hanging in the yon gallows. Therefore, I obliged
to take slavery over death, and again put my mark on
the piece o' parchment by the letters he said meant my
name.

Within a few days we were taken in a large barred
box sitting atop a flat carriage to the port town of
Liverpool. It was in the early spring o' year 1716. That
was nigh on 2 years ago. The prison transport was
ungainly and crowded. We picked up more prisoners as
we made the trek to the coast, and the wooden wagon
was loaded with people sitting atop each other by the
time we arrived. Every man there had spent almost a
year behind bars and they all reeked like a week-dead
goat. My back ached from the harsh, bouncy ride in that
carriage, and the shackles on my wrists made my arms
burn. After being pulled out of the carriage jail by force,
we were herded into groups and marched to the docks. I
remember being led in a line onto the plank and
walking up o'er the side o' the ship. It seemed quite
large to me, as I had never before seen a vessel o' that
size. However, as soon as we were led into the lower
decks, I changed my mind quickly. There were far too
many men for so little room, and only two wee pots to
piss in. It was dark, damp and reminded me o' the
Newgate prison. It was about as cramped as the

carriage we were brought over on, as there were over twice as many men here now and the space was wholly inadequate. There were a total of 20 of us from different English prisons crammed into a tiny hold, and all were still wearing chains and shackles. They wouldn't let us speak openly, but from the little I could glean from the hushed or muffled whispers, the vast majority sounded like Scotsmen, and all had taken part in the rebellion. I recognized most of 'em from the brigadeers battalion at Preston. There may have been several different cells in the belly of that ship, with several other prisoners or 'passengers', but I never saw any others except the dozen plus lads surrounding me. We stayed huddled together for several hours without moving much and my whole body ached. I didn't know how long it would take to get to the new world, but I was afraid that we would never make it and die from dysentery or drown on the passage over. We were to sail from Liverpool to Cork, and there take on rations and other supplies, then head somewhat south and make the crossing over the Atlantic with favorable trade winds to our rear, and eventually arrive in Virginia settlements.

Of the other soon-to-be indentured passengers in the hold with me, I mentioned William and Johnathon who came from Newgate prison with me. Three others were Murrays, along with their cousin James Graham, William Sinclair (a lowland gentleman), and a mountain of a man named Gregor McGregor. I soon befriended two brothers, Angus and Daniel McBean, fine fighters from the highlands around Inverness. I remembered 'em from their exploits on the battlefield at Preston and they were good and courageous companions. They had been imprisoned in Lancaster, rather than at Newgate, before being shipped to Liverpool to meet up with our group of Jacobite prisoners. There were many others who I still didn't know, but one of 'em was named Robert Bruce, after the famous Scottish king of the 14th century. The original Robert the Bruce was one o' the leaders with William Wallace at the battle of Bannockburn where my ancestors so bravely fought. It was lucky for us to have a Bruce among our company. He was a distant cousin (by marriage) o' the captain of the *Anne*, a man named Robert Wallace. The Wallace and Bruce clans had been allies for 300 years since those earliest of battles for Scottish independence. It turned out they even knew each other as both were from the area just above Northumberland. Hence, thanks to Bruce's patronage, we were given sufficient food and water to make the day and a half voyage to Cork tolerable. Bruce was even allowed to walk freely on the upper deck and chat with the crew, as a guest of Captain Wallace. Unbeknownst to the captain however, Bruce had been planning a break with the Murrays and he had been able to obtain (either through purchase or theft) a key to the hold.

We sailed into the bay they call the Lough Mahon and into the port of Cork at dusk on the following day. Most o' the crew went ashore to have their last drinks of grog for several weeks and to have a roll with the whores who lined the docks waiting for sailors. This left the ship with only a few guards on board. At close to midnight, Robert Bruce, who had been placed in the hold with the other prisoners for security, pulled the key from his smock, stuck his arm through the peerage o' the door, placed the pass key into the slot below and opened the door to the hold. The group of Scots crept up the stairs, slunk through the decks and most climbed over the side o' the ship to reach the docks below. I almost fell into the water but was aided by one o' the McBeans, who caught me and helped pull me back up to move to an easier portage using the plank and reach the dock. A few prisoners, including the Murrays, stayed back and dealt some furious punishment on the few remaining English sailors still on board. I never heard their screams, but I was told later that at least one of 'em had his throat slit. Alexander Murray, a rather distasteful man, was probably responsible for killing or wounding the guards. He also must have been able to retrieve some sort of instrument to undo his shackles, and those of his son, because I saw the two of 'em later in the street along the dock and they were walking about without any irons on their wrists. They had also taken the clothes o' the English sailors for their own and were therefore much better dressed than the rest of us. I stayed with the McBeans and Gregor McGregor, and we went in a separate direction.

Unfortunately, our wrists were still shackled, and therefore we could not venture freely into town in view o' the locals. We were planning to get as far away from the ship as possible. I had never been to Ireland, and knew nothing o' the Cork city layout . I had to count on the darkness and sheer luck to protect me and keep me from being noticed by unfriendly eyes. We moved southerly and soon found our way impeded by the River Douglas. We crept along the docks for several blocks and then the buildings turned from warehouses to shops and inns. It was a dark night, with only a sliver o' moon, so we went largely unseen. Most respectable people would have been asleep at that hour anyway.

As we walked further from the wharf, the warehouses slowly changed to houses and apartments. We could not find anything to break our shackles and so we had to hide in a barn for several hours as dawn approached and it became light out. We were still only a few miles from the boat when we heard the alarms go off in the distance. I was frightfully scared and still weak from so many months without proper nutrition or exercise. There were four of us huddled in the corner of this wooden shack, with only some boxes of linens to shield us from anyone who happened to enter the door. We hid there for an entire afternoon. Several times we heard voices as people walked by, but fortunately no one came in to discover us. At dusk that next day, after sleeping lightly on and off for several hours, we slowly, one at a time, left through the door o' the warehouse and down more alleyways toward the west. I was terribly hungry, but we could not risk going into any of the taverns as our irons would have instantly given us away as escapees. With the dark surrounding and shielding us, we were able to move about a little more freely as the stars started to come out later that evening.

One of the McBeans smelled some bread baking in one o' the houses and temptation proved too strong to overpower his common sense. He entered the house through the first floor window and pilfered the loaf from the hearth with a towel he found in the kitchen room. Unfortunately, the woman o' the house came in and spotted him as he was leaving through the same window and started screaming. From all over the neighborhood, people were yelling and coming out o' their houses to see what the commotion was about. I didn't even stop to think, I just started running as fast as I could. I kept running down the same boulevard for a quarter of an hour and after a few minutes I had lost track of my companions completely. How I ran so fast with heavy irons about my hands is a wonder that only God can answer. I whipped passed many curious Irishmen, who probably wondered at my flight, but I was moving so fast they didn't have time to react until I had already passed. After a time, I was completely out o' breath and had to stop and rest to catch my wind. I almost collapsed as I hid on a side street between two barrels. I huddled behind one of 'em and noticed that by this hour, it was getting quite dark. I had been on the run for a full day.

I heard shots in the distance, and from my vantage point a block away, I saw soldiers running in a group down the boulevard in the same direction I had been just minutes before. I decided it was time to move again so I started heading north on the other side o' the street while the soldiers moved west. I found an empty barn about two blocks away and I went up into the loft and lay in the hay. I didn't know what else to do or where to go. I didn't even know in which part o' Ireland Cork was located, or how big the city actually was. I slept for an hour and luckily found some oats in the barn that was to be fed to the horses below. I greedily ate o' the grain. It was terribly dry, but I needed something in my stomach. I took two eggs out o' the chicken coop in the barn and sucked at the insides after cracking the shells on the wall. I even took a long draft o' water in the horse bucket. I felt a little light headed, but decided I need to look around the barn to find something to break the shackles on my wrists. I found a rather sharp scythe and started working the blade on the latch o' my irons. It took almost an hour to see any groove forming, but I was making progress on the rusted metal. While so seated in the loft o' the barn, I heard two people come into the space below. They were speaking excitedly, and when I heard the word "prisoners", I leaned a little closer to listen. I stood mouse-still, hiding behind the wood of the upstairs wall, just near the ladder door to the floor below. I strained intently for several minutes to catch pieces of their conversation.

One said, "I tell you Brian, it was a far crazed day. These three Scots dressed in sailor uniforms were in the tavern huddled over their beers and all of a sudden soldiers burst in with their muskets flashing. They went up to the gents and pointed their guns right at em'. He says: Alexander Murray, you are an escaped convict who has killed the King's sailors. Alexander Junior and Peter Chalmers, you are his accomplices and are also escaped criminals. That's what he says. Then this soldier takes the 3 of 'em outside and this captain fellow comes up. He says take the younger two to the ship, and then he puts this Murray fellow against the wall of the tavern and he and three soldiers all took shots at him. The Murray fellow was filled with musket fire, he was. Blood still all over that tavern wall."

The other man then said that "Three others were caught stealing bread from the Murphy lady less than an hour past. They were also taken to the ship."

The first man then said, "In total, they recaptured all but 4 of the 20 missing convicts. The constable says they are hardened criminals and dangerous, so we best keep on our toes and look out for the others they haven't caught yet. The soldiers said they were to go house to house to find the rest. They shouldn't be hard to recognize, as most were still in irons and looked pale and gaunt from the prison."

I was as sad and lonely as could be at that moment. It sounded like most all highlanders had already been caught. I was one of only a few that had still eluded capture. I looked again at my shackles and worried how I was going to evade everyone who was searching for me, with such obvious signs of imprisonment bonded to my wrists.

The two Irishmen below were feeding the horses and chickens as they talked, and after a little more talk between em' that was too garbled to understand, they left the barn. I spent another two hours on my irons before I was able to break the chains about me. I eventually freed myself by bending the edges of the now bisected clasps on an anvil I found below, with the aid of a blacksmith's chisel laying on a table. I was about to leave the area again when I heard a lot of yelling about a block away. Shortly thereafter, the two men came back out o' the house next door, and walked again toward the barn. I barely made it up to the loft, but I was in no danger of being spied as they remained outdoors. I heard one of 'em say that he thought they must have caught another prisoner and I guess they went down the street to watch what befell one of my fellow escapees. I waited for about an hour before I snuck out o' the barn door and along the neighboring street. It was just after midnight. Despite no visible chains, I was wearing the ragged clothing of a prisoner and my long matted hair and beard made me stick out in a way which was likely to get me captured easily. After another 45 minutes of walking, I found some clothes hanging out on a line to dry. I eagerly changed out of the rags into some breeches and a white cloth shirt. I had seen no one in the last several minutes, so I was more comfortable walking on the street with my new costume. It was almost morning when I reached the edge of Cork. I was especially tired and sleepy after walking so long without much food, but I needed to get out of town and into the countryside as quickly as I might. I hit the main wagon road westward by sunrise and walked for another 30 minutes. I saw some farmers out tilling the fields to my right, but no one else was on the road at that hour. Everything seemed eerily quiet and I finally felt comfortable enough to rest. In the early morning, I decided to lie down and take a nap under a nice shady tree about 100 yards off the road. I felt at ease and thought things were beginning to break my way.

I awoke with a start by something prodding my chest.

"You, get up! What is your name? What is your business here?"

I opened my eyes to find two soldiers staring at me, and one holding a long musket rifle right at my chest. In my shock, I didn't say anything immediately, and that made the other soldier also raise his musket in my direction. He prodded me again for my name and business. I remembered the conversation between the two men in the barn, and that they had mentioned the name of a local woman, so I quickly said "Murphy".

He noticed the scars on my wrists and pointed at them as he snickered at me. "Murphy!" he said to himself with a smile, as he put the musket right in my face. "You don't sound Irish. You're a stranger. I'm pretty damn sure I know who you are and where you came from, so tell me the truth and we'll go easy on you."

Before I even had a chance to answer, he yelled back at the road and said to another group of men standing there, "Sir, I think we found another one!"

I got up and was taken by the two men back to the soldiers on the road. An officer type came up to me, and in a thick Irish brogue, asked me my name again. I figured by that time they would kill me if I didn't start telling the truth, so I told 'em my name was Alexander. He asked again what my surname was and I said Fraser. The first soldier told the officer that I had initially tried to say I was a "Murphy", at which point the officer cocked his eyebrow and several soldiers around him started laughing. He then checked a paper he was carrying and found my name there.

"He is definitely one of the escaped. Quickly, bring him along. Captain Wallace is about ready to make sail. We got all but one."

I was pushed, shoved and led at a run back through Cork, all o' the way to the original dock where we jumped ship. This took over three hours, even at our fast pace and direct route. However, when we reached the docks, the ship was already well out to sea and the space at the dock where the ship was moored was empty. I remember thinking to myself, that things were looking bloody bad and I might be led to a wall and shot like Alexander Murray Senior. One o' the soldiers asked the commanding officer what they were to do with me. When no one offered any possibilities, he suggested they put me in their military stockade. I simply held my head low and stayed silent. There was nothing for me to do but wait and see what fate held. The officer briefly considered the option o' throwing me in their military cell, but he seemed to change his mind after he thought on it.

"I don't want to feed this man, and I'm not even sure what crime he committed. He's too dangerous to let loose."

He had just about decided on executing me, when his faced changed suddenly. As he stared down the dock at a ship in the distance, the officer lightened up and he told the soldier next to me he had an idea. He took off at a swift walk and left me there with two guards. My feet hurt from the march and I was terribly hungry, but at least my hands were no longer bound. I had no idea where the officer had gone or why, but I couldn't believe it was going to be for my good. The officer returned in about a half hour with a smug look on his face.

"Well, prisoner Fraser, this is your lucky day. I would have just as soon shot you as keep you in our jail, but you've been given a reprieve. There is another slave ship in our port this morning, and they are also going to America, but by way of the Slave Coast of Africa. You will be able to share your journey to the colonies with 200 African natives headed to Carolina. Won't that be warm and cozy?"

At that he let out a belly laugh and the other two soldiers joined in. I was not very amused by his joke, nor the prospect of being thrown into an African slave ship. I had heard several stories about the slave ships from Africa. The conditions on board were even more dismal than they were for the Scottish indentured prisoners. I had heard that they stacked bodies on top of each other as ballast for the ship, and that African slaves went days without food or water on the voyage to the Americas. I figured things had just been dealt much to my detriment, but at least I wasn't going to be shot. Not yet anyway."

I stopped telling my tale for a minute while I squirmed about on my forelegs trying to get a little more comfortable. My knees and legs were killing me from sitting up. I had been in this same spot for the best of a day. The Portuguese man did not try to impede my attempts at repositioning, but he didn't offer to let me sit down completely, either.

"If you won't take pity and let me rest for a wee bit, will you at least let me piss for Christ's sake?"

He nodded and motioned for the two natives to help me outside the door. It was getting dark. They held each shoulder as I wet the ground in front of the small hut they held me in. Within a minute I was done and I was shoved through the entrance back to my former position. I really hurt. I noticed the Portuguese man was drinking liquid from a flask, and he noticed that I noticed, but he did not offer me anything to drink. In fact he loudly swallowed and made a point of wiping the liquid from his mouth. Bastard.

I sat down and moved around for a few seconds trying to find a position to ease my pains. When I had finally found a more comfortable posture, I began again with my story.

"I was again led down the dock and up to a rather large galley class wooden ship with three masts, square rigged sails, and a huge deck. I marveled at the eight cannons on both starboard and port sides which extended from the galley decks. I was forced up the plank walkway and aboard ship. We were met on the deck by a captain. He was older and quite gray, and did not seem so dignified as Capt. Wallace of the *Anne,* and he was missing several teeth. He eyed me up and down for a few seconds before speaking to the soldier beside me.

"Welcome back to the *Whydah Galley*, Lieutenant. I stand by our bargain. One more slave under the deck isn't going to matter, but you still owe me 40 schilling for the crossing."

"I will deduct it from your dock fee and loading expenses Capt. Prince."

The salty captain in front of us nodded to the soldiers with me and added, "Bad luck for the captain of the *Anne*. He lost 3 pound sterling on this here convict, and 6 quid more for one missing and the one shot. They aren't going to pay full when he reaches Virginia missing three of their tobacco pickers." He then looked squarely at me and taunted, "Like to escape do you, lubbey? Think you're going to jump ship on me again, boy? I'll lash you to the quartermast first!"

I didn't know why he called me lubbey, and hoped I never had the opportunity to ask him. Something about him looked a little unsavory, even if he was a ship's captain, and he wasn't really dressed for the part. His outfit looked like it had been slept in for several days, and several holes were visible in the sleeves and pant legs. He had the dark, heavily wrinkled skin of one who has spent his life on the water. After looking me over one more time, he nodded at the soldiers and smiled. "We'll put him in the hold by himself for a week or so to soften him up. He ought not to have the strength or stamina to want to leave after that."

Two men grabbed me by the arms and escorted me

across the ship toward a door laying flat across the deck. I passed several large cooking kettles on the bow, which were intended for making gruel for the 'passengers'. One of the men lifted this large wooden plank and encouraged me with a shove to crawl downwards. I made my way slowly down a steep set o' steps toward the cargo hold, and into a rigged shelf in the middle o' the ship that divided the hull into what I presumed was the slave deck. We quickly came to a thick wooden door, which one of the men opened without a key. The door was constructed of heavy oak timbers interspersed with thick iron bars that allowed one to see into the hold before entering. The space beyond was black and the air was very still and heavy. I peered inside. It was dark except for some square grated hatchways on the ceiling which let enough light in to see some o' the surroundings. I glanced at the two large wooden planks that lay next to the door, and which sealed the entrance from this side. It would take a team o' giants to break out of this door when latched. We moved slowly into the slave hold. The ceiling was so low on this deck that one had to bend way over to walk, and then only with bent knees. The heat was stifling down here, and although there was no one in the space but myself and the two men escorting me, there was a lingering stench o' stale air emanating from the hold that smelled of piss, shat and vomit. The feel of death was suffocating. The combination o' the heat and bad odors made me balk at going further into this pit o' hell, but one of the men shoved me onward. I gazed around the wee wooden hold. The two overhead grated hatchways were covered with tarpaulins that blocked most o' the sunshine, but also added to the heat and stifled the air. There was little headroom, and no opportunity to stand up. In fact, this hold had little more than 4 feet between floor and ceiling. I could not imagine how anyone in this squalid space would be able even to sit upright during any part o' the voyage across the sea.

There were manacles and fetters of different kinds, and several leg irons attached together with a large thick metal chain, lying across sitting planks along the bulkhead. They appeared to have been left over from the last voyage. I gagged several times on the smell coming from all sides o' this room. The floor o' the hold was stained with a mixed palate of dark colors, and I shuddered when I considered their source.

One sailor shoved me down to the deck of the hold and both men retreated back towards the entrance. One shut the prison-like door that led back up on deck and latched it with one o' the heavy bars, making a loud thump that made me jump despite myself.

It was another half day before we set sail for Africa. I was getting used to living in these types of conditions, but even Newgate prison guards treated men better than on this ship. It was two days before anyone even remembered to check on me. Without much human ballast, the ship sat high in the water and sailed roughly and haphazardly, even with the slightest of winds. We sailed back around Cornwall and England to the southwest coast of France and then down around Spain and Portugal, eventually reaching the North African coast after about fourteen days. I never really saw anything but wooden walls for most o' the journey.

As I said, for the first two days of sailing, I had no company and no vantage point as I sat in the darkness feeling every swell o' the sea. I retched repeatedly with the wave motion, but I had nothing in my stomach, so no food came up with my vomit but yellow bile. I was miserable and laid down barely conscious. Severe thirst and hunger were constant. I figured it would only get worse when we took on another boat load o' slaves in Africa. I had to look forward to smelling other people's vomit. I would be lucky to survive such an ordeal.

Sometime on the third day I thought the Captain must have finally remembered I was down in the hold, because someone finally showed up to check on me. It turned out to be prudence and luck rather than compassion. The ship's cook had gone down to the hold to sneak a snort of whisky, when he noticed there was someone already laying in the dark. I was all but dead and fortunately for me, he took pity on me."

The Portuguese man put his hand on my shoulder, and said, "Finally! I begin to understand how you came to be in Africa. But this does not explain how you are free and in the mining trade so far from the coast. There is more to this story. Tell me of the slave ship." I only nodded and continued.

Chapter 3: Old Pirates

"I was perhaps quite lucky that it was the cook that found me, instead of one of the other ship's mates. The cook for the *Whydah Galley* was a thin but strong man with whitish hair, and a wiry build. He walked bowed and had a limp. He had a grizzled beard and almost no teeth. I was barely conscious when he appeared suddenly, and I choked when he tried to give me a shot of his whisky. From what he explained later, this happened as we were sailing past the Portuguese coast. He asked me my name but I was too weak to answer above a whisper. I just said, "water" as loud as I could. He left for a time and came back down to the hold to bring some leftover scraps of bread and a flagon of water. He said his name was Nathaniel Turnbull and hailed from the borders region of Scotland, just to the south and east of Edinburgh.

The old man watched me take a long draught of water and clapped my back when I choked on the cool liquid again.

"That's it, boy, drink heartily from the cup. Yer lips haven't touched enough water yet to moisten yer thirst. Soak it up like a sea sponge."

He ladled more water from a bucket, and I splashed some on my face.

"I've seen the negro slaves so heated down here

that they were rabid for drink, foaming at the mouth and desperate to quench their throats, all from the ungodly heat of the hold. Rushed me like maniacs trying to get to the bucket. You're lucky I found ye down here or ye would have died within the week."

I drank greedily once more from the ladle. My throat was so dry it hurt to swallow.

After several gulps, I at least got my voice back. It was barely above a strong whisper. "Was the captain going to leave me to die then?" I asked.

"Captain Prince is a busy man, trying to ready the ship for the middle passage and reach port so we can get all of the crew, cargo and slaves on board for the Atlantic crossing. With all his other goings on, I think he forgot about ye. He don't rightly know yer down here."

"Thanks for your kindness Nathaniel. I do wonder why are you being so nice? You could have just left me some water and some food and treated me like a criminal or another slave."

"You a convict then?"

"Only by chance. I'm a highlander who got captured by the English at Preston. Got to spend some months in Newgate. Now, I get to fancy this passage." I pointed to the hold.

"I pity ye, boy. Traveling the middle passage in the slave deck is not for the gentile. The slaves are treated poorly and many will die on the way over. Don't get me wrong, our captain and crew are much better than other slavers, and on our first voyage we lost many fewer than other slave ships, but I would not begrudge a kinsman a seat in this hold. Though he spent years as a galleon buccaneer, Captain Prince is not the uncaring, cruel tyrant that is the lot of other slaver captains. He understands that fair treatment of Negroes means better profit in the Americas and he don't tolerate mistreating or starving natives. He never adopted the ways of some others. We use loose packing to deliver slaves. Under his rules, fewer natives are transported than the Whydah can carry in order to reduce the disease and deaths among the slaves. The other slave ships use tight packing, which is far more cruel and based on the notion that the more slaves ye transport, the more profit ye could make. In practice, they end up losing a quarter to half of their human cargo and their profits suffer. Captain Prince, well, he has us put buckets out for 'em to piss and crap in, but there ain't never enough to go 'round, so ye can still see the shit stains on the deck down here. Slaves who are close to the buckets will use it, but those who are farther away are apt to tumble and fall over others trying to reach the privy bucket. Captain has to prevent rioting and breakouts so's slaves are chained ankle to wrist, with barely any place to move. Hindered by the shackles secured around their ankles, many Negroes prefer to relieve themselves where they are, rather than to get hurt moving over several other people."

I looked at some of the stains and understood better why they were there, and my nose needed no explanation for why it smelled so terribly in here. My gaze switched to the manacles and the chain that was set across the seating plank next to me. The old man followed my gaze.

"The crew that brought ye down here was too busy, so they must have not bothered to chain you in place. I came down here for a lil' tastin'." He pointed to his flask, and smiled. He told me that he had decided to head to the lower deck, so he wouldn't have to share a snort with other crew. Nathaniel had noticed the plank barrier plied across the door to the slave hold and was surprised to see me down here.

"I might never have seen ye, if I hadn't been thirsty for a snort." He looked again around the hold. No one might have found ye until we hit the Guinea coast. I saw the plank on the door and wondered who be behind it afor' we picked up the natives. Yeah, you were lucky today."

I didn't feel very lucky. I felt hot. "I can hardly breathe down here, and when I do the greeting the stench gives my nostrils causes my own senses to revolt."

I looked around to emphasize how horrid things were when my eyes fell on the square crossbarred hatches overhead. Why the tarpaulins?"

"Those tarpaulins form awnings that keep the sun and rain out, but still give some light. It's not perfect, and I know the air don't circulate well. I've heard slaves complaining of heat down here, and have seen 'em fainting, almost dying for want of water. It's worse in rainy weather when we have to close the hatches off. We do a lot for them slaves just so they stay alive, and try to give 'em some food and water when they need it, but conditions bein' what they are, they still get sick. The natives drink more than normal due to heat and sickness. We only have so much water for the voyage across, so sometimes it must be rationed when we get toward the coast. Especially if we hit some bad winds or doldrums. Thirst and dehydration set in, it's bad for everyone. We still lose a few." He shrugged.

Nathaniel stayed long enough to ensure that I was going to be ok, and then returned to his duties in the galley kitchen.

When we next met the following day, he brought more food and water, and I was much stronger and able to speak with a little more pleasantry. Nathaniel was eager to hear about the 1715 uprising and which o' the clans had participated. I told him everything I knew, glad to actually have someone to talk to for the first time in o'er a year. I recounted much o' the same story that you've already heard. He asked me about several names of which he was acquainted, including kinsmen and friends, but I knew of none. I commented that it was strange for a Scot to be aboard ship and a seasoned sailor in the first place, but even more unusual for a clansmen to be working on a slave ship. I didn't say it aloud, but I was thinking that was something usually reserved for the underbelly of English society, and something the Scottish people held in low regard. His reply caught me by surprise.

"Aye, there were not many highlanders in the naval service or the English India Far East Trading company, but even fewer in the ranks of the buccaneers."

I looked at him with astonishment. "You were a pirate?"

"Aye, with Henry Morgan himself as my captain and admiral. I was with him, as only a tike of a lad of 16, when he captured Santa Catalina in 1760 and still with him when we ascended the Chagres River and sacked Panama. Lawrence, meanin' Cap'n Prince, was one of the buccaneers too. He was only a ship's mate back then. We been together on galleys ever since."

"The captain of this galley is a pirate?"

"The days of pirates is about done with, lad. They are getting hanged and quartered in every stretch of ocean. Only Bellamy is still out there on the open sea, taking plunder from the Spanish and Dutch. The crown has given up their support and protection and there are bounties on buccaneer heads. There is no more profit in it, like there was in decades past. Too many warships huntin' em' down, and no ports to hole up in, even in Jamaica or Trinidad. Slavin' is the only way for us to make money and keep our heads. If I had any money I'd head back to the Borders and live out my days, but I've got no coin to go anyplace but stay with Capt. Prince til I die on this plank. I'm too old and sore to run the rigging and man the lines anymore, so the Captain has me cook for the crew these days."

I looked at him a little closer and thought that he was in fair shape, but then looking at the deep wrinkles and white hair I realized that he was much older than my uncle or father, and probably much older than anyone aboard this ship except perhaps the captain himself. I wondered how someone of his age could handle cross Atlantic voyage after voyage, especially with that limp. Fate had placed him in a situation not much better than mine. He had a life o' hard toil and no chance to get back to a highland farm. Mr. Turnbull promised again to visit me often and when he could, he said he would bring me some scraps from the kitchen.

The next day he stayed with me for over an hour regaling me with tales of the high seas. He apologized for the two days I was left without food or water, but I told him I was just happy he found me. He was right. They might just as easily find my shriveled body laying in the hold once they reached the African coast, since

the captain seemed to have otherwise no thoughts
turned to me at all.

The ship sailed past the Canary Islands and on
to the great bulge of Africa. I don't know what
Nathaniel told the captain or rest of the crew about me
or my condition. I was left alone in the hold and never
allowed to come up on deck, and I saw no other sailors.
By good chance, the seas were smooth for a few days
and the lack of bumps let my seasickness go away.
Unfortunately, we soon moved farther out to open water
to avoid some shallow shoals around some river deltas,
and the seas picked up as we sailed steadily towards the
Slave Coast. Nathaniel explained that Guinea Propria
was the term the mapmakers used for most of Western
Africa 'neath the Sahara and west o' the inland
Aethiopia. Everyone called the area under the bulge the
gold coast, or more recently, the Slave Coast, based on
the trade o' the time.

Nathaniel kept his word and brought me food and
water every day for the next few days. My strength
improved and I actually enjoyed hearing from him about
his days as a swashbuckler in the Caribbean Sea. It
was apparent that he held the captain in the highest
regard and his eyes shone brightly with admiration
when he explained how together they had attacked and
mounted Spanish galleons, conquered the Dutch traders
in hand to hand combat, and looted Incan gold and
silver with Henry Morgan. In turn, I told him stories of
my youth in the highlands, and about my time in the '15
uprising. He was extremely interested in the names of
any clans who participated on each side, and how they
acted in battle. He made me retell over and over
descriptions o' the cowards who slipped away when the

battle became intense. He would smile and laugh when I told him that most were English sympathizers, but he would admonish me if I complained about the battle worthiness of Northumberlings or especially lowlanders, since some of those may have been his relatives. He relished in descriptions of the individual valiant Scottish warriors o' the dragoon battalions, and wanted to know all about my father Hugh and how he died. It was difficult to speak about my father, but afterwards it seemed to help me, as I had not had anyone to discuss his loss with until that time. On one visit, he asked me to speak again in great detail about how the twenty Scots escaped the *Anne* and how I ended up recaptured. He asked about the soldiers that captured me and also about how the other highlanders had been caught. He queried me again about what I thought I planned to do once I escaped Cork and had left the grasp o' the English who had enslaved me. I told him I didn't really know and hadn't thought about it that much.

"Would ye be going back to Scotland then?" he asked.

I replied that I would try, but that it now looked like that possibility was going to have to wait for at least 7 years as I was to be an indentured farm hand in the American colonies for that long.

The old man then frowned deeply and looked directly at me. "Have ye not heard, then?"

I replied that I had been in the hold for my entire voyage and only had met the captain for a brief minute before being thrown into this large empty wooden cell with iron bars on the door portal.

"I haven't discussed this with the Capn', but I don't think ye will be a short term slave when you reach the

Americas, lad. Yer an escaped convict. They won't pay any mind to yer ol' contract. Any agreement ye had with the English courts regarding your servitude is null and void, once ye fled the first ship. Ye are under the terms of the captain now, and will be held under the same conventions as the African natives who will soon be sharing the hold with ye. I'm afraid ye will go on the trading block with the others. They will sell ye for flesh in the Virginia colonies to the highest bidder and he will own ye for yer lifetime. There won't be any freedom for ye after 7 years, unless it is under the good graces of yer buyer. Yer lot is fixed, just like them African slaves."

The reality of what he had said hit me like a blunderbuss. I had followed the other Scotsmen out o' the hold o' the *Anne* into what now seemed like a life of hard labor and toil under the whip. I would never see Ross-shire or my clansmen again. I would never marry, never have children, never own a house or a piece of land. I had reached bottom and I felt wretched. I had given up one temporary enslavement for a permanent one. I looked o'er at the old man, who was eyeing me with extreme pity, and I asked if he would do me a favor and just quit feeding me.

"It would be best if you would take a pistol and shoot me in the chest. I would rather that than to go on living as someone's hound for the rest of my days, to order around and kick at when I disobeyed, or as chattel to mistreat, torture and neglect."

I turned away from the bars that we were speaking through and went to the far corner of the hold. I laid in the dark for hours without moving. I didn't even want to think. The old man called after me several times, but I paid him no bother and he left.

He kept coming back to see me daily, and we spoke cordially, but I was not really interested in conversation anymore and had given up most hope of any fruitful life ahead. Our visits became more and more brief as hopelessness took hold of me.

After a few more days, the *Wydah Galley* was cruising along the western bump o' the African Coast heading south past Senegal and Cape Blanc. We were just about to follow the terrain and turn back east along the coast of Guinea Propria to our destination of Elmina. Nathaniel had told me that we were to dock there, in one of the main cities involved in the Atlantic slave trade. He told me that nearby cities of Cape Coast and Kominda were also ports for slave ships, but our contacts were in Elmina. While I nodded my head in acknowledgement as the old man spoke to me, I really wasn't listening to him for most o' the last day or two o' the journey. I tried to starve myself to death, but hunger pangs drove me to accept some of his offerings, especially since he was now giving me some of his own meal ration rather than galley scraps. Severe thirst pushed me to accept his offers of water, but I was little more than a husk and lacked any ambition to do more than move from one side o' the hold to the other. At last and after many days at sea, we dropped sail and drifted into the busy port of Elmina on the coast of Guinea Propria. I was weak and had lost most of my will to live, but some instinct deep within my soul kept me alive long enough to see what lay in store.

Chapter 4: Escape (again!)

Just before we tied up to the pier, Nathaniel came down to the hold with a mop and a bucket of soapy water. When I asked what he wanted, he whispered for me to be quiet. He unlocked the door to the hold and placed the bucket next to me. He also threw me one of his shirts to wear. I again tried to ask what was going on, but he quieted me again and simply told me to wait and to start mopping the floor as soon as I heard a commotion occurring on the decks above. He whispered that I would understand soon. It made absolutely no sense to me, but I put the shirt on and used a little of the water in the bucket to wash my face. Perhaps I was to gain favor with the captain by doing some of the work of the crew, and in turn would get some deck privileges for the voyage, or perhaps this was my way of earning the few scraps of food that I had received over the past few days. I half-heartedly mopped a tiny corner of the hold, but I didn't see how that was of much benefit to the captain. I wondered why the old man had asked me to wait to start mopping until there was something happening on the ship deck above. I quit mopping and followed his advice and just sat looking at the mop and bucket as if they were fellow passengers. At least I wasn't crazy enough to start talking to the cleaning tools. After about an hour I curled back up against a corner and went to sleep. I don't know how long I lay there, but in the early morning I woke to the sounds of clamor on the decks above. I could hear shouting and the rumble o' heavy feet on deck and planks outside. I did as I was told, and picked up the mop and started swabbing the floor o' the hold with renewed enthusiasm. I didn't have much energy and tired quickly, but I had a large portion o' the front area o' the hold washed down when several people started down the steps to the hold and waited in front o' the thick door. It was then that I realized the door to the hold had been propped open! Oh Lord God almighty, I thought, I have missed my opportunity for escape!

I surmised that the old man was so feeble that he forgot to lock the door after he gave me the mop and bucket! Damn my lack of attention! I could have simply walked out. I wasn't even in chains or shackles. It was dark; I could have slipped away. Then a thought occurred to me. Nathaniel must have purposefully opened that door and when he was with me, he had made sure I wasn't talking. Somehow, he had planned this escape for me. I wondered why Nathaniel hadn't told me he was going to leave the door open so I could flee? Then I realized that it was possible he needed to wait until we arrived at the docks, so that I had a chance to get away. What if he unlocked the hold door and propped it open only while I was sleeping? Why didn't he wake me up so I could get out? And what the hell was the mop for? All of these confusing ideas were swirling through my head, as two white men and a host of Africans moved slowly down the steps and into the open door o' the hold. The old man was trailing slightly behind.

Nathaniel came forward and said loudly so

everyone could hear, "Alex, damn you! What the hell
are you doing? Why ain't you in the kitchen mopping?
Didn't I tell you that the kitchen comes first, always!
Never mind you, come with me and help me get the
supplies you wretched piece of shit!" I told you to finish
mopping this floor before the slaves arrived. They'll just
have to sit on the dirty ground!

One of the two white men looked directly at me
and then back at Nathaniel. He said, in a thick
European accent, "Its fine old man, the slaves don't need
any clean floors. It'll be filthy in here soon enough." He
and the other white man started shoving the slaves to
the back o' the hold with muskets that were pointed at
the front o' the native line. There looked to be over 3
score of the Africans, and among their number were
both men and women. Most looked terrified, and all had
their hands bound with rope. Some men also had rope
nooses about their necks which were tethered to several
others similarly collared. Many were naked and no one
that I saw had any clothing above their waists, other
than the white captors. I could not keep from staring at
the bare bodies of the native women, who generally
looked down when my gaze met theirs. I pitied 'em. My
gawking was interrupted by the shrill voice of Nathaniel
again.

"Alex, pick up the mop and bucket and follow
me upstairs. We got to mop the kitchen before we sail
and first we have to go carry supplies. And then you will
help me peel potatoes in the galley! Get moving you
piece of shit!"

I feared for a moment that the two men with
the muskets would recognize that I was not one of their
shipmates and turn the gun on me, but they seemed to

be preoccupied with moving all o' the black men into the hold. As I moved past the steady line of African slaves moving forward, Nathaniel whispered to me to keep my head low, shut up and follow him. As we passed another white man with a musket and a sailor at the back o' the column of men at the top of the stairs, the sailor gave me a very strange look. I kept my head down, and Nathaniel moved in between us.

He slapped me on the side o' the head, and said loudly, "Damn greenhorn Irish swab jockeys; don't pull their weight on the decks. I'll get work out of this one yet."

I didn't turn around to see how the sailor reacted, but there were another group of slaves which had been shoved down the steps towards the door o' the hold and so I lost track of the sailor in the mass of flesh.

Nathaniel grabbed my hand and said, "Quickly! Lose the mop! Follow me if you want to live!"

I didn't need much coaxing. I stayed close to him and we moved quickly right beside several lines of Africans who were roped together. I saw the captain at one far end of the vessel talking to another white man with a musket, but he was too engaged to have noticed me. We made our way past a few other tough looking white men, but all were eyeing the line o' slaves and didn't even seem to see me. We were halfway down the plank and near to another group of slaves at the place where the plank met the dock when a voice froze me in my tracks. I looked in fear at the sailor down on the pier below who had just spoke.

"Just where do you think you are going?" he had said.

It was Nathaniel who spoke as I was too scared

to even reply. "Let us be if you want any food for the next few weeks. I have to get some supplies for the galley kitchen. They're waiting for us at the front of the dock."

"Captain said no shore leave. No one off of the ship until the cargo is loaded."

"I know exactly what he said. That's why I'm going to get the food supplies. That is part of the cargo."

"Who is this? I've never seen him before."

"Eh? Him. Some stupid swabby we picked up in Cork. Useless. Been cleaning up below for the past 3 days. I think he's damaged in the head. I don't know who signs up these men. Anyway, I've got to have someone lift the crates of bananas and barrels of water. I can leave him here and you can come help me carry all of this stuff up these planks." Nathaniel had hurried both of us down the rest of the plank and had then grabbed the sailor by his collar and tried to lead him towards the end of the dock.

"Let me go old man. I'm not going to help you lift barrels. I've got my own duty here sheriffing these savages on board. Go get your food and get back to the deck as soon as possible. Captain wants to shove off by sunset." With that he turned around and motioned for the next group o' slaves to move up the plank onto ship deck. Another man cracked a whip nearby, and two other important looking white men came up to force the black men up the thin board to the deck above. Nathaniel nearly shoved me to the ground; he was pressing me forward so rapidly. We moved with great deliberation and speed down the pier to where there was a row of ramshackle wooden buildings with a dirt alleyway heading into streets beyond.

"Get out of here, now. Alexander, GO!"

I was bewildered with what had just happened. "Wait, Nathaniel, how can I thank you. Why did you help me? Where will I go? "

Nathaniel stopped and placed his old wrinkled hand in mind as he smiled. "Listen, boy. I did this because I don't have much time left in this world. I miss my home. I miss dry land. I miss the smell of heather and color of thistle in summer. And I don't want one of my kinsmen to live through what these poor savages are going to have to endure. Ye would never survive the voyage. Hell, many of them won't either, and they're in much better shape than ye are now. Ye almost died in front me on the way over. They say slavers lose a little of their soul with every run. They keep less and less of their kindness and grace and lose all of their compassion. Before long they treat the slaves worse than they'd treat their own dogs. I'm not even the same bloke I was before I took the first two voyages. I hate this life. I was a better man and a felt better of myself when I was a pirate! I think Capn' Prince feels the same. We're here for the shillings, but I don't know how much longer either one of us can do this. It's crappy work in a crappy business, and I'll soon smell as bad as the hold."

"Ye have a chance to live here on the Slave Coast. There is work here for a white man. Ye could find a job in the trading houses or stores. If you are smart, ye will stay clear of the slavers markets or on board one of the schooners. If ye can't find work on the coast, go north. The Dutch and Portuguese still work the gold mines in the Ashanti. No one knows who ye are. Ye'll be fine. Who knows? Maybe ye'll find enough gold to become a gentleman. And when ye get enough money, find yer way back to the highlands. See your mother and sis. Marry a big bosomed lass and spend the rest of yer days with yer clan."

"But what of the crew and the Captain? They'll find out I'm gone and come after me! I think that sailor recognized me. I'll be caught again and then just shot! What am I going to do? And they'll catch you too."

"Relax, Alexander. There ain't none on the *Whydah* who remembers who ye were or that you was even down there. If they do, they'd think ye died and that some of the crew tossed ye overboard on the crossing. The men who saw ye today in the hold and many of the men on the deck are slavers, not sailors from the ship. They have no idea who belongs or doesn't belong onboard. Even the sailors on deck wouldn't recognize ye and are too busy to worry about ye anyway. Trust me, they are more concerned with the 200 slaves we have on board now. They don't care about one skinny Scot that the English dropped in our hold in Cork. They have to keep these savages from rioting and hurting themselves, or having too many die and cut into the profits. The crew is busy with their own business. Quit worrying yerself. Now quickly, go!"

I didn't have much time to digest what he had told me, but realized I had to take his word for everything. I moved off at a fast walk down the alley between two shacks and into the city of Elmina as the old man ambled back in the direction o' the ship. I didn't know where I was going, but it didn't require much navigation. Elmina sits on a thin strip of land between a large salt marsh on the north side and the crashing waves o' the ocean on the other. There is a large harbor there, but the buildings, about a thousand or so, are strung out along this strip only a half a mile wide. On the north side, the buildings are mostly factories that process salt out o' the shallow marsh. The town uses salt for major trade to the incoming ships. The center o' this strip of land is looked over by a hill bearing a large white monstrosity called the castle of St. George. It was built by the Dutch and manned by several soldiers and has great cannons jutting from its ballastrae. I slunk past this great fortress and into the surrounding streets and alleyways, moving to the northeast and following the coast. My intention was to put as much distance as possible between myself and the slave ship. I didn't want a repeat of Cork. I passed at least two slave markets where captives were being paraded in front of white English businessmen by a series of heavily armed and ornamented African traders.

After the town of Elmina, I kept walking north until I reached another castle fortress and the town of Cape Coast. I stayed there, sneaking food and water for a few days before traveling further northeast."

As I completed this portion of the tale I noticed the Portuguese man staring intently at me and shaking his head in wonder. At length he said, "Alexander, how long ago did you say this occurred?"

I was impressed he called me by my name this time instead of "Scotty". It wasn't respect, but it was an improvement. I replied simply "About eighteen months past, give or take."

He smiled deviously back at me and said, "I have come to believe that you are either telling the truth about your arrival here or are an incredibly gifted liar."

I looked back quizzically and asked what he meant.

"I have been to the coast many times and your descriptions of the towns are accurate. However, that is not what intrigues me. I heard from some slavers just a month ago that a slave ship named the *Whydah Galley* was captured by pirates in North America only last year, while it was sailing the windward passage near Hispaniola. It seems about a year ago you're Captain Prince of the *Whydah,* let a buccaneer ship led by the pirate captain Black Sam Bellamy board her and take command of the vessel. The owners complained that the takeover was a little too easy, without as much as a flagon of cannon fire. The Dutch slavers who own the Whydah had suspicions that her captain and crew may have been complicit in its capture. Their hunch seemed to be confirmed a few months later when it was found that Bellamy was using the *Whydah* for his flagship and Prince was captaining Bellamy's old buccaneer vessel, the *Sultana* and assisting the Whydah in raids on the colonies and merchant ships. I understand the *Whydah* went down in a gale just this past April off of the shore of the Massachusetts's colony."

He noticed I was greatly distressed at the news of the shipwreck, and let me gather my thoughts before addressing me again.

He finally said, "Don't worry Scotty; the old man who befriended and freed you probably wasn't on board the *Whydah* if he remained with Capt. Prince. He would have transferred to the *Sultana,* and the *Sultana* apparently wasn't with the *Whydah* when it sunk in the gale. No one has heard from the *Sultana* or Captain Prince since the *Whydah* went down. Or at least that was how the story was told to me. I'm sure the owners of the *Whydah* would like to get their hands on Captain Prince, but he is probably hiding out in the Caribbean somewhere and his crew with him. He hasn't been back to this coast."

I was surprised to hear news of the vessel that brought me to Africa, but not so surprised that Captain Prince and Nathaniel had given up slaving for pirating again. I sat ruminating on the fate of the man that freed me. We said nothing for a minute as the Portuguese man considered my story thus far. I noticed he was back to calling me "Scotty". No niceties for long.

"So now we know how you found yourself in West Africa, but I do not yet know why you are in my village and who you have worked for these past 18 months. You could still be a slaver or an English spy." His attitude toward me had changed for the better, but I don't think he trusted me yet, nor was he going to release me. However, he did finally offer me some water after I coughed several times. I accepted the cup greedily as I was parched by the jungle heat and my throat was dry from the long winded tale I had delivered. I would not have traded the water for a tankard of ale or a dram o' whisky.

After gulping down the last of the proffered water, I asked if I could stop for a while. It was getting dark and I had talked for an entire day. I was exhausted, my voice was cracking and my head still hurt from the beatings. It had to be late.

"I need some sleep".

"Alright, Scotty. I will let you sleep for now. But you must finish your story first thing in the morning. It is likely that I will kill you then, but you have tonight to consider the answers to my questions. I'm afraid we don't have any quarters for you, so you are to remain on the floor of this hut and rest there. Don't attempt escape. My two men here are instructed to shoot you and run you through if you try anything to get away."

I lay down on the dirt of the floor and I was asleep within minutes.

Chapter 5: Welcome to the Ashanti

The next morning I awoke again on the floor of the same hut I had been held in. My head was pounding again and my mouth was dry and full of cotton. One of the large native men was at the door and allowed me to go outside and piss into a bush. He held the sword at ready and never was more than a foot away from me. I had no chance for escape. The Portuguese man spied me from the doorway of a neighboring building and approached, still with a pistol in his hand.

"Ah, Alexander Fraser, famous soldier and prisoner, and who now finds himself captive for the third time."

He was mocking me, but I was too worried about my situation to be goaded into an argument or pushed into an outnumbered fight. I would continue to be civil and keep my wits about me. Maybe an opportunity for escape would still arise. I was hungry. He tossed me two oranges and I ate them greedily. I could have eaten six more.

He continued, "I see that you are awake and now that you have eaten, you can begin your story from where we left off. There are so many gaps and unexplained details yet to uncover." He motioned me back into and through the doorway of the small mud brick building I had just exited. His feigned courtesy was infuriating. I liked him better when he showed his menace. As I sat down again in front of the Portuguese man, the other native joined his companion to my side. They seemed bored, but the dark haired man in front of me seemed interested in what I had to say and his eyes were bright and penetrating.

I began the tale anew, explaining how I had wondered for days around the city of Cape Coast looking for work on board ships, and having no luck there (as I had no experience as a sailor) finally made my way o'er to the port town of Accra.

"It had taken me nigh' o'er a week to walk the coastal road from Elmina. I drifted past the immense European castle fortresses and dangerous slave trade o' the coastal regions, northeast to the ancient city of Accra and its huge marketplaces. Once I got there, I spent a few months doing odd jobs and labors for resident Europeans. I think most Europeans preferred to have whites work for 'em. They disliked the easy-going work ethic of the native Africans and perhaps feared, or at least distrusted their intentions."

I went into great detail about each job I had held there for the rich Dutch and Portuguese elite. He did not seem to know any o' the families personally, but recognized some Portuguese names. I told him how I was barely scraping by doing these menial tasks, and how I had remembered the words o' the old pirate about the lure o' the gold fields.

"After a time, I finally scraped together enough farthings to buy some supplies and join a caravan of would-be miners heading for the fields in Ashanti."

He interrupted me with a question. "But why not just book passage back to Scotland when you had acquired some money."

"It was yet too soon after my incarceration. I was afraid that I would be identified back in England or Scotland, or perhaps even in Elmina before I boarded ship, and thereby sent back to Newgate or even put to the gallows. Also, as you have stated, it is quite expensive to travel across oceans by ship, and although I had a few coppers, it was a far cry from the 5 pound note I required to travel home."

He seemed satisfied with my answer, and bade me continue.

"I eventually tired of menial labor and followed the lure of treasure and riches and found my way into the thick wilds of exotic palm forest to find work in the Ashanti gold mines to the northwest."

"And so you became a miner for the guild and have spent the remainder of your time in the fields." He paused for moment before shaking his head and coming to an abrupt realization.

"Liar! Again you persist with outlandish claims! A miner without experience will soon starve or go broke, or both in the Ashanti. It is no place for a greenhorn."

"As you say, mining alone is not fit for an unbroke colt, and quickly and well did I learn that lesson. But the story is true nonetheless. I spent only a few weeks on my own panning the rivers and streams. I found naught but a nugget and nothing in my hands but calluses and blood. At first I had set out into the jungle to mine the land on my own. I had tried like all of the other fortune seekers to find gold working the dirt by myself along the creeks with a pan. I had only been digging and panning in the fields for a few weeks before I almost starved to death and had to face the fact that I was ill equipped to strike it rich on my own. I soon realized that I would be dead from exhaustion and malnutrition before I even laid eyes on the first yellow flake. I was a highlander, with no idea of how to break the earth and find any mineral wealth hidden there.

Hunger and misery eventually sent me yonder to the local mining labor camps nearby. I was forced to go searching for better pastures and in desperation I happened on the Dutch African Mining company and spent many months toiling in their fields. I joined a legion of Africans, mostly slaves, and a few hardy Portuguese, Dutch and English adventurers and worked the large barren fields and valleys, harrowing deep red dirt for the Dutch mining interest. It was dirty, hard physical work that lasted from dawn til dusk. Days basically consisted of shoveling as much sand and rocks as possible, pounding 'em with a sledge, filtering through a screen and then washing and sifting 'em by weight in a long wooden runway that had a constant flow o' water. The slew had ridges in it which caught the heavier metals, while the lighter rocks and minerals washed farther down the plank-like runway. Those who were not bosses mostly worked in the field digging and hauling. We couldn't work after dark due to the risk of wild animal attacks from leopards, lions or poisonous snakes. The ground yielded little wealth, and anything that came up went to the bosses who held sway. I received only food and shelter for my toils, though I was promised a share of profits when I joined. Our accommodations were little more than an overcrowded mud barn, with leaves on the floor for 30 men to jostle over for suitable sleeping positions. Most Europeans thought they would learn the trade secrets o' the mining collective, and then somehow quit the Dutch African company, embark into the surrounding jungle and stake their own claims. As if mining in this wilderness required any claim to overgrown fields of dense trees, palm, grass, swamp and mud. Most white men ended up dead due to the elements, some to snake bite, and many to disease before they could become self-sufficient miners with the chance to strike it rich."

"I am familiar with the Dutch African guild. I have traded with them in the past. Please remind me of the name of the lead foreman."

He was testing me, but I was not to be trapped. For I was telling the truth, if nigh' all of it. "Jan Van Meter was the leader o' the miners in the field. He was a large, bald headed white man, with an angry demeanor and a scar o'er his left cheek. I don't know who owned the company. I never saw him. I boarded with a host of other miners, both African and European, in a great sleeping quarters in the forest near the mining fields. It was horrible work and I was given rations and a space to sleep, but nary much else."

"And so you quit and came here."

"No, as I have tried to explain, I became quite ill with jungle fever and was fired when I couldn't work. I left the camp on foot to try and find a doctor and another job. I was as haggard as wet haggis, but I had enough push left to try to make it to Kumasi."

"Preposterous! Explain to me how it is you survived the almost certain death of the fever when you were traveling alone on foot in the middle of the Ashanti without medicines, a doctor or even a place to sleep and recover."

"I almost didn't recover. I was on the verge o' collapse and close to meeting St. Peter when I was found by some nearby villagers. They kept me in their company until I felt better. When I grew stronger and was well enough, I left the village and headed off along trails until I could find a road to send me back to the coast where I might finally board a ship back to Scotland."

"What was the name of this village?"

I was hesitant to give him the name o' the village I had stayed in. Some things were better omitted. If this man was a slaver, I might somehow lead him and his warriors to my friends and result in their being taken captive. I had to be weary. I figured I could give some, but not all details.

"I don't know. I don't speak Twi, and they didn't speak English, so I never got around to asking."

I could tell he didn't believe me, and his whole manor changed again as he began to see through my caginess and guile. "So you just left the village and came here by yourself." His tone was sarcastic and condescending.

"Aye, that's about it."

"And I suppose you don't know where this village of compassionate natives resides either?"

I couldn't say to him that I didn't know a location or he would immediately realize I was lying, so I carefully worked around his question. "Well it lies to the East and somewhat to the North of the mining camps. It is in the deep jungle." That was actually the truth but would not provide anyone enough information to ever find it.

"So you were able, with no compass or prior experience, to get from this village to Akrokerri traveling by trail after trail through the densest forest of the Ashanti. Remarkable."

I nodded and thought that he had finally accepted my story, when he reached over and picked up the dueling musket and cocked the flintlock mechanism. He pointed it again at my head.

"You, Mr. Fraser are a liar. May I remind you, that I know when you are being deceptive, and this musket ball fits nicely between your eyes." He seemed pleased with himself.

I acted as nonchalant as possible to his response, and simply shrugged.

"I must admit, Scotty, that you almost had me. I actually believed your incredible story for a time. But you made a mistake when you tried to conceal all of the details about your home village and your accomplice. You see, I know you are lying when you say you came here alone. I already captured the young Ashanti man that accompanied you. My warriors have beaten him for answers. He hasn't agreed to talk to them yet, but he will crack soon enough. So you see your loyalty to the village and your little dark friend is misplaced. Deceit will only result in causing them more pain."

He could see the horror reflected in my face. "You have taken Kofi hostage as well?"

"Yes, and we will knock him senseless until he explains his intentions and answers our questions."

"Portuguese Bastard." I said softly through gritted teeth. "You didn't need to beat him. He's just a wee lad. He was simply helping me reach Obuasi. Go ahead and kill me, but let the young villager go. He's done nothing and he is just a simple farmer. He's a harmless boy."

The Portuguese man was no longer smiling at

me, but was instead staring at me again intently and he moved the pistol away from my forehead. It was still cocked.

"You are a most intriguing man. You grieve for an old pirate you hardly knew, and now you try to protect a native African as if he were a family member. I would not expect that of a former criminal or a military man..... to show such compassion."

"I am no criminal. I was a prisoner of war."

"Just so. You are still not what I expected."

"Sorry to disappoint. What are you to do with the native lad? Please let him go."

"I may let the boy go if you answer all of my questions and quit stalling. I do not have days to waste milking the tale out of you. Firstly, tell me what happened with the Akwamu slavers we found south of here. You have already admitted it had something to do with you and the boy. I already suspected as much. One of my scouts spied you hiding beside the road near to where the Akwamu lay dead."

I was alarmed by the fact I had been spotted near the dead Akwamu, but tried not to show it outwardly. So he knew for sure that I was involved. It didn't matter. I had already admitted as much. I hoped they were not his friends or colleagues. I could just try to placate this bastard, but I was still mad as haggis piss o'er the fact he had taken Kofi too. Scottish emotion took over.

"You are going to kill me and my friend anyway. You obviously work with the Akwamu. I'm not sure what difference it makes now whether I finish the tale or not." I was beginning to think my strategy of stalling was never going to work. If he held Kofi captive, we were both knee deep in a hog wallow. I had only served to keep us alive for a couple of days after capture. I suspected he would kill us both as soon as I quit talking.

"You have spent the better part of a day and a half telling me your entire life story. It is only fitting that I hear how the tale has ended. Don't withhold the finale from the audience." He laughed at his own wee joke.

I glared at him and my lips barely masked my contempt. I thought about it for a minute, but realized there was really no option but to stick to the complete truth at this point and finish the story. If he had Kofi, I was powerless to do anything to help my companion, and escape was pointless if it meant sending my friend to his doom.

"No, I will tell you everything. I was just trying to protect my home village from a future slaving party, but there is no hope for em' if you wish my friends harm. They're doomed anyway."

"You misunderstand my motives and my position in the Ashanti. I do not wish to harm your native friends in the village, unless of course they are helping you spy on my activities. But I must know everything you know. If there are other spies to be apprehended, they must be flushed out of their hiding places."

His assurances regarding Kofi and his fellow villagers did not leave me much comfort, but I had little choice.

"I ask you again, what was the name of the village and how did you arrive there?"

"It is named Tontokrom, and if you give some slack to your reigns and permit me to continue, I will explain how I came to call it home."

He glanced at one of the two natives behind me
and I saw that one nodded at the sound of Tontokrom.
He must know of it. The Portuguese man then waved
his hand for me to go on.

"The long hours and back breaking work at the
mining site, with intense heat, thick humid air and
constant swarming o' mosquitoes took its toll on me. I
became weaker and weaker as the months wore on,
until one day my piss turned blood red when I relieved
myself. I remember when I finally decided to head to
Kumasi to find a doctor, after the Dutch boss of the
mines fired me for "laziness". I could barely stand and
couldn't lift a shovel or a pick. I hardly cared what
happened at that point, but I remember one o' the
Portuguese miners who befriended me telling me I had
to get to Kumasi to find someone to treat the fever. I
only knew that if I didn't reach a doctor soon I would die
in the jungle. I had no idea how far I had to go or how
long it would take. For two days I followed the thin trail
to the northeast, doing all I could to lift each foot in turn
to move my slender frame forward. The trip was
surreal due to my poor physical state. My mind
wandered freely as I walked. I remember marveling at
how green everything looked, so different from the
whites, browns and greys of the Scottish highlands. I
remember staring in wonder at the short hills on either
side o' the trail and wondering what lurked behind the
tall grass and dense stands o' brush and trees. The
canopy often covered the trail yielding deep shadows.
The smaller trees and bushes were dwarfed by the
occasional tall Odum trees with their thick white trunks
devoid of branches until just near their tops, which
reminded me of a woman's parasol. I stopped by

stagnant, brown pools of water to take a drink, and noticed exotic birds overhead with their strange haunting calls. I was constantly followed by a flock of black and white banded ravens. I began to feel like they were waiting for me to collapse so they could share in tearing the eyeballs from my sockets. By the third day on the trail, I fell further and further into a daze, and don't remember removing my clothes or shoes. I just remember looking down one afternoon and noticing all o' my clothes were gone. I was walking only in my undergarments. I must have made quite a sight.

Near the end, I remember seeing a dark spotted cat-like creature in front o' me on the trail, growling and hooping more like a fox. It had dark black spots, a black band across its eyes, and a bushy foxy tail, but it was twice as large as the foxes back in Scotland. I worried it was some kind o' cross between a wolf and lion. We had no lions in Scotland, but I had been told about 'em from the bible and the escapades of Daniel in the den. At that time I had ne'er seen one in the flesh. All of the miners I roomed with worried about lions at night, although no one got attacked by one. I wondered if this spotted creature in front of me was some form o' that beast. I remember the hungry look it gave me and its remorseless toothy grin as it slowly paced towards me. I remember thinking, "It won't make much of a meal o' me." And I wondered if I would ever be missed back in Scotland."

The Portuguese man interrupted me to tell me I was describing a jungle cat. "Only a jungle cat has those stripes. They are much smaller and aren't as vicious as a lion, but they have killed young children in the villages and are certainly imposing enough to do harm to someone who is already incapacitated. How did you escape?"

"I didn't really have the strength to escape. I dropped to my knees and in my stupor waited for the inevitable. I hoped it wouldn't hurt and I would pass out instead o' having to watch it devour me. I seem to remember hearing screams or yells before everything went black."

The Portuguese man stopped me again. "So you were wounded by this wild animal? Is this seeping wound on your leg from the animal attack? How did you survive? "

"Please, wait to ask your questions until you hear more. My bleeding leg wound came much later. The animal attack happened months ago. Be patient, set back in your stirrups and I will explain."

He seemed skeptical but let me continue.

"Like I told you, I fell unconscious. That seems like an age ago, now. Days or weeks went by. I don't know how long, as I was deep in sleep from exhaustion, sickness, dehydration and depths o' despair that come from wandering the jungle by yourself. I only remember the day I finally opened my eyes and slowly stirred from my long period of slumber and weakness.

I remember I had been dreaming of a bed in Bunchrew manor. I imagined I was invited to a gala put on by the Laird Lovat himself, and had stayed o'er as a guest. I was surrounded by finery, linens and the soft down feathers lining the bed of a Scottish clan chief. I could see the old thick oak in the yard, out o' the large glass window of my manor bedroom, and beyond, the shores o' the bonnie Beauly Firth. The sky was grey, as it always was, there was a slight drizzle, and white caps were visible on the water from the force o' the Scottish wind. A great, grey fuzzy dog with lean features lumbered alone along the rocks lining the bank o' the Firth, and he stopped to look at me from a distance, with his warm dark brown eyes and waggy tongue. From that great distance, I could still hear him bark twice as if to wake me. My eyes opened suddenly and I roused from that deep sleep. I realized then that I had been dreaming. I wasn't in Bunchrew House, nor was I in Scotland. There was no dog and no Firth from my homeland. The shock of awareness startled me forward."

"I'm still in the depths of Africa!" I thought to myself, with no wee measure of remorse. My thoughts then returned immediately to that large spotted cat that was pacing hungrily towards me just before my eyes closed, and I jumped in alarm. I may have even yelled out. But as the room came into focus, I realized I was no longer on the trail to Kumasi either, and I saw no animal in front o' me. I was lying on a bamboo and palm leaf cot in the corner of a tiny mud hut. Other than another Spartan sleeping surface on the adjacent wall, there was no furniture in here and no window. I looked up at the ceiling and examined the intertwined waxy green and brown leaves that made up the roof. It was raining and a steady drip, drip of water was making its way through the roof thatches onto the mud floor o' the domicile. The splash was getting me wet, but I remember thinking that at least it was warmer than rain in the highlands. My head hurt like I had placed it between a cooper's hammer and an anvil. I tried to get up but fell back suddenly from dizziness and passed out again. It was several hours before I woke to the tender hands of a young native woman, wiping my forehead with a moist cloth.

"Ye te sen." she said with a concerned look.

I blinked twice and tried to tell her I didn't understand her, or even where I was. I started to rise up but she pushed me back down onto my back.

"Wonye Asante. Yefre wo sen anaa? Wote asee anaa?" She asked again, but I could only shake my head in misunderstanding.

"Woye Portugesini anaa? She said quizzically.

That one I guessed at correctly. "No, I am not Portuguese. I'm a Scotsman, from the highlands."

That evidently meant absolutely nothing to her, as she just stared blankly at me. She reached below the cot and from the floor, picked up a wooden bowl filled with broth. It smelled somewhat putrid, like rotten flesh, but I was famished and thirsty so I drank the bowl down despite the foul odor. It tasted much worse than it smelled, like rotten meat, only with a bitter aftertaste that reminded me of tree bark. When I had finished slurping down the liquid, I looked at the bottom o' the bowl and noticed there actually were remnants of wood bits along with what looked like bones from the head of a trout. Even the poor in Scotland didn't stoop to making fish-head tree soup. I tried again to ask her where I was and how I got there, but she pinched my lips with her fingers and wouldn't allow me to speak. When she rose, I blushed slightly as I stared at her chest. I had just realized she wasn't wearing anything above the waist except a necklace of wee white shells. Her dress was made o' simple patterned brown cloth and covered only to her mid-thigh. It was tied with a cord made of some kind of plant material. Although this

attire would turn heads in the highlands, I had seen
many female captives along the African coast similarly
clothed. I wondered if she was a slave, and if so, who
she belonged to. She was in her mid- to late teens, and
her breasts were little more than oyster shells poised on
her dark lean body. My eyes lingered over her chest a
little longer than necessary and she noticed my glance
and smiled briefly. I felt somewhat ashamed that she
caught me staring at her nipples, and I forced my eyes
up to her face. She wore a thoughtful expression and
her hair was very shortly cropped in the fashion of
European fancy lads. She had a bonnie face with a
pretty little nose and a broad chin with full lips. Her
skin was dark and shiny with sweat. In the highlands
she would have been only a few years away from
marriage, but I had no idea how things worked here. I
at first thought she might have been the matriarch o'
the house. I glanced again at her breasts and her belly
and decided that she was not yet a mother, and
wondered again if she was someone's slave.

My thoughts returned to my time living along
the coast in Accra. I pitied her station in life if she was
indeed indentured. Male slaves in West Africa had a
terrible lot, but girls of her age suffered even greater
torment. Young ladies could be kept as captives from
other tribes and lived as slaves within the conquering
village. They were often molested multiple times even
before they reached their first bleed, and some of the
wee lasses were impregnated before they were old
enough to handle it. They suffered ruptures when they
delivered babies that young and many died. A worse
fate could occur if they were sold to slavers on the coast.
Those that made it to the slave ships often died in route

before ever reaching the Americas. If they did get to the colonies, they faced a life o' hard labor and torment on the plantations. There would be no potential freedom after 7 years, as was the case for the indentured Scots in the new world. Most were left to die if they became ill or injured.

She handed me a cola nut to chew on. We had these to eat back at the mining camp. The nuts had medicinal properties and made one sleepy but also provided some relief from pain. I ate one and savored its mildly bitter taste, knowing it would act on my system like a dram of whisky. She gave me a bowl of water to drink with the nut, which helped a little. The water had some leaves in it which made it taste bitter, but it quenched my thirst.

The young maiden then left through the door. I assumed she went to retrieve something or someone, but I was still extremely weak from lack o' food, and the strain of sitting up had left me completely spent. I shivered uncontrollably for a few minutes before I faded off to sleep.

I awoke again, but I did not know how long I had remained unconscious. I felt better, and at least the shivers were gone. It had apparently stopped raining as there were no longer droplets o' water filtering down on the floor o' the hut. I looked o'er in the corner to find the maiden lass was again in the room, but she had been joined by an older tall man, probably in his late thirties, wearing a thoughtful expression and the hint of a smile. He wasn't much older than me. I pulled my head up to look at him and he gazed back at me with wonder and curiosity. His teeth were perfect and brilliant white, which contrasted sharply with his extremely dark skin and dark eyes. He had just a touch of gray in his short, curly black hair and unkempt beard. In contrast to her, he was wearing an off-white woven shawl with black stripes that fit very loosely around his waist. It looked a little like a wee lasses' party dress with the sides torn out. He had a similar shell necklace to the maiden, but shorter and tighter fitting around his neck, and a matching bracelet of white shells. He had a tan linen loin cloth in place of his trousers. The combination of shawl and loin cloth would have brought a chuckle to me, if I hadn't then immediately looked down to see that I was wearing a similar outfit. I was about to ask how in laird's ghost I had got into this native dress, when I was interrupted by the man standing over me.

"Akwaaba. Tena. Me paucho." He gestured for me to sit up.

I slowly rose from the cot and braced myself along the mud wall behind me. I was sore all over, and every joint hurt like I had been beaten with slaver's sticks. The skin of my arms looked so pale I was afraid I had already died and was hallucinating all o' this, and there were dark blotches all over my skin. My gaze returned to the native man and the lass beside him.

"Thank you. For helping me. For feeding me." I didn't know what to say. I had no idea how long I had been there.

"Meda ase." I repeated it in their own tongue. It was one of the few Ashanti language words I knew and meant "thank you". They both smiled at me and nodded in understanding.

I was still disoriented, and he noticed my confusion. I wondered what had happened to the big cat? I checked all of my limbs to make sure I hadn't lost a foot or hand and nothing had been eaten. It was all there, to my relief. I put my hand to my face and felt the whiskers, the bags around my eyes and the sallowness of my cheeks.

"Wonksa. Enye. Tumba. Da." With that he made gestures like a bug flying, then landing and crawling on his arm. He then took two fingers and tapped on his wrist and looked to see if I understood. I didn't. He repeated these hand signals again and again and then put his hands to his head, closed his eyes and lay down and pointed to me. I guessed at that point that he had tried to tell me I had gotten sick from some kind of bug and fell asleep.

"Aye." I said, "Jungle Fever". I repeated his hand movements and said, "Jungle Fever."

Both he and the young lassy laughed and tried to say jungle fever, but it sounded much more like "Jongo Peebee" when it came out o' their mouths.

"Wote asea Twi anaa?" he asked, but I didn't understand much of what he said. However, my time with the slaves in the gold mining fields had made me aware of the word "Twi". It sounded more like "Chree" when they said it, but I knew it meant the name o' the dominant native tribe language in this part o' West Africa. These were the Ashanti, a proud warrior race. I had learned from other miners a little about these people and their habits. Their warrior tradition was impressive. Unfortunately, I had not yet learned much o' their native tongue.

At that time, I did not know exactly where the village I was staying in was located, but I knew it was likely to be somewhere near to the Ashanti stronghold of

Kumasi, where the king resided. Hence, the risk for being sold into slavery by competing tribes or neighboring villages was probably lessened as the village I was in was surrounded by many other Ashanti villages and near to the might o' the King's palace and army that could help defend 'em. Indeed, as I looked at the two villagers standing before me, it was hard to believe they could have anything to do with the slave trade. They looked like farmers who knew nothing of war or unsavory activities founded on greed, like human abduction and bondage. In any case, they were kind enough to help me out.

"Wote asea Twi anaa?" the old man asked again, breaking my momentary lapse of concentration.

"I'm sorry. What. Oh, well, uh.......Debi, Debi Twi." I said in a pitiful attempt to use their tribal language. I was trying to tell him I didn't speak or understand his native tongue.

I can speak Gaelic, English and some French, as could most highlanders, but I had no talent for native dialects. Much of it sounded like bird chirping. African miners were fond of saying "debi, debi" which meant "no, no", but that and a handful of other phrases was about the total extent o' my Twi language skills. The native lass giggled at my ineptness and the clumsy use of her language. The older man eyed me nervously and smiled, but his grin seemed forced.

After some pointless exchanges of English, Gaelic and Twi, the native girl went outside and soon returned with a bowl o' some more awful smelling fish head- tree bark soup.

I waved her off and said again, "Debi, debi!"

The man shook his head and countered, "Ani,

wonom". He pointed at the bowl and then said "enye. Tumba." He slowly went through the same pantomime routine with his fingers making the stinging bug on his arm.

I didn't really want any more o' the bloody fish-head tree bark soup I had previously tasted, and doubted the concoction would help any ailment, much less jungle fever, but he persisted until I drank the entire draught again. After the bowl of nastiness was finished, he gave me some yellow fruit that looked like an apple but had soft orange meat. I devoured it, and he brought me another. After that I was given another medicinal cola nut. When I was finished I could barely keep my eyes open, much less stay upright, but it suddenly occurred to me again that I had almost been eaten by a large cat-like creature. Had I been dreaming that in my weakened state? I asked him about it by doing the same pantomiming he had demonstrated. I put my hands up in front of me like talons and growled and hooped as I remembered the 40 pound cat did when it wanted to eat me. I made a mask with my fingers and tried to demonstrate a bushy tail. I pointed outside, and then asked "Where? How did I escape the bush cat?"

"Ahhhhhaaaaa. Kakanii." The man said with sudden understanding, as he gave me another toothy smile.

He said a whole lot of words that I couldn't begin to try to pronounce as he described what happened, but of course I didn't understand a word of it. At least until he got up and went to the door and grabbed a big spear. He yelled loudly in a voice that seemed to harken to the screaming I remembered hearing just before I passed out, and then proceeded to show me how he had stabbed it several times. Apparently when it tried to run off, he had thrown the spear and he pointed to his own chest to show where the spear had punctured the cat. He grinned widely at me and then pointed to the soup bowl below me.

"wo di Kakanii."He pointed again at the bowl and said "wo nom".

I was reasonably sure I was going to be sick at that moment. From what I gathered of what he had just said, I surmised that I was eating bush cat stew and from the smell of it, the beast was sacrificed more than a few days ago. I had been asleep with weakness for most of that time. Bile rose up in my throat and I burped bitterly o' the fish-head and bush cat tree soup. It was not long before I gagged again and heaved several bits of dark fluid onto the floor by the cot. I was still really weak with Jungle Fever, and the effort o' communicating had sapped what wee strength I still possessed. I passed out soon after and woke again the next day, where I was literally force fed another bowl o' the bitter bark concoction. A large ankle bone was sitting in the soup this time, with bits of raw flesh hanging from it, and the smell was even ranker than it had been the previous day. Fortunately, there was also a great deal more bitter bark in it, which actually made the taste slightly more bearable. Surprisingly, I felt stronger and could at least sit up, if nigh get to my feet.

That evening I was introduced to a young lad, slightly older than the native girl, but still only in his late teens. He apparently also lived (or at least slept) in this hut. At first I thought the young man might have been her beau or husband, but from the way they acted and spoke to each other, it became clear very quickly that they were brother and sister. The young lad was tall and thin and lightly built. He was dressed in a shawl-like dress of tan with black stripes that extended to his knees and was slit on the side. He was bare-chested and barefooted but had a shell bracelet and a leather necklace with what looked like a large animal tooth hanging from it at his chest. His hair was black and wiry, closely cropped and his dark eyes peered deeply into mine. He had no hair on his face, and it made his eyes shine ever that more brightly.

He pointed to his chest and said, "Me ye Kofi. Ye frewo sen? ".

I thought I understood part of that, since many male Ashanti are given only one of 7 names, based on the day of the week they were born. Kofi was a common name for a laddy born on Friday. He was telling me his name and likely asking mine.

"Ahhh. Me ye Alexander." I pointed to my chest.

"Al –zander." He said slowly. He grinned at me and reached for my hand in greeting, but when I tried to shake it in the standard Scottish fashion he withdrew it confused. Instead, he took my hand and clasped it thumb to thumb as if we were doing highland arm wrestling. He then grinned and said "Akwaaba madanfo". I repeated the gesture and the word "madanfo", hoping it meant something like friend or guest, and not "we are going to put you in a pot and eat you tonight."

The native lass pointed to her own chest, and said "Amma".

I repeated "Amma" and pointed to her chest in understanding. I tried not to look at her breasts when I did so, but my eyes passed o'er her nipples anyway and I blushed despite myself.

She grinned widely and said, "Ani. Ahhaaaa. Me ye Amma."

It was also a common name, given to one of the female grace born on Saturday. Their father was apparently a traditionalist.

I glanced around again at the room and wondered what village I was in, or if there even was a village surrounding this house. I had not been outside yet, and could only see jungle through the open doorway. I hoped again that there weren't any cannibals in the Ashanti."

Chapter 6: The Village of Tontokrom

"For several more days I slowly gained my strength and with the help o' the tree bark soup and cola nuts (I made 'em forego the bush cat and ate fruit and rice instead), I could wander outside o' the hut and enjoy the open air. I didn't have the strength yet to explore the village, but I at least saw that it consisted of huts on a large hill. My appetite increased daily. I could finally stand up and walk far enough outside of the hut to look out past the village and to reach the trees to relieve myself without falling. One afternoon, I stood behind one of the giant palm trees and pissed for what seemed like minutes. The urine was dark, but at least it no longer looked like the color o' blood. My hands were actually shaking when I was finished, either from the relief or just from continued weakness. I breathed in my surroundings as I closed my eyes. The air was cloudy with the smoke o' village fires. They seemed to keep the fires burning all of the time, at least a wee ember by each hearth. I didn't know if the constant fires were for cooking, for heat (it was certainly hot enough for me at night even without the fires) or to keep wild animals at bay. I noticed it also had the added benefit of keeping the number of flies and mosquitoes down. The hut that belonged to Kofi, Amma and their

father was located at the far end o' the village, which
was why I could not see any other huts from the door.

It was really the first chance I had to explore my
surroundings. I looked off to the southwest and gazed at
the huts in more detail. Most other houses in the
village were just like the one in which I was staying.
They were simple one story, one room structures with
thatched roofs made with some kind o' palm or wide tree
leaves. They were composed o' mud bricks made from
the dark red soil on which the village stood. There were
chickens, sheep and goats running freely all around the
village, and several wee children wondered about. It
really wasn't that different than the highland villages I
grew up in.

A well was present in the village center that was
lined above ground by a circular expanse of large rocks.
It had a wooden bucket attached to a rope-like vine of
some kind sitting beside it. At various times throughout
the day there would be a woman dipping the water into
the bucket and then pulling it up and pouring it into her
own large shallow bowl. She would then put her own
bucket atop her head and carry it to one o' the huts. I
was amazed by the size and weight o' the objects the
women put on their head and carried. They carried as
much as the highland donkeys put on their backs.

There were about 30 of these wee houses placed
in a clearing embedded deep within the jungle, which
was surrounded by a grove of banana trees, cassava
bushes and beyond that, a low swampy area which
looked like a rice paddy. To the other side there was a
broad stand of banana trees and short broad leafed trees
that provided the cola nuts from large brown pendulous
fruit. I could also make out a few trees with round

yellow fruit on branches, and some shorter trees resembling palms that held clusters of a delicious orange fleshed fruit they called "popo". The village sat atop a ridge of high ground, but a larger or higher hill covered with dark green foliage rose behind it to the southeast. A creek could be discerned in a swampy lower valley between the village and the hill beyond, which is where the rice was grown. The forest was thick, but not impenetrable, and except for the snakes and wild beasts, I could imagine heading out cross country and through the swampy terrain to see what was atop the hill above.

My thoughts were interrupted by the strange call of a bird to my right. It made a series o' seven to ten loud tweets, would then pause, then sing another set of identical tweets and this was repeated again and again. I struggled to see it in the brush until it lifted from its perch and flew directly o'er me. It was a large bird, but smaller than a falcon or hawk. It was white and grey and had a huge pale curved beak which dwarfed the rest of its body. I don't remember seeing any such bird when I worked in the gold mines, but then I was usually pre-occupied with a shovel and pick, and my head was almost always facing the ground. The mine fields didn't have any trees in any case, as they were always burned down before we started turning the dirt and working the slew. I saw another few colorful birds including a little starling shaped bird with a bright red body and black wings, and several swarms of brightly golden sparrows that flittered wildly around the trees. A bright blue bird with a bright orange beak sat atop one o' the huts in front. I thought how beautiful things were there with birds with their fancy plumage, and all o' the trees with their flowering fruit.

I noticed a collection of adult African men at the other end o' the village, which included the tall older man who had protected me from the bush cat and the younger man named Kofi who I believed was his son. They saw me and yelled something unintelligible, and gestured for me to come forward. I moved slowly and cautiously along the well-worn dirt path, past several other huts and a corral made of wooden stumps that held some goats, and one o' the skinniest cows I had ever glanced upon. There were a few dogs sniffing around for scraps. When I finally arrived at the group o' men, Kofi came up to me and put his arm around me. I must have looked a little shaky.

"Akwaaba Al-zander" was shouted in a cacophony of hellos from all around me, and all o' the men swarmed up to me at once, and each shook my hand in the manner that the young man had done previously. Each man in turn slowly and carefully tried to give me their names, including several middle names and a last name, but I got lost after 4 or 5 words and had no idea who was who or called what. Except for the younger man who shared his hut with me. Before he could give me his name again, I pointed at his chest and said, "Kofi!"

That seemed to make everyone laugh and they all patted me on the back for my clever insight and there was another round of "Akwaaba". When it came time to reacquaint myself with the father who was my host, he told me his names, but I missed most of the words (which seemed to go on and on), but I caught "Japhet". I would try to call the older man that name whenever we met again. It bothered me to keep referring to him as the older man, since he was probably about my own age and neither of us had yet reached our fortieth year. I had a lot of grey hair despite my relatively young age, and I thought it was he who should be calling me the "older man". Maybe he did call me that. I wondered if "Akwaaba" was the Twi term for "old white man." I pointed around at all of the houses and tried to ask what the name of the village was. It was important to me to know where I was at. After several miscues, one finally understood my question and what I was pointing at and said, "Tontokrom". I smiled back. "krom" was usually the term for city and many village names in the Ashanti ended like that. My home was now Tontokrom.

Since there was virtually no room in Japhet's hut to sleep with three occupants living there already, only a few weeks after I arrived I moved into one o' the older huts which had been abandoned. It lacked a roof and one wall, and was being occupied by a couple of goats, but within a few days, I had replaced the thatch roof and added a fresh wall of baked mud bricks. Unfortunately, I did not share the native skill of thatching, and my roof leaked badly the first time it rained and I got soaked. The cottages in the highlands had peat for roofs, and I would have had much better luck with some highland building materials and tools I was used to. Fortunately, Kofi and Amma pitied me again. With their father's help, they replaced my ceiling with one that was far more water tight. Apparently not only the size and type of palm fronds were important for this purpose, but also the particular way they were weaved together. Their skill and speed in such things were a marvel to watch.

My strength improved steadily over the ensuing weeks until I could run at a good clip and had my color back. I hadn't had any tree bark soup in several days and my headaches were gone. Once or twice a week Amma would make redred, a porridge made o' beans and peppers, which I loved, and often we would have bananas cooked in palm oil, which was also delicious.

Several more uneventful weeks went by in the Tontokrom village. I helped where I could, making and carrying mud bricks to repair huts damaged by the force of constant spring rains, digging trenches to allow the sewage to drain from the village where there was a communal latrine, and harrowing and pulling foliage in the wet swampy rice paddies. I learned many new skills, including trapping bats at night for food and stripping away the bark of the Kyenkyen tree to harvest material for clothing. I refrained from cleaning the bats or eating the nasty creatures, even when cooked, since they closely resembled the rats we had back in the highlands. I worried they carried some kind of plague. The villagers loved 'em. The Kyenkyen (pronounced chen chen) bark was shaved off in long wide strips, pounded until soft and didn't require spinning like the wool back home in Scotland. It lacked color, and most patterns were either the natural white or light cream tan color, or geometric variations of black and off-white that were made from a natural ink. I wore my Kyenkyen cloth every day.

I slowly picked up some of the native Twi language, and what I couldn't say or understand I could make out with hand gestures. Over time, the people in the village and I began to understand and converse with each other. At least once every two weeks there would

be a festival of some sort, which involved eating
something unusual, drinking copious amounts of a
milky white beverage that didn't get you drunk but
made your mouth numb, and lots of singing and
dancing. This village really liked their dancing and
some women were amazingly good singers as well. The
singing was always accompanied by the beat o' drums
from the men. We also had drummers in the highlands,
but the Ashanti seemed to delight in drumming of any
kind and used it for every occasion. Sometimes at these
festivals a fetish priest would come from a nearby
village to bless someone or to help heal an ailment. He
would wear a terrifying wooden mask that was in the
figure of a demon and he would dance around even more
vigorously than the local villagers. As I understood it,
the Ashanti believed in a single supreme God they call
"Nyame", but they had other lesser deities or angels
they called "obosom" that inhabited certain buildings in
the region that priests lived in. I never quite understood
to what angel this priest was inclined to or how the
magic was supposed to work. He was highly venerated
by the inhabitants of Tontokrom and they welcomed his
visits with great fervor.

The Portuguese man interrupted me again. "Yes,
we have had dealings with many priests like him. If
they can be persuaded with money or gifts, they can be
quite helpful in garnering favors from the local village
chieftains. I have utilized their talents in my own
ways."

He paused for a moment, and finally said, "It
seems you really cared for these people as if they were
your own family. You do surprise, Mr. Fraser. Tell me
more of life in the village. How did you adjust to life as

an Ashanti farmer?"

I perceived the Portuguese man's tone had definitely softened and he seemed to be genuinely interested in my time as a native. It did not go unnoticed that he had referred to me as "Mr. Fraser". I didn't know what that meant. Was he being kind or just mocking me again? His tone was definitely different and not as harsh towards me. As I answered him, he kept shaking his head in disbelief as I described my encounters in Tontokrom.

"I was treated just like one of the village men. I might even have taken a wife if one had been available. Amma was easy to look at, if a little young, but all of the other women were already betrothed." This statement was not entirely a true representation of my feelings for the girl, but I was not going to delve into my lustful thoughts and emotions with this stranger. They were none o' his business.

"I remember one morning I was asked by Japhet to join the men on one of their frequent hunting trips into the forest. It was the first o' many such forays I did with village men. Most o' the time they came back from these hunting trips with a deer-like creature or small rodents, which they cooked up for the village as a group feast. I was thrilled to have the opportunity to get away from Tontokrom and see the surrounding countryside. Japhet tried to hand me a long pointed lance, but I was a rather poor shot with the spears they used for killing prey. Instead, I chose a short, thick and wide straight blade they used as hacking swords to cut away dense foliage along game trails. They were sharp enough to easily cut bamboo into thin lengths. These bladed weapons reminded me of some o' the short swords we used in the highlands, if not a wee bit smaller and thicker. The blade was about as wide as one's hand, had a curved tip and the hilt consisted of two rounded wooden orbs with a skinny flat piece in between, where the hand rested. The hilt was made out of one piece of wood from the fiber tree, and was quite hard but lighter than oak. The blade was embedded fast and far into this handle.

I had for days began practicing swordplay with one o' these straight blades, and had modified the blade handle by whittling down the wooden orbs on the hilt so that it was easier to manipulate at speed, and more closely resembled swords I was used to handling. The week before, I had found soapstone and a flint in the forest and had sharpened the edge to a fine line. The flint also had the advantage, when combined with a borrowed iron arrow tip, for using as a fire starter. When the other men saw my choice of weaponry they were amused and laughed openly. They seemed confused as to how I was to catch prey without a spear. I don't suppose they ever hunted with a short sword. I really had no idea what I was doing with this type of hunting. However, I was more comfortable with a blade in my hand than with a pike or halberd, and I wasn't even sure what kind of game we were going after. I just knew it would be more fun than loitering around the village huts. We marched as a group for a few miles on a thin game trail through the forest. The vegetation was incredibly dense and the trail was difficult to follow. I used the blade to clear some of the brush.

We were accompanied by three dogs from the village. These were not the large majestic deerhounds o' the highlands, which could bring down a stag and were swift o' feet. These were wee, light brown, short haired mutts that were sized little more than a barn cat. I was unsure how much help they would be in a hunt. They looked as if they hadn't eaten much in months, but all three dogs seemed excited and happy to be in the hunting party, with tails a waggin'. They stayed right with the man in the lead and never wavered from the trail.

I was glad I had the blade to clear some of the tall grass and branches. There were many waist-high, nasty nettles that held troublesome barbs that stung horribly and drew welts. I wondered why the others were not similarly bothered until I heard one of the men, named Yeboah, curse and pull out some thorny stems from his legs. That brought chuckles from the group, but for the most part everyone remained quiet for the length of the hike. After an hour, we entered into a clearing where there was no canopy of trees and the underbrush was only knee high.

I noticed that another young laddy, to whom everyone called Kakra because he was short, had brought along a bow and quiver of arrows. It was short and light, as compared to those I had fought with in the highlands. The arrow tips were formed from sharpened stone rather than metal, but it looked lethal enough. The shafts appeared to be made of thin strands of bamboo. I was unsure of the material of the drawstring. I gestured for him to show his weapon to me.

"Yaso. Eye ho ye." he said as he showed me the bow, telling me it was a good piece of work, and he handed me an arrow. All of the men then crowded around and pointed at a nearby stump. I think they wanted to see whether I could hit a target with it. I notched an arrow

to the string and ineptly dropped it as I was pulling
back. It was not my fault as the back of the arrow had
two feathers but virtually no notch to hold the shaft in
place, as opposed to the long bows with which I was
trained as a lad. It didn't stop the men from some more
good natured laughs at my expense. I tried again and
drew back as far on the bow as I dared. My release was
accurate this time, and at least I hit the stump, if not a
little low and to the right. Kakra retrieved the arrow
and patted me on the back.

"Wo ho eye." He said, inferring I did well.

"Meda ase." I thanked him in reply.

At this point, Japhet and three others started
moving to the far side o' the clearing. I tried to follow,
but Kakra and Kofi both grabbed me and gestured for
me to remain there. I watched as the other men split up
and followed separate paths spreading out to the left
and right They soon disappeared through the brush,
with the dogs all staying with the man in the lead, who
took the middle path. We waited for quite some time
before I heard rustling in the bush beyond the clearing.
The men in the distance were yelling and coming this
way, judging by the increasing volume of their voices
and the nearby barking o' the dogs. All at once, a very
large hog came crashing through the brush, squealing at
the top of its lungs. I called it a hog, as if it bared
resemblance to the wild pigs we hunted in Scotland, but
this was an 80 pound African warthog. I had seen, and
even eaten these in my time with the miners, but most
had been wee piglets. This was a large ugly animal
with grey hair that was covered in mud and had a short
tail with a coal black tuft of hair at its end. A similar
black tuft of hair ran in a line along its head and neck.

Two large tusks were protruding from its snout. It was running right at us. Kakra and Kofi were hiding behind brush on either side o' the trail and did not yet show themselves. Warthogs were not particularly vicious except when cornered, but judging by the sharp tusks and huge heads, they could inflict nasty wounds if one strayed too close to their mouth.

Two of the dogs had moved to both sides o' the hog and were keeping it from veering away from the trap by constant barking and nipping at the warthog's legs. The other dog and the men were running behind the hog with spears raised. As if on cue, the two younger men near me rose up in unison, and the spear and an arrow were driven into each side of the hog before it even realized it had been surrounded. It turned around quickly to back away from the three of us (I had now also stood up and was brandishing my blade), but the animal was confronted with a flurry of 3 spears being forced at it from the other direction. It squealed loudly and long, as two spear thrusts hit their mark. It turned again and ran right at me, an arrow visible piercing its shoulder and two or three deep gashes visible on its body. I had a momentary rush o' fear as the hog turned slightly and was close enough to brush me with its whiskers. I swung the blade hard and caught it across its shoulder with a deep gash that almost removed the right front leg. At the same time, Kakra had let loose another arrow. The warthog fell to the earth on its side but not before it gave me a slash of its own with a tusk to my shin. That was going to hurt, but the exhilaration of the hunt kept me from barely noticing the blood trickling down my leg onto my feet and woven sandals. For a few moments, I was transported back to the highlands, back to my youth, when I remembered hunts with my father and our own dogs. Before war, before prison, before slave ships and hard labor in mining camps.

The cheers and whoops from the village men and loud barking from the dogs brought me back to reality. I think they decided that I must bring luck, because we got a warthog on my first hunt. They were not easily caught. We tied the hog to two spears and it was carried between four men back to the village to butcher. The dogs never shut up on the entire trip back, eager with anticipation for some entrails once the carcass was opened. Everyone was in great spirits, and after smoking the hog o'er a large fire pit for several hours, everyone in the village shared in the bounty o' the hunt. I enjoyed the meat immensely. It was gamey and tough, but the flavor was not as strong as I expected and much better than bush cat."

My reflections on my first hunt were cut short. "Is that the scar from the warthog?" interrupted the Portuguese man. He pointed to the large long raised, pale red mark on the front of my shin. It was not far from a recent wound on my thigh that was scab encrusted and still oozed blood.

"Yes. Amma tended to my leg, after putting a few coats of red mud on it to stop the bleeding and carefully rinsing it in well water. She wrapped it in strips of Kyenkyen cloth. It healed nicely. I greatly appreciated her kind attentions and tender treatment of my wounds. I've seen battle wounds fester and rot a leg off."

"The Tontokrom villagers seemed to treat you as family."

"I was very fond of both Kofi and his sister, and their father cared for me as a brother of his own. Kofi was enthusiastic, inquisitive and eager to prove his maturity, and he was devoted to his family and village. He and I enjoyed spending time together and we became fast friends. Japhet is a loving father, and his family and community ties were strong. Their compassion is ingrained in their nature. It was a supreme act of kindness to take me in and treat my ills. I have not traveled beyond the borders of Scotland and England, except as a prisoner and my travails in the Ashanti, but it seems that these primitive people could teach cultured aristocrats a lot about love and compassion."

The Portuguese man shook his head in disgust and disagreement. "Most natives, especially in the Ashanti bush, are too stupid to teach us anything. They lack the conviction of the white European and will never understand those types of emotions. They can fight, they can fuck, and they can be trained to do simple tasks, but they do not share our intellect or capacity to love. They have their place." He looked up at the two natives beside me but said nothing more.

I was not surprised by his answer. The Europeans I had met in Africa acted, for the most part, superior and condescending. If they heeded the natives at all, they tended to disrespect 'em. They treated all natives as slaves, even the village elders and the local chieftains. The whites underestimated the depth of personality in the villagers and always would. This man probably felt the same about the Scottish. The same way the English always had. I knew different. I saw the clever ways the villagers solved problems without the use of many of our tools. I observed that they were generally happy people with happy lives. Probably happier than the arse that sat cross-legged in front of me. Before I got angry again and said something rash to my captor, I decided to restart my story.

"Several months went by as I became more comfortable in my African home and I joined their hunting parties more and more often. The villagers accepted me and did not appear to have any expectations of my leaving. Kofi and I became as brothers, and I taught him several sword fighting moves. We practiced daily. He began to carry a short blade like mine rather than a spear, and would often copy some of my speech, even if he didn't know what the words meant. O'er time, he became as proficient as I with a sword, despite his young age. He gained prowess among the village with both the blade and the bow during the weekly hunts in the forest. He started wearing a set of bird feathers in his headdress, fancying himself a true Ashanti warrior. Many other village men also came to me for weapons training, and we practiced trading blows with spears. I taught the men the basic blocks, thrusts and counters I had learned when using English and Scottish pikes back in my soldiering days. I hoped I gained their respect as a warrior, and at least I was trying to repay their kindness. I thought that if slavers ever came, perhaps with the training I gave they could defend themselves against enemy war parties.

After several months, I finally decided it was time to leave the village and go seek my destiny elsewhere. I was bored and driven to thirst for something that could not be quenched in Tontokrom. I needed to make a name for myself, or at least make some money. I couldn't do that in this village. I think I was homesick above all, and missed family and the comfort of women. I had no idea where I was headed in the short term, or what I would do when I got there. Somehow I needed to find a way to eventually return to Scotland, and it was ne'er going to happen if I remained in an Ashanti village for years onward. I didn't want to return to a life of doing odd jobs in the big coastal cities, and I had no intention o' going back to the gold fields or joining the slave traders, but I needed to earn enough farthings to somehow book passage back to Europe. I would find a job on the coast for just long enough to make a few pounds. I thought that if I could get to France, perhaps I could then make it back to Scotland on one of the many frigates moving freight across the channel from Calais. I hoped by this time, my name and crimes against the English would be forgotten and I could live a quiet life among the heathers and glens of Culbokie, along the firth with my clansmen. I would never see my father again, but I still had family that I longed to be with, and hoped that I would be able to see my sister, mother and the land o' the Frasers again."

Chapter 7: Journey through the Bush

"When the day finally came and I decided to leave the village, I was not alone. Kofi was outside of the hut waiting for me, packed, with a knapsack of fruit and berries, a gourd canteen of water, and both a sword on his belt and his own bow and quiver around his shoulder. He was wearing his best (and only) striped cloth shawl draped o'er his upper body, and had a hunter's kilt-like loin cover below, all made from the Kente cloth of the Kyenkyen tree. The villagers called the shawl a "fugu", but I didn't know exactly what that referred to. It was considered their most fashionable dress, and an indication of status and respect. He wore the sandals typical of Tontokrom adult men, and had his warrior's feathers on his head.

He addressed me in his own broken English dialect. "Al-zander go. Kofi go too." He smiled then said, "You….See! mete Borofo." the latter statement implying in half English and half Twi that he spoke English and therefore would have no problems accompanying wherever my travels led.

"Debi, Debi, Kofi" (No, No Kofi!). I tried to explain in short English sentences and broken Twi that I didn't know where I was going, that it would be dangerous, that he needed to stay with his father and sister. I was also very aware of the tradition amongst the Ashanti for a young lad about to reach manhood to leave his village and go on a great quest to achieve a name for himself. I think Kofi had decided this was his opportunity to prove his courage and virility. I was not surprised when Japhet ambled up to both of us as we were arguing at the edge o' the village. He smiled and took my hand as if to say goodbye, then placed it in the hand of his son. He pointed at Kofi, then pointed at me, and said, "Al-zander ne Kofi, wo' m'adanfo", which I now knew meant we were friends. He then just said "Wo kor", meaning "you go".

I considered all of my options for returning to the highlands, and I couldn't figure one choice which would have included a teenage Ashanti companion, however mature. Since I couldn't really speak more than 50 words in their language, it was virtually impossible to talk either of them out o' this and I knew it. I eventually resigned myself to have Kofi accompany me. I shook Japhet's hand in the Ashanti manner, and simply said "Meda ase" for "thanks". There was no way to thank him properly for all that he had done for me during the past several months. He had saved my life, and received nothing in return. Now he was gladly sending his son with me on a trip to hell knows where.

As I started to turn around and move toward the trail back to where I thought Elmina and the coast were located, we were interrupted by someone yelling behind us. Amma was running toward us at full speed, and yelling loudly waving her arms. Tears were flowing freely down both cheeks. She wrapped her arms around her brother and kissed him several times and then did the same to me. I blushed crimson at her display of affection. I hugged her back and then hugged Japhet once again before we proceeded down the trail."

"You were attracted to this girl." It was a statement rather than a question.

"I cared for her, but as I told you she was young."

"And you never took her or the other village women to bed?" He seemed dubious.

"I never really had an opportunity to do so, nor the desire." This was not true at all, but I wasn't going to offer anything further. I told him I could definitely see the advantages of having a wife around, but life's turmoils had intervened.

"You've never been betrothed?" he asked, surprised considering my mature age.

"No one is interested in a poor miner, and especially one that was a convict."

I had never had the time to consider settling down with one of the neighboring lasses in Culbokie, always thinking there would be time to start a family when I had finally established my own farm. That never happened. I had reached my late thirties with no prospects, no farm, and in the recent past, I was living like a native in a foreign land. Amma was much younger than me, but she was pretty, and she seemed to brighten when in my presence. She was quiet and caring, with a strong maternal drive. I never knew what had happened to her mother, but it was obvious that Amma had taken on that role since she was but a young lass. I had really liked her, and I had to admit to myself that I was attracted to her, but my chances had past when I left the village. Maybe I would find another pretty young native here in Africa, but I wasn't sure I was going to get the opportunity. Outside of Tontokrom, most native women were fearful around whites and trysts were limited to whorehouses and mating between owners and their young slave girls. That latter thought disgusted me for some reason. Was it the difference in races? I decided that wasn't the problem. Many of the miners in Guinea Propria had bed the native women without a second thought and the thought of sex with natives didn't bother me. No, I think it was the idea of forcing oneself on a servant. It went back to my highland disdain for slavery and domination. Rape was rape, and not the kind of lovemaking I desired. I did long for the company of a woman. If I thought about it very hard, (and at night alone in my hut sometimes I did), I decided I would be just fine with a nubile, bonnie young wench who smiled and looked cute, even if she was a native. She didn't need to understand anything or even open her mouth to speak. I thought I would relish the possibility of a future tryst with one of these bare-chested village women. Aye, I realized again that I would have liked to take Amma to bed, but lamented again that I had missed my chance when I left Tontokrom. As I silently considered those possibilities in my head, I realized it was probably lucky I had not consummated the relationship with Kofi's sister. It was not really just her age that had kept me from a randy tumble with her. The friendship I shared with her father and brother was one I didn't want to lose, and a brief romp in the heather might have complicated things to the point of souring our ties. Although she might have been willing, it was respect for Japhet that had probably held me in check, and prevented a rash act that might have ruined our family-like friendship. I was relieved again that I had not brought her shame or disgrace due to a casual romantic encounter. I wondered if I would ever see her again. It occurred to me in a flash that I might not see anyone ever again. My daydreaming was broken suddenly as I looked into the face of my captor. He was staring and probably wondering what I was pondering in silence. Of course, I expressed none of these feelings of lust and longing to the Portuguese man, but he probably could guess at where my memories led. My affections were none of his business, but he had obviously noticed that I had been thinking hard on something and it was a little awkward that we had not spoken out loud in over a minute or longer.

"We'll forgo the explanation of your sparse love life. Tell me of your journey from the village here. This is the part of your tale I have been waiting for."

"We wanted to make our way to Elmina. I had only a vague idea of how to get to the coast, but looking at the sun through the gray clouds o'erhead, and knowing Tontokrom had to be northwest of Accra, we headed down the trail back towards the mining camps of the southern Ashanti with the morning sun to our left front. The mining camp that I had worked in had been located west of Obuasi. That meant Tontokrom should be located a few days walk north and somewhere between Obuasi and Kumasi and to the west. I thought if I could get to Obuasi, I reasoned there should be a well traveled road we could follow south to Accra or Elmina.

As we started off on our trek, Kofi was absolutely beaming with excitement. I am not sure where he thought he was going or if he had any measure of how long we would be gone, but he seemed carefree and unconcerned about any perils we would face. He was singing and chanting and taking note of everything he saw.

We travelled with good speed and covered a lot o' territory in the first several hours. The trail at first snaked south and then headed more to the east. I figured we were well on our way to Obuasi. Kofi abruptly stopped me in my tracks in the late afternoon. He noticed movement in the trees and raised his bow with arrow drawn. We slowly made our way to the moving trees, when we spotted two large gray forms grazing on two medium sized fig trees. They were elephants! I had heard of elephants when I was a wee lad in Scotland, as the legendary beasts involved in the Punic wars of Carthage and Rome. These were the colossal creatures that the famous general Hannibal had used to traverse the Alps and win victory against the Roman Legions. I had always thought they were myth until I was reminded again while mining. One o' the Dutch miners told a story about a friend who had been trampled to death by elephants while panning by himself. He tried to explain to me how large the beasts were, and describe their attributes, but I failed to believe him. Now, here I was in the African bush and I was face to face with two of these huge creatures. Their long snouts were muscular and used as arms to tear leaves off low hanging branches. Their color was almost red from mud staining on their bodies, and which matched the color o' the surrounding earth. I was fascinated and could have stayed and watched for hours, but for a look of warning from Kofi. The larger o' the two beasts had noticed us and gave a trumpet-like call and they were both grunting and turning to face us. Their ivory tusks gleamed brightly in the midday light, and I was reminded o' the wound I received from the tusks of the warthog months before. That hog had only weighed as much as one leg of these creatures and the tusks were less than a tenth o' the size of the elephants' two amazing protruding tusks.

"Che!" he yelled, and I didn't take any time to translate in my head as we both ran as fast as we could down the trail. I heard a trumpet call and some grunting, but I never looked back to see if the elephants were following. My legs were moving as fast as a céilidh piper's fingers. I was filled with fear and excitement at the same time, and I never slowed. After several minutes, we were both out o' breath and we finally had to stop. I was panting madly and I needed a drink of water. We pulled the cork on a gourd flask and shared a draught of cool liquid between us. I tried to tell him how impressed I had been with the creatures, but he seemed to be more concerned and frustrated with himself that he had not figured out what they were before approaching so close. A few missteps and we could have been trampled. After a few minutes we continued down the trail.

Before long we had crossed a large trail with a well-worn dirt red surface that headed in a more north-south direction. We turned right to move toward the coast and walked somewhat more leisurely for another two hours. At length, I decided my legs could not take much more exercise for the day and we halted just off road; in a clearing that looked like it had been a way stop for many travelers heading on this route.

We were about to go to sleep for the evening as the sun had set and twilight creeped in, when we heard a low rumble in the distance to the south. I was not particularly concerned as it sounded like thunder. I looked up to notice that there were indeed some clouds in the sky. However, lightning and thunder are actually uncommon in Ashanti as the rains tend to be more of the slow drizzle type, even in the wet season. Much different than the summer rains in Scotland. I heard the rumble again and Kofi almost jumped out of his skin. He was on his feet quickly and had picked up both spear and bow.

"Gyata!" "Gyata!" he added again for emphasis. I had no idea what that word meant, as I had never heard it used in any of my time on this continent. Was it a strange weather pattern, some animal, or some form o' human musical drum? As if on cue, we heard it again. He looked at me with wide eyes, and made his hands into claws and opened his mouth wide. "Gyata" he said again and grabbed my arm. I wondered if it was another o' the bush cats that I had encountered just before I came to the village, but I decided the bush cat I had encountered probably could not have made such a sound. We collected everything we had and he moved swiftly to the road and north away from the sound o' the rumble. I tried to stop and to explain that we were moving in the wrong direction and away from the coast, but he put his finger to my lips to quiet me. He looked terrified. I did not know what a Gyata was, but I had been on many hunts with this young man and had never seen him show fear of any kind. Whatever a Gyata was, it was bad. And it was close.

We moved as fast as we could in the dark northward along the wide trail, distancing ourselves from where we had heard the rumbling sound. After an hour the trail turned slightly to the right and headed in a more northeasterly direction. The air was clear and clean that night, but the storm clouds obscured many of the stars. I could just make out part of the big dipper constellation in the far north, and so even in the dark we could find our way. I did not like travelling at night in the jungle. I had only been on the trek for one day and I had already met elephants and heard the sound of a "Gyata", whatever that was. I tried to get Kofi to stop and make camp, but he waited until we found a clearing and a tree that he could scale. We climbed up several feet and each took a rest on the branches. I was worried that I would fall during my sleep so I kept my back against the trunk. I did not sleep well that night and woke several times. In my dreams, I kept imagining I was falling from something: sometimes a tree, sometimes a cliff, sometimes from the rampart of a castle wall. We woke again in the early morning to the rumbling sound of another Gyata far off in the distance.

Kofi was anxious as we climbed down the tree at the break of dawn and headed out again on the trail. We moved slowly and cautiously to the East towards the upcoming sunrise. The sky was a bonnie purple hue and there were clouds forming. The temperature was as it always was in the Ashanti, hot and sticky, but at this time o' the morning it was not yet uncomfortable. We walked in silence for almost an hour when Kofi stopped me again. I looked around to see if there were more elephants and I strained to see if there were any trees or bushes moving off to our side. Instead the young man's eyes were fixed in the grass to the side of the trail, where there was an outcropping of dark slate rocks.

I couldn't see anything there. He slowly put down his bow and moved even more cautiously back towards me on the trail. Kofi motioned for me to remain still. He searched the ground around the trail and finally and carefully picked up a rock about the size of my fist. In his other hand he had his flattened sword held high. He moved lightning quick back toward the rock outcropping and tossed the rock with one hand just beyond the boulders. Out o' nowhere I saw a light grey-green snake launch itself from the underbrush around the outcropping at the fallen stone, and just as quickly I watched as Kofi leapt and struck down swiftly with his blade, severing the head of the sinewy serpent. He swung the blade two more times until the snake's head was completely decapitated. I was proud of how far his abilities had progressed, and confirmed then that his prowess with the blade had probably surpassed mine. I walked up to him and examined the snake lying in front.

It was one the miners called a puff adder, one o' the more common snakes in the Ashanti. As it was packed with poison fangs, it was a snake that had killed many miners working in the camps to our west. Its triangular head was large and the fat body was almost 3 feet in length. Kofi opened its mouth to show me the fangs with his blade forcing the jaws apart. I thought we were going to leave it, but he smiled at me and picked up the body to show me.

"Wo ne Me di. Aduane ye de" he said, and then translated for me in his broken English. "You, I eat. Meat sweet." He nodded his head with a devilish grin, proud of himself for the swiftness of his battle and victory o'er the snake, and the bounty o' food we would share.

First we needed to make a fire to cook the snake.

I was glad it wasn't raining. The day was fairly clear and dry. The winter haze that accompanied the dust of the dry season was still a few months off, so one could see for miles in any direction from the hilltops. Starting a fire in the jungle can be problematic when it is raining, and wet tinder made the process difficult. The Ashanti utilized a common African tribal technique. A long thin wooden stick was placed in a flat board which contained a round hole in its center which was depressed about a half inch. The board was placed down on the ground and the long stick placed between two hands outstretched flat. The hands were then rubbed together such that the stick spun very rapidly within the depression on the flat board creating friction and heat. Wee bits of dried grass were used to spark flames. The technique works surprisingly well and is quite fast. When I tried to show the Tontokrom villagers fire starting with flint and steel, in the fashion o' the Scots, they were not very impressed, and thought the highlanders used the less efficient system. In practice, the village always had a fire going, and embers could be shared, but the bar and pestle technique was handy out in the field and when on a hunt. I was never very good at it, so I kept a flint and steel in a pouch on my belt.

I was not that thrilled with the idea of a main course of snake that day, but once we cooked the meat and tore into the flesh, I had to admit it tasted bloody good. The bones were tiny and troublesome, and I kept having to pick fragments from my teeth. We restarted the trek after finishing the snake meat. Several black and white ravens flew down and joined us in the feast, eating the leavings and picking flesh from the backbone.

I had renewed energy especially after taking another long draught o' water from my gourd canteen.

The trail was moving progressively eastward and only slightly north. I guessed that if we could cross to another trail moving south, we would have another two days of walking before we would reach Obuasi, and then a two week journey to the coast. The afternoon was uneventful. We crossed a pleasant stream where we were able to drink freely and fill our canteens. My legs were tired and I was beginning to get some blisters as the day drew to a close.

We finally crossed a wide expansive road that looked to be the main thoroughfare in this part o' the province. I guessed that Obuasi lay somewhere directly to our south, but I had no idea exactly how far that might be. As nightfall approached, I thought it safer to make camp just off to the side o' the road. We did not sleep in the trees that night, as there were none of sufficient size around to hold us both, and also because we had not heard the rumblings at all today. Hopefully the gyata had left for better hunting elsewhere.

It was very early in the morning on the next day when we heard noises and we both were awakened. There were voices on the road, and the sound of metal clanging. I rose to go see who it was and where they were going, but Kofi cautioned me still. He bade me move carefully to the road and to observe what was there. We saw several black men and women in native dress in single file one behind the other, but their necks were bound by two parallel tree trunks that acted as poles binding each person to the one behind 'em. All their wrists were bound. The poles were lashed together by several fashions of rope. In addition there were another half dozen men who had no poles about their necks, but wore leg irons on their feet that were all chained together. These dozen or so natives were being driven forward by three warriors in full battle dress. One of the warriors held a long musket in his hands, while two of the others each held spears and had knives protruding from their belts.

"Akwamu." whispered Kofi to me. He frowned and spat on the ground.

These were slavers, fresh from a war party, and they had hostages. I did not know where they were from, but the poor captives looked miserable. One o' the men at the back of the line of poles turned in our direction and both Kofi and I immediately froze. It was Yeboah from our village. When I looked closer, I could see that the woman in front of him was his very pregnant wife Pesaata. He had left the village only a few days before us to go to a neighboring village called Datano that lay to the northeast, in order to reach a midwife. There were none in Tontokrom who were versed in the arts of delivering babies, and it was the tradition of the village to go to Datano shortly before births and have the midwife help them deliver safely. It was only a three hour journey on foot, but that is certainly far enough for a woman 9 months pregnant to have to travel. I gathered from Kofi that it was safer than delivering a baby in Tontokrom.

Now they were captives of Akwamu slavers. Obviously, they had not reached their intended destination and must have been bushwhacked somewhere on the trail. Pesaata looked absolutely dreadful and in pain. She was moaning with every step. I told Kofi that we had to do something, but he was

already planning an attack in his head. I saw him draw
and shaft an arrow and move to his right, down along a
hedge line to follow the party in secret. I drew my blade
and readied myself for whatever followed.

Suddenly, Pesaata stumbled and fell to her knees
causing all o' the captives in her line to stop and wait for
her to get back to her feet. Unfortunately because of
their neck bindings, all they could accomplish was to
bend slightly, to make it a little easier for her to rise.
She stayed in a crouch, held on her feet only by the
bamboo shoots on her shoulders. The entire line of
captives were straining to maintain her weight. They
kept looking at their captors to see if they would be
whipped or beaten for her lapse. Her husband helped
lift her from just behind. One of the Akwamu took the
opportunity to walk over and slap her brutally on the
face. He then jabbed her with his spear in order to try
to make her stand up and straighten her legs. The
other warrior with the musket then turned his weapon
toward the column.

The slap was just about all Kofi could take. He
ran several steps forward and let an arrow fly. It found
its mark, hitting the slapping warrior right in his back,
but he did not go down. Kofi continued his advance, this
time with his blade held high. There was momentary
confusion as everyone in the slaver's war party was
trying to understand what had just happened. I focused
on the man with the gun. I came running right at him
as he slowly turned the flintlock in his hands to face us.
I saw him cock the trigger back and aim at me. I
watched as his finger was placed to squeeze on the
trigger.

From my service in the dragoons I knew that

there would be a musket ball hurtling toward me at any second after the musket was cocked. At the last possible instant, and as the powder charge ignited on the flintlock, I dove to my left. I heard the shot crack just above my head and to my right, missing its mark wide. I had no time for recovery, as I knew the warrior would be trying to reload. Even if he was a well-trained English soldier, it would take at least one or two minutes to pour the powder, place the ball and pack the charge. I rolled across my shoulders and back to my feet and headed back toward my foe. He realized that he had no time to reload his weapon so he grabbed the barrel o' the gun and brandished it like a club. We were on each other in seconds. He swung the musket in an arch, and I used my left arm to block the stock before it landed. I followed with a downward blow of my sword in my right hand aimed at his wrists. I was just out of range and missed, but I scared him. He pulled the musket back and held it aloft by his shoulder and backed up several feet. I quickly turned to see Kofi and noted he was busy in hand-to-hand combat with the warrior who still had an arrow protruding from his back shoulder. I didn't know where the other warrior was, but I didn't have time to scan for him, as the Akwamu in front of me noticed I was distracted and had again taken the opportunity to swing the musket like a bat. I was in too close to back away from the blow so instead I immediately dropped to my knees with my left elbow shielding my head in case the weapon came lower than expected. It swung briskly but harmlessly close o'er my head and whooshed past me. This threw the warrior's balance off and his right side became exposed. I wasted no time and brought my blade down on his back right side. I created a deep gash from his right shoulder to his hip and he cried out in pain. I followed the downswing with an arc up to my own right to block his flintlock from hitting me. Unfortunately, the parry with my smaller blade was no match for the force of the long flintlock musket being swung at full measure back across the warrior's body, and the weapon and my own blade hit me in the side of the head with enough force to knock me to the ground. He raised the musket high again and meant to hit me on the head with the stock. I surprised him by rolling to my side and then frontwards and tackling him to the ground by grabbing both legs about his hips, blade still in my right hand. He lost control o' the musket, but unfortunately, my blade was pinned under his back. His eyes were wide as he saw me on top of him. I refused to let loose o' the weapon in my right hand, and instead I punched him repeatedly in the face with my left hand. He was trying to punch me at the same time and got several blows to my face but as he had no leverage, they were not of sufficient strength to do damage. I decided my punches to his face were not doing any harm either, so I changed tactics and started punching his right shoulder with my free left hand. The shoulder wound was still bleeding profusely from the sword impact. He screamed in agony and rolled to his right to protect his wounded arm. Just enough pressure was taken off o' my own right arm that I was able to pull out the blade, slash his other arm with a downward swing of my sword blade, and follow it with a backslash across his neck. The last blow cut major vessels 'neath his jaw and he was vanquished. I rose as he gasped for breath and quickly bled to death.

I was just turning around when I felt a burning in

my thigh. The third warrior had come to help his
companion and had tried to shove his spear into me. I
had only been saved by the fact that I was rising and
turning around, and my movements had taken his aim
off slightly. Instead of going through my waist and
puncturing me through and through like a wild boar in
a hunt, the strike had glanced off o' the front of my
thigh. Although inflicting a rather long wide wound, it
was not too deep and I had not been seriously hurt. I
stumbled and turned to face my attacker. He looked
down to his dead companion and then back to me with
an intense hatred in his eyes. My leg was smarting and
a thick ooze of blood was gathering on my skin, but I
was back in the fight.

I gave out a highland yell (which was the Fraser
battle cry of "Je Suis Prest" followed by a string of
Gaelic curse words) and raised my blade high. He tried
a straight ahead thrust again, but I parried the shaft o'
the spear with a strong downward blow of my sword,
and sidestepped to the left. The thrust moved safely
past me on my right side. This was pike warfare from
the highlands and I was as comfortable in this fight as if
I was practicing with my clansmen. I made a circular
motion of my arm to my right with the blade o'er my
head then continued the swing down to my leg, so as to
wrap my right arm around his spear and trap it in the
crease of my armpit before he was able to withdraw the
thrust. I locked it there with my right arm, and
transferred the sword blade to my left hand. The
warrior looked alarmed as he realized he no longer
controlled the movement o' the spear and I was gliding
down its shaft directly toward him. I slashed at his ribs
with the blade in my left hand but wounded him only

superficially. He dropped the spear and picked the hunting knife from his belt. I let the spear fall from my right arm lock and at the same time swung upward with the blade in my left, catching him in his groin squarely. As I intended, his eyes had followed the falling motion of the spear to my right and he had briefly forgotten the danger lingering in my left hand as he greedily eyed the grounded spear. His knife was not long enough to stop the momentum of the strike from my wide blade. His eyes bugged out as he realized I had delivered a mortal blow. I had to pull the blade back with force as it lodged in the man's pelvic bone between his legs. I delivered one last arc of the blade to the man's neck for good measure. He fell lifeless to the ground. Out of breath, I turned to Kofi to see how he fared. He was repeatedly stabbing at the man's chest with a spear, although the man looked to be already dead.

"Kofi! Stop! He's dead!" He turned to me and he had tears in his eyes. I doubt he had ever felt rage like that before and I'm sure he had never fought a man to the death. He was taller but much lighter than the man he had killed. Although the Akwamu warrior fought with an arrow in his shoulder and therefore was at a great disadvantage, I was still proud of the young Tontokrom villager. He had fought and survived his first battle. Were we in the highlands, we would have shared a bottle of whisky that night and lay drunk til morning. As it was, we needed to free these captives and get off o' the road before other Akwamu followed.

I picked up the flintlock from beside the first warrior I had killed. It was a tremendous piece of workmanship and surprisingly a newer model. He also had a leather satchel bag about his waist containing musket balls, wad linens, and a nicely carved hollow goat horn filled with gun powder about his waist. I had not had the luxury of owning a flintlock for two years, so I was pleased with this new prize. I marveled at the craftsmanship of this weapon, which was better and more expensive than any I had used in the highlands. The ornately chiseled steel hammer lined up perfectly with the frizzen, so that the flint would strike directly and prevent misfires. The mechanism was beautifully curved and inlaid silver on the stock and face plate were equally ornately embossed. High quality was even evident in the roller riding on the taut spring. The flint barely scraped the face of the frizzen, meaning it would perfectly cut steel and spark well. In the satchel I found a 'cow's knee' of oiled leather to fasten around the lock area to keep out rain and moisture. Even the lead balls were well made, and the flints appeared to be of the best tan colored French variety. The warrior who had owned this weapon was either very rich or provided for by someone with a lot of money and power. There were few muskets to rival it in Europe, much less in Africa. I looked down again at the man and wondered who he was.

My attention was then drawn to a growing commotion. The captives were yelling "Kofi, Kofi, Kofi" and Yeboah was also adding "Al-zander" to their cheers. It took several minutes, but we were able to use our blades to free the men and women from the poles by cutting through the ropes that bound 'em together. Most sat down dazed and rubbed their sore necks, but others ran off immediately. Yeboah walked up to hug both of us, but he kept looking back at his wife with great concern. I moved closer to examine her and noticed a wet bloody stain on the cloth she wore on her waist and a puddle 'neath her.

"Cripes, Kofi, Her water's broke!" I said. She was gasping, and obviously in great pain and discomfort. One o' the other ladies sat by her and looked at me with great concern. She said a whole series of things in Twi that I didn't understand, but it meant something to Kofi.

He said, "Move Pesaata." He pointed to an area to the side o' the road. Several men came toward us to carry her. I helped lift her up and as I did I looked 'neath her cloth skirt and noticed her privates were dilated widely. She was about to deliver. I was overwhelmed with how things were getting out of control. I had never helped deliver a baby, and by the looks o' the others here, no one else had much experience either. Most were fairly young. The six men were still chained together by leg irons, so I tried to search the warrior's bodies for a key, while two women and Yeboah and Kofi cared for Pesaata. Soon enough, I found an iron clasp key wrapped with twine around one o' the warrior's loin cloths. It was the one who was holding the musket, and I surmised he must have been their leader. I proceeded to spend the next several minutes trying to remove the shackles from the captives' legs. It took several tries as the locks were quite rusty and even when unlocked were difficult to bend away. We threw the irons to the side of the road, and then carried the dead men into the brush on the opposite side of the road from where Pesaata lay. I looked at the road and saw there were multiple blood stains left there. If anyone was passing, they would know there had been battle, but perhaps they would pass at night and a rain would wash the evidence away before tomorrow when more warriors would come this way. I wanted to take leave o' this field as soon as I could, but we couldn't leave Yeboah's wife in the throes o' delivery."

Chapter 8: It's a Boy

"I did not reckon myself to carry a weak stomach, as I had fought with the dragoons and had seen much war and human carnage, but I didn't really want to watch my friend's wife deliver the baby. Instead, I let the others bare that problem, while I strode up and down the road, keeping an eye for trouble. What kind o' trouble, I wondered? I decided it could be just about anything or anybody. I did not feel the least bit guilty for killing the three warriors. Yes, we had ambushed 'em, but they were holding our friends captive, and I was content that they deserved whatever they got. We were in a dangerous part o' the world at a dangerous time, and these things happened. At least that is what I told myself, but I wondered how this would be handled by local constables if viewed from the side of the law. I didn't even know if there was a sheriff in these parts. I figured no constable, no convict. That meant whoever survived was in the right. In the highlands, the Macshimi ruled on such matters. The head o' the clan was the sheriff, judge and jury and would meat out justice where and when necessary. No clan justice worked liked that out here.

I wondered who these Akwamu were and how they had acquired their captives? Yeboah and Pesaata were, until at least a few days ago, free villagers, who as far as I knew had no quarrels with anyone. Therefore, I

129

didn't believe the captives were taken by "legal" means, whatever "legal" meant in the Ashanti. I was more concerned that there had been slavers as close as a half day's walk from Tontokrom. If more Akwamu came down the road, or any other persons who supported the slave trade, and they discovered what happened there, Kofi and I were likely to be drawn and quartered and the other men and women put back into bondage.

The silence was interrupted by the large wail of a child. It was crying, but it was alive. One o' the women was saying her prayers repeatedly to herself, at least that was what it sounded like, and the men were all congratulating Yeboah on his new addition. Kofi came up to me smiling.

"Boy." He paused, then said "Laddy" again in perfect English with a hint of my own Scottish brogue and grinned broadly at me. He was mocking me and making a good natured joke. I was happy for Yeboah, and happy that Kofi was getting credit for helping his fellow villagers.

I looked at Kofi and said, "Great. Now we go!"

He shook his head, and said, "soon." He went back to check on the baby.

I was just beginning to think everything was likely to be alright when I heard something that sent chills through my spine. Again. It was the rumbling of a gyata, and it was coming from close by, just to the west, beyond the spot where we had laid the bodies o' the slain warriors.

"Haggis Piss. What now?" I exclaimed to myself and anybody who was close enough. A gyata was nearby and I knew it was some great beast of legend: a lion or a bear or a wolf.

The male former captives had been stripping the warriors o' their clothes and other items. All looked up in terror when the sound o' the gyata shook the air again and almost everyone jumped to their feet.

"Wo suru" said Kofi as loud as he could muster but it came out as a hoarse whisper. I knew what that meant ---Danger!"

Two men came up to us with the Akwamu spears and stood next to me with concerned looks on their faces. They held their spears pointed toward the sound across the road. Several other men and women who hadn't yet departed just started running down the road in both directions. Yeboah was with his wife and newborn trying to wipe the blood off and tie off the umbilical cord. One of the women had stayed and was helping. Kofi was moving to my position quickly, and I had men with spears on each side. The native man to my left was babbling in Twi at high speed and I understood nothing o' what he was trying to tell me. He finally pointed to my musket and I understood. I needed to load it. It had been two years since I had last loaded and fired a musket, but due to my training, it might as well have been yesterday. I poured the black powder, reeking o' sulfur, from the horn, packed the wad and used the ramrod to force the musket ball I had pulled from the satchel down tight covering the wad and powder. I carefully cocked the hammer to the half position, primed the pan a third full with powder, covered the pan with the frizzen and aimed across the road as I leveled the weapon and pulled the cock full back.

I was astonished to see two large cats move into the opening, their noses sniffing the air. They saw us, but did not approach; instead they circled around the bodies o' the three dead warriors. They were huge with enormous legs and paws and were colored a dusky light brown. I was fixed on their fangs which were long and as wide as spear tips. They made no noise but stalked back and forth inspecting the surroundings, and especially the dead bodies. I now knew what a gyata was—a lion. As I told you before, I had never seen a lion face to face, but there were pictures of these creatures in the bibles in my chapel at home in Beauly. These creatures were surely the most powerful and dangerous on Earth. They were well within 400 yards of us, and things would get ugly if they charged. I stood transfixed, as they each dropped to the ground in a prone position and started chewing on the dead warriors we had left there. They must have smelled the blood and followed the scent here. They took large chunks o' flesh with every bite. I was sickened, but fascinated.

Kofi went back to Pesaata and tried to help her up to her feet. She appeared faint and pale and rose only with great difficulty. I pointed south for the group to try to head toward Obuasi while the lions were preoccupied with their meal. Everyone agreed and we began to move very slowly in that direction on the road. As we did so, I heard a crash to my right side in the brush near the two lions. Suddenly, another lion appeared through the brush at the side of the road and moved onto the embankment near the trail just in front and to the right of us. It was close enough that I could see its back teeth. It was larger than the other two and had a huge ring of dark brown hair around its large face. It looked right at us and moved a few feet onto the road and toward us by a few steps.

"Boy gyata." Said Kofi, but I had already figured that out for myself. The two men with the spears were already stepping backward rapidly and Yeboah and his wife, with the baby in his arms, were almost running on the road to the north in the opposite direction. Kofi moved next to me with his bow raised and an arrow already notched.

"What do we do?" I said out loud but in hoarse dry whisper. They didn't understand me but didn't need to. We all slowly backed up and I noticed the male lion moved a few steps closer. I was afraid he would charge. I motioned with my head for Kofi to move quickly backward and I raised my musket.

Instead, Kofi moved forward and the two other natives with spears raised their weapons and moved forward at the same time so that we formed a wall of weaponry. They chattered in Twi and I gathered from hand signals that everyone was to fire on the animal together. We spread out in a semi-circle around the male lion. The two female lions were still busy eating the bodies of the dead Akwamu warriors and did not seem to heed us. The male lion, on the other hand, was watching carefully as the four of us started to circle and he became more and more agitated.

The lion started to charge and I fired the musket right at him. Unfortunately, I missed. Kofi did not miss and his arrow found its mark in the animal's front shoulder area. Both of the spears were thrown and landed, although only one of the spears remained embedded in flesh. The other spear hit the lions head and glanced off the bony hard crown on the lions face. It was enough to break the charge. None o' the blows caused serious damage, but they stopped the forward progress and forced the beast to fall back and try to dislodge the arrow and the spear from its body. He sat down, rolled and pawed at his shoulder until both shafts fell to the ground. The lion looked at me for what seemed like several seconds and roared. The sound made the hair on my skin stand straight up. At length, he turned sideways and slowly walked to where the other two lionesses lay and squatted right between the females. There was some blood at his shoulder but he wasn't hurt and if he decided, he could still charge and kill all of us. My musket was not loaded, and both spears lay harmlessly in the middle of the trail.

"Wo kor! Mmrika! Run!" I yelled, and Kofi took off. I was backing up two steps at a time with the musket outstretched. Even though it was unloaded, I was fairly sure that the lion did not know that. Maybe the sound had startled it enough to be wary. After several steps I was able to meet up with Kofi who looked at me expectedly and said, "gyatas, bad". He held up three fingers and nodded with dismay. The men who had thrown the spears were a few yards ahead of us.

"Yes. We go this way." And I pointed north. We moved very cautiously back stepping, keeping an eye on the lions the whole way. It was about a half mile when we caught up with Yeboah and Pesaata. I don't know where any o' the other captives were. Pesaata was very pale and was bleeding badly. They were moving very slowly and the two men had to help her walk. I was afraid the lions would be tracking us, so I kept looking backwards as we went.

A long discussion ensued between Kofi and the others in Twi. I could only understand a few words, like "san", "yera" "fa" "mmrika" and "pira, which meant "return", "lost, "take", "run" and "hurt" as well as the word "Datano" which they repeated several times. Thus, from what I gathered and due to his hand gestures, Kofi had suggested they return on this road to Datano, but everyone else was very reluctant to do so. Pesaata really needed a doctor or at least a midwife as she was bleeding badly. I didn't think we wanted to head south to Obuasi past the lions again and all agreed. Several more minutes of Twi dialogue continued as we slowly moved to the north on the road. They were certainly afraid of encountering more Akwamu slavers on the road, but there appeared to be more to it than that.

It took a very long time for Kofi to use hand gestures and his limited English vocabulary and my few Twi words to carefully and slowly explain to me that Yeboah and Pesaata had originally made it to Datano, but the local chief had demanded money for the cost o' the midwife services. They had brought an akoko (chicken), as was custom, but this was refused. Yeboah had called him a cheat and the chief had claimed he was dishonored. Apparently, there were some slavers passing through the town of Datano, and had several captives with 'em. The couple had been held as prisoners, then sold to the slavers by the chief. I assumed they were afraid that if any of 'em returned to Datano they would be taken captive and sold again.

I couldn't understand everything they said but I sure could understand their fear and concern. The danger of recapture was real, but we couldn't risk taking a bleeding woman back within yards o' three lions. I remember wishing I had a map and knew our exact location. I guessed that we were likely somewhere

north of Obuasi, and at least twice that far south o'
Bekwai. Kumasi was another two or three days journey
past Bekwai if I reckoned the road properly. The group
didn't want to go back to Datano, and no one wanted to
go towards Obuasi then, so Bekwai was a logical choice.
Kofi tried to explain to me that one o' the men with the
spears said they had passed two villages on this road.
This encouraged me that there may be a midwife or
someone who could help within a short hike."

"They were referring to this very village and the
one only a short walk that way." I pointed to the ceiling
and then towards the south. The Portuguese man
nodded.

"We walked a little bit further and crossed a
river. The water was not deep but went up to our mid
thighs. I had no idea whether lions swam or not, but I
figured this would at least pose a mild barrier between
us. I hoped the lions would have full bellies from their
Akwamu feast and would not pursue us.

Once we crossed the river, Pesaata had to stop.
She was exhausted and weak, and could go no further.
We helped her cross to an area about a block off the trail
and she laid and rested. She had just enough energy to
try and breast feed her baby for the first time, who was
now crying loudly. She was too dehydrated and hungry
to have more than a few drops of milk in her breast, and
it didn't satisfy the infant. One of the men was
motioning to us that he wanted to depart. Kofi thanked
him for his help and the lad then headed off down a thin
overgrown trail to the northeast. I don't know what
village he belonged to or where he intended to go, but I
think he had had enough o' the road and its perils, and
he was alarmed by the baby's cries. No doubt he, like I,

feared that the baby's wails would give away our position to either man or beast. There were dangers every direction here.

Yeboah and Kofi spoke again and I gathered that they decided that someone would have to go for help. Pesaata could no longer walk. We left the other lion fighting man to stay with Yeboah and his family, and Kofi and I headed north. We needed someone to speak Twi, to explain the situation and find a healer. I went along for a different reason. I think Kofi believed that as long as he was with an "obroni" (white man), he would be unlikely to be picked up by slavers. That was especially so, since I was carrying a musket. And as that thought occurred to me, I decided it was prudent to reload my flintlock. I felt stupid for not doing it earlier, but I supposed my mind was preoccupied with many other things at that point. After a couple of minutes o' preparation, it was loaded, but not primed or cocked, and we pushed north. It was just beginning to get twilight as the day waned. I was glad I had not heard the rumbles o' lions to the south, but I had no illusions that they weren't capable of stealth, and could sneak up on us at any time.

Moving with great speed and intent, it took us less than an hour to get to the point where we could see the fires of a village from the road. We found a connecting trail and worked our way forward to some buildings in the distance. The village was laid out much differently than the one we were used to in Tontokrom. There were several huts arranged randomly without a central road or plaza, and the roofs were deeply pitched. There was a central dwelling that was quite large, with a wooden and thatched roof that was supported by 6 large pillars, but lacked any visible walls. It had a dais at one end. I wasn't sure if it was a church, a town square, or a place of business. A few men were in the doorways of the huts we passed, and they eyed us suspiciously. Many glanced long, with fear or envy, at the musket in my hands. Kofi went up to the first man he saw and spoke with him. I understood almost nothing, but I knew what he had to tell him. The man just shook his head and apparently told him to go somewhere else. We repeated this with two other natives, neither of which would even talk to us. Finally, we saw a woman pounding rice with a club outside of her tiny hut. We hurried to her and Kofi spent several minutes explaining our dilemma. She listened patiently, but answered negatively. All I heard was Debi, Debi, Debi, but I knew from those words that we weren't going to get any help in this village. He spoke again to her briefly then rejoined me by the large airy structure after she explained something and pointed to the north. She had offered us some rice and some bananas, which we ate greedily.

Kofi explained to me in his fractured words that the woman had said no one here would or could help Pesaata, but that there were obronis (whites) in the next village up the road. He said that it was only a few miles by her reckoning. However, I could tell from the woman's tone and the looks leveled in my direction that there was something else to her story that she was withholding. Kofi concurred that he thought there might be danger there, although if he knew what kind of danger he was not able to describe it to me in English or Twi words I could understand. I thought it prudent that if I went on to the next village, I go alone. We could

meet up later." As I said this, I noticed the Portuguese
man had leaned closer to me and was eyeing me very
suspiciously.

"We decided to head back out to the road and
split up. It took only a few minutes to reach the road
and we were about to turn and part ways when we saw
the man who had helped us fight the lion running
toward us from the south. He was out o' breath by the
time he reached us and seemed excited. After taking
some water from Kofi's canteen, he explained in Twi
what happened. I didn't understand much, but I
understood the word for death "owu". Pesaata had
apparently bled excessively and had died soon after we
departed. Yeboah had wanted to bury her, but had
feared for the health of his newborn son from the
elements and the lions. He had instead taken off on a
trail to the west, in hopes of returning quickly to
Tontokrom. He was going to walk all night and day to
reach it. He asked the man to find us and to please
bury his wife before the lions ate her remains. After
translating as much as he could for me, Kofi thanked
the man for his help and we watched as he jogged on
north toward Bekwai. He was a big man, although only
in his early twenties, and I hoped he would not find
trouble. He had showed much more courage than other
captives, and had stared down a charging lion. I wished
I knew his name.

As we watched him go, we turned back south.
Kofi started to sing a song of lamentation for Pesaata.
It was a soft and sad tune and although I couldn't
understand the words, I could feel the remorse and care
in the melody. It reminded me o' the bagpipes and
music we played in the highlands when a clansmen had

passed beyond.

We no longer had great haste to return to the spot where we had left Yeboah and Pesaata, and it was getting quite dark. Had I not had a musket and had we not been on a fairly wide road that made it difficult for ambush, we probably would have simply slept for the night on a clearing by the road. I wasn't keen on moving closer to the lions, but I thought as long as they were on the other side o' the river with full bellies, we were probably fine. We ambled slowly back and Kofi continued his song. By the time we reached the clearing it was quite late. Pesaata lay to one side of the clearing with her arms crossed in front of her stomach. We used our blades to hack at the ground as we had no shovels or picks. Fortunately the red clay gave way easily and we were able to hollow out a 2 foot by 5 foot resting place that was about 3 feet deep with our swords. We scooped the broken earth with our hands. The tomb was not deep enough to keep the animals from digging it up, but there was bedrock underneath and we could dig no further with the broad sword blades we were using.

It took only a short while to cover her remains with the upturned red earth. Kofi said some semblance of a prayer o'er the shallow grave, but I didn't even know what religion to which he belonged so I don't know what kind of rites he presented. I said a few words of my own in the habit of the Scottish Presbyterians, but the words felt empty. I didn't know what religion Pesaata belonged to either. I had no idea if she had ever heard words of the bible or anything about the God of Moses and of Jesus, but from my time in the village, I knew most of the Ashanti believed in some form of God. She followed "Nyame", and it had something to do with the fetish priests, but I knew nothing more. Maybe it was the same God, with a different name. I wasn't sure whether that even mattered, and I wondered for a brief moment how my God would judge the primitive tribes that hadn't ever got a chance to hear about his word. Did they go to heaven, or were they condemned to hell without ever having a chance? It somehow didn't seem right to me, but I was no religious scholar and these kinds of questions were well beyond my limited religious knowledge. Hell, I couldn't even read. I looked sideways at Kofi and hoped there was some kind of salvation for the lad and his family. Heaven would be a boring place if it held only the English and the other Europeans.

We decided that it was still too dangerous to cross the river and go south towards Obuasi. I was still intrigued as to the reason for the presence o' white men in the village north of the one we had visited. I thought it perhaps was a mining camp. I also wondered about the worried look the woman gave us when she talked about this village and Kofi's hesitation in coming here. I sent him off back to his home village. I had a momentary pang of fear for his safety in traveling alone with lions about, but it soon passed and I headed back north on the road. I made camp only a mile or so from the grave site, due to the late hour, in a wee glen just a few hundred yards from the road. It had been a very long day and I was exhausted. Once I lay down, it took only a few minutes for my eyes to close and I fell fast asleep. I dreamed of lions and snakes and large battles with Akwamu warriors, and therefore I did not rest comfortably. I awoke in the early morning shivering with dew on my face, arms and legs. I was hungry again, but I no longer had any edible provisions. I was hoping there would be more food in the village I was heading for.

It took a couple of hours of walking to reach the village we had visited the night before, and I was careful to hide in the scrub to the side o' the road if I thought anyone was coming. I was extra-cautious and jumped into hiding only to find oncoming sounds came only from birds and suspicious shadows represented only clouds, instead of a war party. Once, I saw a group of lightly armed Ashanti go by. I don't think they spotted us, but one o' the men gazed for a few overly long, tense moments at the bush where I lay hid. However, they passed without incident and I was soon back on my way. I eventually saw the unwelcoming village to my right in the distance, but I did not stop and instead moved ahead towards the next village on the road. Taking directions from the woman we spoke to the previous evening, it should have been located only a few miles north.

The village I am in now that you call Akrokerri is not what I expected it would be. Instead of mud huts and bamboo stalls, I saw several buildings made of stone with wooden roofs, and a central road lined with stone gravel. This cottage is quite spacious compared to most Ashanti dwellings I have been in."

I pointed to the ceiling.

"Few inhabitants were visible outside the few huts I saw, and unlike most villages in the region, there were no goats or chickens lulling about. Instead of huts, this village looked barren, but clean.

I looked back at the Portuguese man and said,

"Now we come to the part of the story you already know. I walked a bit further and saw a sign that said "Loja" and another building that said "refinaria de oruo". I gathered from the pictures on the signs below the words that these were your general store and a gold refining and processing station. Further up the alleyway there were several other official looking structures, but little activity. A third said "Restaurante y Pub". I knew that meant a place for food and drink, so I thought I would go inside. And yes, I really did want to ask for directions, as I told you two days ago! I was hoping to find my way to Kumasi or at least Bekwai. Once I opened the door and strolled in, the native barkeep seemed alarmed by my presence and he looked into a corner at a white man that I suppose now had to be you." I pointed to my inquisitor.

He smiled and dipped his hat as if he was introducing himself for the first time.

"Of course. I had known of your presence in the area due to your activities in the neighboring village, but I was even more intrigued when you came to Akrokerri and strode into my own pub."

"I remember I was about to walk up to the barkeep and introduce myself and see if I could get some water when the door opened behind me and these two natives came in." I motioned to the two beside me.

"I had just started to turn to see what they were about when one decided to hit me across the back o' the head and neck with a damn Ashanti war club. Even the English are civil enough to attack from the front."

The barb did not bother him. "Just so. You let out a long curse word as you fell." He laughed, and I flinched as he reached out to touch my head.

143

"So, here you are."

"Here I am, wherever here is."

Chapter 9: Bondage in Akrokerri

The Portuguese man seemed somewhat confrontational now in his tone. He remained standing and still had a dueling pistol. "I captured you because I had to know what you were after, Mr. Fraser. It might interest you to know that the warriors behind you now are Ashanti, not Akwamu or Akyem, and that I trade with everyone, from many tribes and many lands. You see, I own this village and all of the stores and shops within it. I trade with miners, with slavers and with anyone else who regularly travels these roads between Kumasi and Obuasi or even those who travel from Elmina on this trading route. I also own the only gold refining station between Obuasi and Kumasi. You may have wondered how or why an adventurer from Lisbon could speak English fluently. I speak 6 languages, which helps me provide services to all of those in need. I am all that is civilization in this region."

I was still dubious of his intentions and didn't trust his new found civility. I almost preferred that he call me "Scotty" instead of "Mr. Fraser". This sudden formality made me uneasy. Why bother with cordialities? I didn't really care about his language abilities, nor was I impressed, if that was his intent. I was preoccupied with my current plight and especially that o' my young companion. Where was Kofi? I had to

find a way to get out o' here, and despite the
pleasantries in the man's temperament, his eyes
gleamed with a sinister look. I was afraid I was
running out o' time or options and might yet be killed.
My story was finished, and I might be too.

"So tell me again about your motives for
disturbing our little peace here and killing some of my
potential clients."

"The Akwamu deserved to die." I said in
exasperation.

"Please explain your purpose in disposing of
them, in greater detail." He wasn't arguing with me, he
seemed genuinely interested in my reasons, but then he
said, "especially tell me why three dead slavers that you
claim to have never met, now lay dead on the road by
your hand. You say it was vengeance for taking your
friends captive, but enslavement of natives happens
with regularity in the Ashanti. You see, if someone
went around killing all of the Akwamu slavers in the
area, I would lose lots of business for my stores. I would
have to start trading with the Akyem, and they are too
violent to be trusted."

So I relayed again the story of how Kofi and I
had originally eyed the captives being led down the road
by three Akwamu warriors and how cruel the captives
were being treated.

"We were going to let 'em pass, but then we
recognized two captives from Kofi's village. We couldn't
stand by and do nothing while they were being beaten
and forced unfairly into slavery. One woman was
pregnant and about to deliver! You heard my story. The
strain o' the march ended up killing her. We buried her
this morning. You must have seen her when the slavers

brought them through this village from Datano yesterday. Aye, she'd be the plump, slow one and easy to spot."

"I'm afraid that I did not see the captives on the road to the slave market, but I did meet one of their Akwamu captors in my pub as he stopped on his way to Manso Asiado. In fact, he was sporting the same ornate musket that we found you with. I didn't know they had come from Datano, though that would have worried me little. By the way, your musket is a fine weapon, indeed." He smiled wickedly.

I realized now, too late, how he had known (before I had even begun the story), that it was Kofi and I who had disposed o' the three Akwamu slavers. He must have recognized my musket. Damn! To change the subject, I asked, "Manso Asiado?" "Where's that?"

"It is the slaver's town you and your native boy visited last night, asking questions. It is only a few miles to the south." He noted my look o' confusion then explained, "Manso Asiado is a slave trading center. It was built by the Asantehene, King Osei Tutu, to make it easier to trade slaves with the Akwamu from the coast. The great building you described there is not a church, it is a slave trading pavilion. The Ashanti, Akwamu and Fantu bring their captives into Manso Asiado from throughout the kingdom and from points distant. They are bought and sold under the great pavilion and transported by the Akwamu back down the road to Obuasi and on to the slave markets on the coast to sell to English, Dutch or Spanish slaving ships. There was no slave market happening there either yesterday or today, so I assume the Akwamu just decided to move their captives on to the coast for sale directly. And if you are wondering how I knew you visited there last night, you should understand that I have many men in my employ, including many in that village."

"I realize the king is making money from the slave trade, but why would King Osei Tutu want to trade Ashanti slaves with the Akwamu. He has been at war with all the neighboring tribes for almost twenty years. Why would he trust the Akwamu, or they the King?

"I see you are not totally acquainted with the Asantehene or all of the history in this land. The king is not at war with the Akwamu and never has been. They are allies and strong friends. He was even raised by the Akwamu on the coast, and his current spiritual priest and second in command, Okomfo Anokye, is also of the Akwamu. The roots of the slavery tree run deep here, but it has not always been so. The Dutch and Portuguese have been mining the Ashanti region for better than a hundred and fifty years. My Portuguese ancestors here actually had a distaste for slavery, not because of any moral outrage, but because they thought it would interfere with the gold trade, of which they were heavily invested. I, myself, have no qualms over the slave trade. It has made me quite rich, though I don't sell the natives themselves." He gestured to the surroundings, but all I saw was a dismal little room with pale walls and virtually no furniture. Not exactly a palace, and the fact that he wasn't a slaver himself didn't make up for the fact that he still made money off of and from slavers. He was still a slug. I stayed quiet and let him continue.

"Many local tribes, especially the Akan tribe known as the Denkyira, became adept at goldsmithing and there was general peace in this area for a generation, with both white and black men separately prospering from the mineral wealth it provided. At the same time in other parts of Africa, slavery was booming, and humans, not minerals, were the driving commodity and the two races came into conflict. About 40 years ago, around 1680 in the year of our lord, the English arrived on the West African coast. Despite their early efforts, they were unable to break into the gold trade. This was a consequence of Dutch control, but also because the Akwamu tribe completely controlled the coast from Elmina to Accra, and the English could not gain access to the mines of the Akan tribes without military confrontation. The Fantu controlled the coastal lands to the west of Elmina which prevented the English from entering the interior of the Gold coast area farther west. Both Portuguese and Dutch had also already built large fortresses along the coast, to protect their own economic interests. You have seen these castle fortresses in your travels here."

I nodded.

"Thus, the English could not openly or successfully attack the resident Europeans or even the native tribes on the coast."

I commented that I wished the English had such reluctance about invading the highlands of Scotland. I would never shake my hatred for that pompous race. The English knaves had devastated my bonnie homeland. I had long ago given up on vengeance, but forgiveness came hard when everything you ever had was lost because of a rival people.

The Portuguese man nodded his head with equal disgust as I disparaged the English. He continued, "After about 25 more years of trying, or about 5 years into the reign of the Asantehene, the English finally gained a foothold here and began trading in slaves with the Akwamu along the coast. The enslaved come from throughout the continent and are sourced from far away African tribes using war scouting parties. This village is a conduit on a mighty trail of slave trafficking. Some hostages are taken from neighboring villages in these foreign lands, or sometimes they are purchased from village chiefs selling their own subjects and relatives. The captives are then herded into the Ashanti and sent down to the big coastal Akwamu cities."

I knew most of this already, but I was content to let the Portuguese man talk. It meant he wasn't in the act o' killing me.

"Let me tell you of the Asantehene, the first king. Many are misinformed about his history. About the same time the English started gaining ground here, Osei Tutu as an Akan warrior king conquered the neighboring tribe of Denkyira and its gold-rich region. He has fought battles and vanquished many tribes and kingdoms, but not all by force. Many joined his legions by choice. When the Asantehene first came to power, he united the Juaben, Mampong, Kwaamen, Nsuta, Bekwai and Kokofu tribes under one Ashanti banner and allied them against the Denkyira, which as I told you he eventually also conquered. He considers the chiefs of these six states all Ashanti and 'his peoples', but the Denkyira he still considers 'the vanquished' due to many previous years of oppression of the Ashanti by the Denkyira. He is as motivated in trading Denkyira slaves for guns as he is for scratching the fields for gold. His domain has become a rich kingdom of mineral wealth from the ground, and even greater income derived from the practice of slave trafficking. He has become the major supplier of captives for the Akwamu slavers to his southern border. Not all of the Ashanti clans or tribal groups have converted to income from the slave trade. Many Akan villages have simply kept their original way of life. Denkyira stayed on in the region's mines, and most have continued their goldsmithing crafts."

He smiled broadly. "In that I am grateful, for trading with the Denkyra in gold and smelting their ores has been quite profitable for me."

I only grimaced. I had briefly tasted the life of a miner. It couldn't be any better for the Denkyra.

"Other tribes assimilated into the Ashanti kingdom but have maintained farming as their way of life. However, many of the region's assimilated natives have still remained in constant fear of being captured and turned over by neighboring Akan tribes to the slave markets on the coast. The Fantu and Akwamu tribes, which are not considered under the Akan banner, have continued to abduct captives from as far away as terra Nigreterrum, western Athiopia, and even the lands of the Sahara sands. Alongside the Ashanti and closely related Akan, those two tribes have become rich and powerful in the process. All slaves, from throughout the continent, eventually end up coming down this road to the coast, and spending their profits in my stores. Unfortunately for the local Akan tribes, local tribal chieftains have recently found it profitable to sell whoever comes their way. Understand, Osei Tutu grew up around the Akwamu slave trade and has no qualms selling men for profit. However, the Asantehene is honorable in his own way, and values his Ashanti subjects. He would much more likely trade Denkyira or Fantu slaves than any of his own matrilineal clans, or especially not fellow nton of the Ashanti. He prefers to deal with slave traders from tribes from much further afield and extract bounty for passing through his lands."

I interrupted him. "Ntons?"

"Ah. The Ntons are spiritual groups passed through the father's line, whereas Ashanti clan lineages are inherited through the mother."

I still had no idea what that meant, but didn't bother to ask again. I decided to press him on another issue.

"But the King, Osei Tutu, does support the sale of his own Ashanti people to the slavers on the coast. The Datano chief sold Yeboah and his wife to the Akwamu when they went yonder to Datano only for the service o' the midwife!" I became angry again, when remembering the injustice.

"I do not believe the Asantehene had any knowledge of the capture of your villagers in Datano and their sale, and I doubt he would condone it. I'm sure the King would prefer not to trade in his own people and he strives to keep raiding parties outside of the Ashanti borders, with exception for Denkyira slaves. Unfortunately, some of the lesser chieftains and local elders within the kingdom are not so inclined. I am afraid it has been the Datano chieftain's habit of late. If this chief continues to sell Akan tribesmen to the Akwamu, the neighboring villagers are going to rise up against him. I have cautioned him against such tactics."

"You know the chief who did this?"

"Only through business. He is an ass."

"If the king would not condone such behavior,

someone should tell Osei Tutu of this breach o' trust and hospitality to his people. The chieftain should be punished."

"Perhaps. The Asantehene is a fair and just ruler and is capable of righting the wrong."

"You speak as if you know the king personally and befriend him."

"Yes, I have met the King, and remain in his graces. It is quite profitable for me. Osei Tutu loves his gold, and is very generous to his friends and colleagues. The Asantehene has rewarded my allegiance. Do not judge me by this small building in which you are kept. As I have told you, I own many dwellings and businesses, here and elsewhere. Interlopers such as you have tried in the past to crowd into my domain and claim that power and influence...unsuccessfully." He smiled wickedly.

"I have no desire for your slaver buildings, your slaver stores or even your slaver money. I can't see how anyone would bother to acquire this town. What's the attraction? All o' this?" I gestured around the room.

He didn't appreciate my sarcasm. "There are many who would be jealous of what I have achieved. I am a wealthy and powerful man, even by Portuguese standards. Some have tried to take it by force. Slavers from both north and south would like to control the market of Manso Asieda, for it is quite profitable. But Manso Asieda is officially the dominion of the Asantehene and I do not own the market there. I only watch over it for the king, but managing his business reaps great material reward. Of course, I am obligated to use ruthless force to maintain my own holdings and to fight off enemies. That is why I hold you here. I

153

must be sure you are not part of one of those factions aligned against me." He glared at me as a Newgate jailor does at the inmates.

"Of more direct concern, the English have, in the past 10 years or so, increasingly tried to force their way into both the slave and gold trade on this coast. That may eventually be a problem for my business. As the Portuguese have lost strength and prestige in Cape Coast and Accra, so have the English tried to weasel their way in to gain access to these valuable commodities. If not for the strength of the Dutch and their forts, the English would have long ago tried to take the region by force. They are much more involved in slaving than are other European powers, by virtue of their interest in the American colonies and need for plantation labor. And the English do not value or trust the Asantehene. They are jealous of the wealth he has accrued in acting as landlord over the slave highways. My alliance with the Ashanti King also makes me a target of the English. So when we found a white man skulking around these villages, I had to assume you were doing reconnaissance for a future inland English incursion. You have your own experience with the English war machine and realize the devious potential machinations of the crown."

"Why do you still think I am a spy? You must realize the English are the last people in the world who I would entreaty with."

"I believe from your story that you may not be aligned with the natural enemy of your people, but that does not mean that you are not a spy for someone else."

"Well that's just absurd."

"Possibly, but a stranger in Akrokerri is still

under suspicion until proven fair. And there are circumstances which make your appearance here a trifle curious. So tell me again, Alexander, how you and a young farmer were able to surprise and subdue three seasoned, armed Akwamu warriors?"

I reminded him again that I had rushed one of the warriors that held the musket, and that Kofi had pierced one of the other warriors with an arrow when that man had threatened me. He was interested in every single detail. I explained again how I had subdued the man with the musket with my blade, and was able to fight the second man hand to hand. I told him that the third man was killed in mercy by Kofi after the arrow had mortally penetrated his back. I am not sure he believed the entire version of events, because he paused for a long time to consider the story and its merits.

"And you still maintain that you are telling the truth?"

"Aye, as much as I can remember it."

Would you explain how and why we found your young friend at the edge of this village. He did not, in fact, go back to his village did he? He accompanied you here that night we caught you."

"OK. You have me. I admit he accompanied me. I was only trying to protect my friend from your fury and any further harm. I didn't want you accusing him of being a spy too... Aye, he did come with me to this village after we buried the woman. I wanted him to go, but he would not leave my side. Once we approached Akrokerri, he hesitated as we entered the town. When we saw the buildings, Kofi looked at me with a concerned facial expression and whispered, "Slavers!" It was a guess more than a statement of fact, and one based on the appearance of things, but we were both worried."

"With reason." was all the Portuguese man said as he smiled.

"I motioned for Kofi to stop and stay still, and then decided it was better for him to wait for me outside of town. I didn't know at the time that he was at any risk of becoming a captive. Even so, I realized that he would not be so blessed as I if we actually ran into slave traders. He could be taken prisoner and sent to the coast like any other stranger in the village. It took some persuading, but he finally understood my meaning and went to hide just outside of town. Please don't hurt the boy. He really is of no threat to you. As far as I know, he stayed hidden on the outskirts of your village."

"And that is exactly where Yaw here found him. Yaw is an outstanding tracker. Your friend was taken by surprise without a fight."

I looked up at the native to my right and said, "Then you are indeed a good warrior, Yaw, because my friend is also a great tracker and not easily crept up on unawares." I don't think the large native warrior understood me, as his expression never changed.

"And so the entire truth finally bleeds out. I was waiting for you to finally admit that you and the native boy worked together. It makes it easier to apply leverage when we both realize you are wont to protect the boy." He smiled and set back.

"Now, I have to decide what to do with you both. It is getting late, and I am tired from two days of your interrogation. I must say you tell a good story, and I believe most of it is the truth, based on the evidence we have. I don't think you are a spy, but you are a very dangerous man, and letting you free would be foolhardy. I may kill you in the morning, but for tonight, you and your little dark friend may sleep in the company of my guards. Rest easy. I need to think on what I should do with you. We'll speak with the native boy and see if your friend agrees with your story, then decide. Firing squad, I should think." He laughed as he exited.

He left me there on the floor. I did not sleep well, if at all. I worried for both of our fortunes. I tossed and rolled and worried myself through the dark hours. I felt sick. Early in the morning on the next day, the Portuguese man strode in to the room.

He stared at me for a long while without speaking. Finally he said, "Regardless of how much help you received from the young Ashanti man, it is clear you are a courageous and valiant warrior, and a dangerous man with or without a weapon, Mr. Alexander. My scouts tell me that even with the evidence obscured by the lions, it was clear there was a great struggle in which you obviously persevered. I can see that you still show marks from your earlier wounds." He pointed to the bruises and still seeping spear wounds on my thigh and shoulder.

"Experienced warriors are a scarce commodity in the bush. I could use a man of your talents around this area, Alexander, particularly with the recent unrest caused by attacks from Akyem warriors. They travel here from outside of the borders of the Ashanti kingdom and wreak havoc. Another man skilled in weaponry would be a boon to my guard. How would you like to work for me as a soldier?"

"You have me knocked unconscious, held captive,

threaten me with a dueling pistol, have my friend held captive and beaten, and now you want to hire me? You have a funny way of doing business Mister. I don't even know your name!"

"My name is Aurelio Bras." He bowed in a mock show of courtesy.

"It is a little hard for me to trust you, considering the circumstances. You could just be leading me to a firing squad. Your words, not mine."

"I understand your lack of trust. However, I think you and I could come to a comfortable arrangement in which you could make enough money to afford a trip back to your homeland in time."

"Do I have any choice? It is a fact that you have pointed a gun to my head several times during the past two days."

"I'd like to think this is an opportunity for both of us."

"And I think this is much like being an indentured plantation worker in the colonies, or even the equal of being forced to work in the mining fields for meager food, but no pay."

"But I would pay you a fair wage!" exclaimed the Portuguese man.

"Yes, but I would be submitting only under force."

"You imply that I still have leverage over you. I suppose you mean I still hold your young friend."

"Don't you?"

"Of course. Your friend is my prisoner, and as long as I hold him, I own you too. I guess I have to agree with you that I have the upper hand."

'So I have no choice in working for you, even

though I distrust you. I would not make a great or very motivated employee under those circumstances. I don't know if you would ever trust me."

"I begin to understand your position. I probably would be forced to have you under suspicion....always. Trust would come only with time, and then perhaps never..... So instead you would prefer that I kill you both?"

"No, of course not. I just mean that if you wanted to hire me you could have treated us better from the beginning."

"But then we never would have gotten at the truth, would we?"

"Perhaps not. Is there another option? I don't suppose there is any possibility of just letting us go?"

"I'm afraid that might not be wise or profitable. Profitable. Hmmmmm. There is another possibility."

He sat quietly for several minutes without speaking, thinking things through in his head. I said nothing while he considered his options.

Finally he said, "Maybe I should just kill you and get it over with, but I may be able to profit from this another way. I will make you another proposal. One I suggest you agree to. I will offer your services to the Asantehene in Kumasi. The king is likely to be very impressed with your skills and background, and may take you on as one of his elite warriors. King Osei Tutu pays his guards handsomely, so after a time, you could potentially earn passage back to Scotland. As for your young friend, you are going to need a Twi interpreter wherever you end up, so I will request the King take on both of you. Of course, there is a possibility he will not be interested in your services, in which case you may be shot immediately or sold into slavery."

My eyes went to the ceiling as I pondered yet another brush with death.

"Don't fret, given your history of military service, your escape from not one, but two slave ships, and the current difficulties with the Akyem nation, I think that he will rather be quite welcoming."

"I don't understand. Why help us? You have held us captive. It doesn't make sense to me. What are you getting out of this? I thought you wanted to hire us as your own soldiers."

"I am inclined to agree with you that you would not be my most trusted guard, and one that I might not consider putting my back to. I might still make money off of you, however. I am to meet with the Asantahene on another matter in 3 days, regardless of whether you accompany me. If he is pleased with my unrequested and unlooked for efforts to bring him a new, well trained personal guard, I am likely to be highly rewarded. Perhaps even more so than if I kept you on as my own soldier. I am likely to be paid well enough to more than cover the inconvenience. I may not be able to trust you, but the King is a different matter. You would be foolish indeed to consider any traitorous acts around the Asantehene. He will earn your loyalty and you his trust. And, the king pays his friends in gold dust. We would both profit. What do you say, Alexander Fraser? Do you use your talents to attend to the safety of a burgeoning kingdom or do you go back to chopping wood, digging in the dirt or cleaning bed pots for others in Accra? Or do I just shoot the both of you now? Do you want to return to your homeland or not?"

I briefly considered his offer, but decided I had no

other options and I would have to agree to go to Kumasi with him. There was a possibility that if I didn't accept either his employment or the possibility of working for the King of Ashanti, that Aurelio Bras would simply kill both Kofi and I even before leaving. I could accept my own death, but not that of my young acquaintance. I did not trust Bras, but I could learn to trust the King of the Ashanti. I also thought that if I did meet the Asantahene, I might be able to tell the King of the problems with the local Chieftain in Datano and the issue of selling innocent loyal subjects to slavers. He might seek vengeance on the bastard chieftain who was responsible for Pesaata's death.

"I will go with you to see the King."

"Excellent. I will send for your young friend."

I was relieved, but still far from trusting the Portuguese man. I wasn't entirely comfortable until I saw Kofi brought through the door of the cramped room I was sitting in.

"Kofi." I greeted him.

"Ye te sen, Al-zander." He tried to smile, but his lips were swollen as were his eyelids. He was limping. Anger boiled up inside me, but I quelled it. Things could have been much worse. The Portuguese man led us to a room where we could sleep, and brought us a wee morsel o' food consisting of stew and some fruit. It was now almost midday. We were allowed to walk around the town, under guard and to have some more food and drink. We slept soundly that night and were treated hospitably for an additional two days. The two native guards who held us even brought me our weapons, although they maintained a guard outside of our hut in case we attempted to escape and back out on our agreement, and our walks through the village were ne'er unescorted. They also neglected to include the horn of gunpowder or musket balls in the return of our weapons. I could not have used the musket even if I tried, and Kofi's quiver was also nowhere to be found. Kofi asked me if we were going to attempt a breakout, but I convinced him that we would instead follow the Portuguese man to Kumasi and see where our fortunes led. Neither of us had ever been there, so it was to be another adventure. Of course, I had already had enough adventures for two lifetimes.

We were awakened by one of the native guards early on the fourth day since I had been brought in front of the Portuguese man. We were led to a line of several men forming a sort of caravan. They were heavily armed with a mixture of spears, bows and muskets. The Portuguese man walked among the others barking orders and checking supplies. One of the warriors brought my ammunition satchel and Kofi his quiver. I guessed they figured we were surrounded and outnumbered and were unlikely to try to flee. After long minutes, we finally got underway and walked without speaking for almost 6 hours. We passed by or through several tiny villages and one large town (Manso Bekwai) where the trail split into another large road to the southeast which I was told went to Accra. We continued on the northerly portion of the road. It was much faster going on this well kept road than on the jungle trails we had traversed near Tontokrom, and although we still had to spend a night camped by the road, we made it to Kumasi in only two full days of walking. We met few travelers on the road, and none that appeared to be slavers. Had anyone seen us, I think they would have hidden in fear. Our party consisted of some 15 strong, all warriors, and we marched with purpose.

Chapter 10: Meeting with the King

On one of the following mornings, the Portuguese man finally approached me with some advice. "When you meet the Asantahene, do not speak unless spoken to. You will speak only to his advisor and then he will enjoin the king. If you are asked to sit down, do not cross your legs, for it is considered rude. The king has many wives. Do not look at any of them if you can help it, nor to the queen. If he offers you anything, you are to accept it graciously. If you fail to follow these rules, you may lose your life and the life of your native companion. The Asantehene will be sitting on the golden stool, the symbol and representation of his power. According to legend, it was summoned down from heaven by his high priest Okomfo Anokye to land in the lap of the king, signifying his divine rite to rule. Beside the king, the queen, who is his older sister, will be seated on her own stool. Avoid her gaze.

"He married his sister?"

The queen is not one of his wives, but helps him legitimize his rule. He does not share her bed, but she is wise in her own right and very powerful. The cultural quirks of the Ashanti cannot be understood by the average European. You do know of the Akans of which the Ashanti are a part?

"As I understand it, the Ashanti are one of several Akan tribes that have lived in this region for centuries, like the Mampong and Nsuta"

"Exactly." He reminded me again how the King had assembled various Akan tribes under the Ashanti banner, including the Juaben, Mampong, Kwaamen, Nsuta, Bekwai and Kokofo, in addition to the original members of the Ashanti, and how he conquered other Akan tribes such as the Denkyira. The Akan tribes maintained their tribal identities, but he tried to teach me again about other equally important familial bonds. Ntons were inherited through the father and focused on specific religious beliefs and practices, but in addition, every Ashanti belonged to a group of families or clans inherited through the mother. These clans were important in a person's standing among the Ashanti, their caste in society. They also helped the king establish the royal line. It was similar to the lines of lords in England, but inherited through only the mother. He told me of the eight clans representing the various maternal lineages.

"I still don't understand something though. Are the tribes different than the clans or nton?"

"The tribes that one belongs to are regional in nature, and can be independent of the clan, which is inherited. Despite this, tribal bonds are very strong, and most marry within their own tribe, whereas there can be intermarriages of clan or nton. In practice, clans and nton are more important to the original Ashanti themselves and less so to the other assimilated tribes like the Mampong, Nsuta or Bekwai. However, with these intermarriages, clan lineage is becoming more important and is a means of cementing power between families or groups. You will see evidence of the clans when we visit the palace."

I was still confused so he explained further that each clan was represented by a totem animal represented in the King's throne room. They were depicted as figures on the head of 8 great golden staffs. These included the dog for the Aduana clan, the buffalo for the Ekoona clan, the parrot for the Akona clan, the leopard for the Bretuo clan, the bat for the Asenie clan, the pie crow for the Asona clan, and the vulture from the Asakyiri clan. He told me that the king and his sister were descended from the Oyoko clan, which was symbolized by the eagle. They were related to the abusua subgroup of the Oyokos and so future kings would also come from that group according to maternal inheritance.

"I thought clan politics in the highlands was confusing. I'll never be able to keep this all straight."

"You won't have to. I tell you this only to emphasize that the king has many rivals, both from other tribes that he has assimilated or conquered, as well as other clans within the Ashanti themselves, and from some within his own family. Think of it as an African War of the Roses."

He walked on in silence and spoke to one of his scouts, as I tried to comprehend his history lesson. I would have to ask Kofi about all of this if I ever learned more of the Twi language.

When we came to the edge of Kumasi we were hailed by border guards, who were alarmed by our show of might. We were challenged by the sentries, who apparently were not used to seeing a large group of warriors entering the city. This caution relaxed when Bras was identified by one of the King's lieutenants, and a portion of the group were escorted to the palace. Bras sent several of the other men off on various errands to get supplies for his village. I was immediately impressed with Kumasi. It was a large city, even bigger than Accra, although not nearly as ancient. The houses, which reached for a mile in any direction, were largely made of stone rather than wood or mud, and had tall roofs consisting of parallel layers of thatching. There were several markets selling food and wares.

The palace was surrounded by a gated stone wall. Inside there was a very large courtyard, to rival those of the European kings. In front of the arched palace doors, which were immense and made of carved wood, a strange tree with odd branches and dark green leaves was planted. Bras explained to me that this was the wisdom tree, and a reminder to guests to hold their tongues and watch their speech when in the presence of the King. He reminded me again to speak only to the King's herald and not to the Asantehene himself. We passed two guards at the doors standing at attention, dressed in black and white flowing robes and both holding spears, with large flat bladed swords with embossed gold handles hanging from their belts. We were escorted through the doors and into a receiving chamber, where a few chairs were placed. There were paintings of battle scenes and intricately designed tapestries hanging on the walls.

We waited for several minutes for the King to arrive and then Bras was led away by himself for a private audience. Kofi and I were left in the receiving chamber for more than a half hour until we were finally escorted into the throne room. Waiting for us were Aurelio Bras, the King and Queen both sitting on a very strange throne, three personal guards dressed in white robes and carrying spears, and finally a man I took to be the King's advisor standing beside the royals. The king and queen were seated on short wooden and metal stools that were placed atop a large wooden stand, almost like a stage or pulpit. The king was a big man, with very dark skin, dark eyes and a blunt nose. His eyes shone brightly and he had an air of confidence and countenance. Unlike the guards outside and in this room, the cloth that the king and queen were wearing was beautifully patterned and of many bonnie colors including yellows, greens and blues. It was not unlike the flowing full length kilts of the highland clan chiefs. On his head he wore a red brocaded cap. There were many golden armbands and wristbands around both arms, and a single golden bracelet around each ankle that had some sort of intricate square designs. He was wearing golden sandals, but his feet were sitting astride two elephant tusks.

I had heard a rumor when I was a miner that the Ashanti King's feet could never touch the ground or the kingdom would collapse. I wondered if that had something to do with this strange practice of having his feet resting on tusks. There was a bag of amulets or magic charms that also sat under his feet, that was covered in elephant hide. I only knew what the contents of the bag were when Bras caught me staring and whispered the bag's secret to me. I had heard of magical charms of course, but I never met anyone who held 'em in Scotland. The queen was similarly arrayed, but her most striking feature was her age, which seemed older than the King. There were strands of grey in her coal black braided hair.

I gazed about the room and was amazed by the

amount of gold present. Next to the King was an
ornately carved wooden stand, which held a large round
golden vessel. I discovered its use when the King took a
golden ladle and used it to draw water from the vessel
and quench his thirst. I also noticed the eight golden
staffs of which I had heard earlier, each with its own
animal totem at its tip. I could identify the raven, the
leopard, the eagle and several others even from across
the room. They were richly painted, and sat next to a
series of large brown earthenware jars and pots. I had
no idea what the pots contained. Two men entered with
multiple drums and they began beating and chanting
and just as suddenly stopped. The King's advisor, who I
now took to be his herald, then began speaking. Bras
whispered the translation quietly into my right ear.
Kofi appeared to be struck deaf and dumb and was
gazing at the royals in wonder.

Bras translated as the herald went on, "All hail
his royal highness, the Kusamihente and Asantehene,
Otumfuo Nana Osei Kofi Tutu Opemsoo, holder of the
golden stool, keeper of the sword of heaven, and bringer
of peace and justice." Everyone in Guinea Propria knew
the story of the stone-embedded sword, as well as the
tale of the golden stool. Even I had heard the tale of the
famous sword. Apparently it had been placed in a stone
in the ground by the high priest Okomfo Anokye by
divine rite within site of the palace, and it was said that
if anyone could pull the sword from the stone the
kingdom would collapse and they would be crowned
Asantihene. So far, none had been able to withdraw the
sword. The tale sounded very much like one I had heard
of the famous King Arthur of the Welsh, and I wondered
maybe if this sort of magical sword was common

throughout the world. The sword embedded in the stone
in Wales had been lost for centuries, but I had been told
that this Ashanti magical sword was located only a
minute's walk from the King's palace and was sheltered
under a tent with a constant guard for protection. I
decided I would like to see the spot where the sword was
embedded in the ground. The golden stool was also said
to be brought down from heaven by the fetish priest
Okomfo Anokye and fell at the King's feet, further
legitimizing his divine rule. Each of the other Akan
tribes had a chief who sat on a stool, including a silver
one indicating second in command, but he who was
enstooled on the golden throne ruled the Ashanti. I
supposed the stool was the same as the throne of
England or the stone of scone in Scotland which was the
seat of power of the kings. I didn't think the thrones in
my homeland were sent from heaven, but I didn't really
know much about such things. It seemed the priests in
this part of the world held great mystical powers. The
same had been said of the druids in my highland home.
They had long since left Scotland for parts unknown,
but certain locations were said to store remnants of that
former wizardry. I had no knowledge of magic myself,
and it made me a little nervous to be so near people who
could wield such power.

The king spoke no English and when he did
begin talking, he spoke only to his herald, who then
relayed his words to us. It didn't matter. I couldn't
understand anything anyone said anyway without the
help of Bras or Kofi.

Everyone was standing and at once repeated the
Twi word for "all hail."

The king looked at Bras and then at me and Kofi

in turn. He said something to his herald who then relayed the question to Aurelio Bras, who bowed deeply. He spoke to the herald for almost 5 minutes in what sounded like fluent Twi. I was impressed with the Portuguese man's command of languages after all. When he was finished the king asked him several questions to which he replied to the herald. The queen never said anything or looked at anyone other than the king now and then. She looked bored.

After the herald said something to Bras in Twi he finally smiled and leaned close to me and said, "The Asantehene is very pleased. He is impressed with your exploits on the battlefield. He has seen many obronis (white men) in his rule, but you are the first white warrior he has met, and he appreciates the fact that you have lived with the Ashanti as one of their own. He wants to know how many lives you have taken."

"Tell the king that I do not count them." He relayed this to the herald and the king laughed deeply after it was repeated to him. He said something to his herald, who then repeated it to Bras. The Portuguese man smiled again.

"The Asantehene notes that only the bravest and most honest warrior would reply to a King with such a humble answer. You have been accepted in the royal guard, as has your young ward. You are to be placed in the upper east quadrant of the Ashanti Square to help fight the Akyem and protect the kingdom from invaders."

I had no idea what that meant and told Bras as much.

"The Ashanti use a square defense pattern with concentrations of soldiers on the northeast, southeast, northwest and southwest corners. It is quite effective in maintaining a defensive position around Kumasi at its center, without the need for a complete but very thin line of soldiers needed to encircle the kingdom. Each square protects one quadrant. None of his enemies have found a way to defeat his military strategy. No matter. You will soon learn all of this."

"Please thank the King for his good graces on my behalf."

"I won't have to. We are to smoke the peace pipe together to seal this friendship."

"And I suppose you are to be well paid for your part in my hire?"

"Of course. With a handful of gold, no less, but I believe you will also be well paid, especially if you perform as you have previously indicated in battle.

With that, a long thin painted wooden pipe was produced, at least as long as my arm, and decorated in blue and white figurines. It was filled with tobacco from the new world. I could not even guess how much gold it must have taken in trade to pay for the tobacco. Even the knights and lords of Europe could scarcely afford to get their hands on much American tobacco, though it was now all the rage across the continent. When the pipe was given to me, I inhaled deeply of the rich smoke. Within no time my lungs burned as if on fire and I coughed repeatedly. However, the sensation was warm and relaxing and I felt as if I was back in a pub in Beauly after a night of heavy drinking.

The King's guards were hailed and Kofi and I were escorted to soldier's quarters within the palace grounds. There were many guard ranks in the palace, and we were among the lower levels in prestige-- not very far above common Ashanti foot soldiery. Nevertheless, Kofi was, as usual, extremely excited and fortified by the experience. He had to translate virtually everything that was said, and since his English was very limited, I was generally unaware of anything that was happening. We were given uniforms o' the king's guard which included Kente cloth drapery about our shoulders, torso and legs. It was black and white and had the royal crest of the Asantehene, which looked a little like a black rooster with many arms. We were allowed to keep our weapons, but the warrior who seemed to be in charge was amused at the modifications to the swords. He asked Kofi about why I had carved off much of the round wooden orbs around the hilt, and sharpened the tip of the blade to a point. Kofi answered simply with the Twi word for "warriors" which was "asafo".

We trained every day in marching, fighting with spears and swordplay, and we also were present for royal protection and control o' the masses when the king and queen were escorted around Kumasi for their social gatherings. We were allowed one afternoon off duty per week for our own leisure. After a few weeks Kofi and I were even able to visit the magical sword embedded in the large black rock. It was indeed under a tent and at the bottom of a 10 foot deep pit. The blade wasn't visible and the hilt was driven into the stone down to the crosspieces. Various offerings to Nyame were strewn about it within the hole. I had the urge to attempt to give it a yank, but the looks from the two guards and the fear in Kofi's eyes dissuaded me.

My drilling skills were hampered by lack of explanation o' the maneuvers, so I simply stayed in formation and followed the lead of the commanding warrior, who was known as D'onoso. He was a fiercely proud man who was strong as a bull and a good fighter. He was from the same tribe and maternal clan as the king and queen and had their utmost loyalty. He seemed to like me, but I don't think he completely trusted someone he could not communicate with. At least he respected my prowess with the sword, and showed Kofi equal admiration.

Chapter 11: The Akyem

After about four weeks o' training, Kofi informed me that there was another Akyem uprising to the northeast where several light skirmishes had occurred. As I understood his broken speech, we were to marshal to the area at the upper right defense square and repel the Akyem incursion there. It took us about five days of marching through the jungle on very sparse trails to arrive at our destination. The spot where we were to be housed was not exactly a fort, but more of a loose collection of huts designed to allow the soldiers to live and do patrols in the area. There were a couple of women who cooked the meals in a giant iron cauldron. The food wasn't great but it was better than much of what I had tasted in Tontokrom and much better than the gruel I received in Newgate prison. It consisted of yams and rice, and was supplemented by fried plantains, fruit and occasionally cassava root. The water in this area was taken from a dirty creek, and hence my bowels were loose for several days. It didn't help when I had to march out on patrols for hours at a time. The other warriors chided me and gave me a nickname in Twi which Kofi told me meant "brown bottom." He at least still called me Al-zander out of respect.

On the sixth day out on patrol we were ambushed by the Akyem. We were moving in a line along the trail when we fell under an attack from trees to the right. They had a few muskets and the man in the lead of our unit was killed by at least 2 shots to his chest and abdomen. The next in line was hit in the shoulder and fell after he also received an arrow to the chest. Kofi and I were in the rear guard, as was our usual position since we did not know the trails or villages in this region. Everyone scattered and dropped to the ground finding what cover they could. I was facing to the rear thinking we would soon be surrounded. My flintlock was loaded with gunpowder and had a wad and ball in the barrel, but I had to place a wee charge of powder in the pan. I kept it in half-cocked position. Kofi signaled for me to follow him and do a flanking maneuver. We circled around carefully to the right rear, and maneuvered stealthily to the right for about an eighth mile and then looped back left. We could hear some shouts to our front and still some gunfire. By sheer luck we saw three Akyem warriors running toward us. Apparently their sniper attack was meant to fire only one or two rounds in a quick ambush, and hit as many Ashanti guard as possible, then to retreat into the safety o' surrounding jungle. They were looking down at their feet to avoid entanglements and not gazing far in front, and so they almost trampled on us before we were observed. I raised my musket, fully cocked the hammer back, and fired at close range. I put a large hole in the second Akyem warriors' chest, while Kofi had already buried one of his arrows in the lead warrior's neck.

Without even stopping, we rushed past the first two and with our swords flailing, slashed to either side o' the oncoming warrior as he tried to raise his bow and arrow in aim. He was at too close quarters and could not fend off blows from both sides and get off a shot. He was hacked to death in seconds from the joint effort of blades to both sides. We gathered the dead warriors' weapons and moved forward another 200 yards, and after only a minute or so, we encountered more Akyem. They had heard my musket fire and dropped to the ground realizing there was another Ashanti party behind them. A musket ball hit the tree beside me and both Kofi and I dropped to the ground. Thankfully, these Akyem snipers were using older model muskets, and their aim was not as true as the more modern flintlock I carried. Beyond 60 yards, they were hard pressed to hit their target. It was also raining softly, and older muskets were sensitive to moisture. It tended to cause misfires or complete firing failures as their powders got wet. I was lucky my flintlock had a 'cow's purse' to cover my firing mechanism and keep the pan dry.

Kofi held up four fingers indicating the number of enemy he saw, and then yelled something in Ashanti at the top of his lungs. I didn't hear all he said but he mentioned both of our names, and I understood the Twi word for three (abiasa), four (nnan) and warriors (asafo), so I assumed he was telling the other Ashanti guard still alive that we had killed three Akyem and had four others cut off if they would pursue. From a distance I heard a "Yaso" from Kufu Tati, who was our patrol leader and who was standing just in front of Kofi when we were attacked. Nothing happened for several minutes, and it provided me time to wipe the pan and frizzen from my musket with my robe and reload. I packed the muzzle with powder, wad and ball, rammed the barrel for tightness and placed more powder in the pan after placing the hammer at half position. When I saw a glimpse of Kufu Tati stealthily moving to our far left, I fully cocked the hammer, awaiting what would ensue. He was carrying a drum, which seems absurd in battle until one was exposed to the cunning way in which it was utilized. He quietly snuck up to the left of where the Akyem were ingrained in their positions in front, and instead o' pounding the drum, he used the tail end of the L shaped drumstick to scratch the leopard skin o' the drum face repeatedly. The effect was startling as it sounded exactly like the rumble of a lion or leopard, and it was loud. I heard an Akyem scream "Gyata", and one of 'em actually flung himself up to his feet to run away. We shot him where he stood with a combination of Kofi's arrow and my musket ball. If I had not been exposed to this technique in the previous several weeks of training, I would have jumped up and run for fear myself. Two other Ashanti warriors by this time had moved up behind the Akyem and started firing at their rear, as Kofi and I advanced with our swords. The rear Ashanti killed one of the three remaining Akyem. Kofi and I were almost upon them when the remaining two Akyem threw down their weapons and surrendered. We confiscated two older matchlock muskets, several bows, quivers and musket ball satchels and paraded the captives back to our base camp in the upper east square. I supposed they would be sold to slavers on the coast, and wondered that dying in battle might not have been a better end. Kofi and I were then sent back to retrieve the bodies o' the fallen Ashanti warriors who would enjoy a week long burial and mourning service in Kumasi.

D'onoso was still at base camp when he heard the reports about the battle from the remaining Ashanti warriors. He marched up to Kofi and me when we arrived, and gave us a big hug and a handshake. Our stature in his eyes had jumped greatly that day. After a few more days, he had to return to the palace, as was his station, but while he was present and in command, he made sure all soldiers in the upper east treated us with honor and respect. We were sent out on several more patrols daily to quell the Akyem insurgency, although it was three more weeks before we joined a pitched battle. We were told that another group of Ashanti soldiers patrolling this quadrant had surrounded approximately 30 Akyem warriors about 10 miles to the northwest of our base camp, near a village called Agogo. The Ashanti had called for reinforcements, and now outnumbered the Akyem five to one. Unfortunately, our enemy, as we had learned at great cost, made up for lesser numbers by having a fierce fighting spirit and the Akyem were great marksmen. It took us greater than a day to reach the battle. By the time we arrived and greeted our fellow warriors at the base of a great hill, there were already many Ashanti dead. The Ashanti guard had tried to overrun their positions, thinking that superior numbers would prevail. Unfortunately they were cut down quickly each time, as the Akyem held the high ground. They waited until the Ashanti were almost upon them before discharging their weapons. They had a few muskets, but many bows. Hence, they had conserved their ammunition and did not require much time to reload. Only a few Akyem were even wounded. We could hear 'em taunting us from their positions, or at least it sounded like that. I didn't speak their language but it reminded me of calls I had heard from the English during Preston, just before the onset of fighting began each day.

The Ashanti leader in charge of the battle was again Kufu Tati. He was not willing to waste any more men on open charges. After spending the better part o' the day trading shots from a distance, I finally went to him, with Kofi interpreting, to explain an idea I had. I hoped to use a tactic I had learned from the English. Rather than shoot flaming arrows into their midst, which any soldier would consider the height of cowardice and one even the Ashanti thought dishonorable, I instead explained (with Kofi's help) we could use fire as a smokescreen. We would try to conceal our charges and force the enemy to waste ammunition firing blindly. With Kofi's help in translation, the Ashanti general approved the idea and said we would try it as soon as it became light. The Ashanti troops nestled into their positions and slept uneasily that night. Kofi and I took turns on guard duty, but the Akyem never left their entrenched positions and the evening went by without further incursions by either side. We gathered as much kindling as we could find under cover of darkness.

Early morning o' the second day, when the fog was already thick, I started a fire with my flint and iron in some dry embers and stoked the flames with wood tinder and moist grass and passed some smaller branches o' fire to others. Kofi and Kufu Tati then instructed the other warriors in my unit to throw these flaming branches and bits of embers in front of us between the Akyem and ourselves, and we covered these flames in the grass with wet mulch from the surrounding forest. Soon flames were rising up to waist high in several places in front of us, and there was deep thick smoke mixed with the fog. We then started yelling and whooping as loud as we could from all our positions on this side o' the hill. The Akyem could not see our positions due to the smoke and fog and started firing blindly into the grass in front of us. We ducked down in cover, but I screamed and yelled as if I had been hit, and so did Kofi, followed by several others. We then waited two minutes for the Akyem to reload and for the smoke to become even thicker as we added more and more wet grass to the flaming ground in front of us. The flames died down, but the smoke became ever thicker.

In most battles, musket shots are delivered in a volley, all at the same time. This is to ensure that one man's sparks didn't ignite the powder of the warrior next to him, as he was in the act of loading. When a flintlock is fired it sprays a shower of sparks forwards from the muzzle and sideways out o' the flash-hole. If you are unlucky enough to be loading your flintlock when a spark hits your pan from your fellow soldier, the ball can go off in your face or the flash o' the powder can burn you.

As the smoke rose up and outward, we hooped and hollered again as if to do a charge, and again it was answered by a strong volley of shots from our enemy. We again yelled like we were hit and moaned as if wounded. This time without warning or waiting, I started crawling along the ground in between burning grass and hedges with my musket beside me, loaded and half-cocked. Kofi saw my plan and followed, as did several other warriors from our group. It took several minutes to reach yonder near their positions but the smoke was concealing most of our movements. We moved closer and closer in silence and thanks to the Ashanti hoops behind us on our original line, we heard and felt another volley of shots fly above our heads. Fortunately, no one was hit and from the angle of the shots I surmised that the enemy did not know they were near to being overrun. As smoke thinned near their line, I simply yelled "Now!" and at once we stood upright and charged directly at the enemy position, running as fast as we could. A man in front of me raised his weapon and pulled the trigger just as I was upon him. I held my breath as I waited for the explosion of his musket that never came. He looked aghast as he pulled the trigger again and nothing happened. Much to my fortune, the powder never ignited to launch the ball into my flesh. "Misfire!" I said out loud as I sped forward, amazed that I was still alive.

I did not have time to raise, cock and pull the trigger to get off a shot with my own musket, as I instead hit him with my sword across his neck as he bent to try to get his firing mechanism to work. Thank God for dull flints, soft frizzens, weak springs, or a clogged touch-hole. That was why we Ashanti warriors cleaned and maintained our weapons so carefully. The misfire would cost this man his life. He fell from one hard blow of the sword in my hand.

I had not yet fired but several Ashanti to my right and left had got off a shot and at least one or two had hit their mark. I jumped o'er a fallen tree in front of me that was being used as a blind by another Akyem warrior. I swung my sword at the man's head, but it impacted his flintlock and caused it to fire prematurely.

The shot went wild with a trajectory straight up in the air. I retreated three steps behind me towards the rear, fully cocked my flintlock, pulled the trigger and fired into his face at point blank range as he was getting up to rush me. The smoke and black powder stains from the muzzle hid the damage to his features, but judging by the amount of blood spraying everywhere, he was mortally wounded.

I had no time to look for my companions as I moved to my left toward another Akyem and swung the sword at his body. It missed him, but hit his musket and kept him from shooting me. He had not had time to cock the weapon so it provided him little help at close distance. I heard other gunshots but didn't know if those came from the enemy shooting at me from elsewhere, shooting at other charging Ashanti or our warriors shooting at them. I was not hit. I fought the warrior in front of me desperately from arm's length. My sword blade was moving quickly from side to side and o'erhead as fast as I could work it, so as to disallow the Akyem time to aim and fire. He was just a breath away from cocking the hammer and pulling the trigger on his musket, but as long as he had to use it to fend off a sword, I had the advantage. He finally dropped his musket in disgust, and took out his knife. He was dangerous at this distance and even with a sword I could take a lethal blow. He allowed me to back up slowly. That was a mistake, as from one and a half yards apart he could not reach my body with his knife and I could still hack at his arms and shoulders with my longer blade. He tried to rush me so as to close the distance and get a penetrating thrust in, but I was ready for it and hammered his head with an o'erhead strike. The blow cleaved his forehead, one eye and part of his nose, and dropped him to the ground. After another thrust to his chest, I grabbed both his musket and my own, as his flintlock was already loaded. It was an older model, with an old fashioned mechanism, but in principle similar to my own. The flint looked much worn, but since he was using it in battle, I assumed it was still in good working order. The hammer was in half-cocked position. I was correct that I had been only seconds from being shot at close range.

I moved slowly further to the right and saw two warriors fighting. From close distance, I aimed the Akyem's flintlock, pulled back on the steel hammer and pulled the trigger. I shot the Akyem a few yards in front of me as he struggled with one of my fellow Ashanti. As the Akyem fell from his grasp, Kufu Tati looked at me with gratitude and I tossed him the musket I had just fired. I didn't know if he had an arming kit or not, but he could find one close by next to the fallen Akyem warrior. I followed a line of thick hedges that offered some protection and spied another Akyem who had retreated farther up the hill and was aiming at me from behind a tree with his musket. I saw him cock the mechanism. I dropped to the ground just as he fired. The shot had missed me so closely I could smell the burnt gunpowder and both of my ears were ringing. Without hesitation, I sprang to my feet, ran forty yards up to the man with my sword drawn again and tried to cut him from behind a tree. However, this warrior was seasoned and tough and he used the tree to his advantage, keeping the trunk in between himself and my sword. He meant to trap my blade between the tree and his arm if he could. He pulled his own blade from his belt for a hand to hand blade fight. Neither of us could use our unloaded muskets, and mine lay useless at my feet next to this thick Odum tree. I saw Kofi out of the corner of my eye to my left in the distance and noticed that Kofi also acknowledged me. Instead of swinging with my blade, I picked up my musket with my left hand, as I dodged in a feint to my right and moved a few steps higher up the hill. Seeing that he would be flanked around the tree, the warrior did as I expected and kept the tree between his body and mine to keep using as a shield. In doing so and moving to his left, however, he turned his back to Kofi who was now squarely behind him and remained unnoticed. It was less than a second before the Akyem fighter had an arrow in the middle of his back, and he fell. He tried to get up and fight again with his blade, but I had now moved around the tree and struck him repeatedly with right and left slashing blows of my sword blade.

I had blood covering the better part of my legs and arms and I smelled of smoke and gunpowder. I was beginning to tire, but I still had a musket, although it was unloaded. I waved at Kofi, who by now was hunting the remainder of the Akyem. From all around the hill, Ashanti had converged on the smoke filled west side where the fires had started and where the Akyem defenses were breached. Warriors now flocked in to the softened defenses, and were firing muskets, shooting arrows and hacking and slashing their way through the last o' the defenders on all hillsides. I saw several pairs in fierce hand to hand combat.

I decided this was the only chance to reload. I placed my flintlock barrel down on the ground and poured the measure of powder down the barrel. I looked around for enemy snipers as I wrapped a lead ball in a wee piece of cloth and used the ramrod to force it down the barrel on top of the gunpowder to a tight fit. I half-cocked the hammer, carefully placed a wee bit of gunpowder in the flintlock's pan, and snapped the steel containing frizzen in place o'er the pan.

Suddenly, an arrow buzzed past my head and hit the tree next to me with a loud "thwap" as it slapped the bark. It came from above me near the top of the hill. I could not see the bowman, but I figured I had a scarce few moments to catch him before he pulled another from the quiver. I turned in an instant and cocked the hammer of the flintlock to the full position. I saw movement above me as I aimed and pulled the trigger. Sparks and smoke rang out from the front and side of the musket and I saw a man drop but I didn't know if he was hit by my shot or not. I ran up the hill in his direction, dodging trees, bushes and downed logs as I went. Suddenly, a man jumped up from one behind a fallen log to my left and sliced my leg with a sword as I tried to leap past. I lost my balance and hit the ground losing my musket in the process, but holding on to my sword with my right hand. He jumped on top of me immediately and meant to put the sharp end of his sword into my chest. My shot must have missed him completely, as he looked unhurt and was fighting like a man possessed by a demon. I held my own sword with both hands out at my chest, and he was cut as he fell on top of me, but not badly. His sword had hit home, and the impact o' the point of his blade still made a two inch long, quarter inch deep cut just below my left nipple. Had my outstretched sword not protected me, my heart would have been skewered. I did not get up, but instead

rolled sideways quickly to maneuver on top of him as I
locked his legs with mine. I grabbed his sword hand
with my left. He was grabbing my right sword arm with
his own left hand. We sat for a few seconds in a
stalemate. He was taller but I was stronger. With my
legs tied around his, my head only reached his mouth. I
took my head and butted his jaw as hard as I could. My
forehead was much denser and his jaw broke with a
crack. I repeated it again and as his hold on my right
arm weakened, I turned my blade toward his neck and
drove it home, just below where my head had bashed his
mouth. It didn't bleed much until I twisted the blade
around in a circle. Soon there was a torrent of blood
pouring from the wound in his neck and his eyes glazed
with a lack of recognition. I sat up, my hair and face
now as bloodied as the rest of my body. I was also
bleeding from the wound in my chest. I was out of
breath so I just sat next to the dead warrior looking at
him. I saw the bow with a notched arrow lying by the
trunk where he had sliced me. I hoped this was the
bowman who had just missed me. I was lucky I wasn't
wearing an arrow in my chest from this brave lad,
rather than just a knife wound. These Akyem were
tough and as well trained as the Ashanti. It occurred to
me that the Akyem were as vicious with swords as the
Scottish highland regiments, although they fought in
much smaller groups and mostly relied on musket and
arrow skirmishes instead of swordplay.

I heard a few more shots ring out as I picked up
my prized musket. The smoke was beginning to clear as
the morning wore on. The Ashanti had won a complete
and overwhelming victory and there were no Akyem left
alive. Ashanti guards were picking up guns and bows

from the vanquished and stripping bodies of anything o' value. I found myself trembling. I didn't know if it was from excitement, fear or exhaustion. I could taste and smell blood. I was sick to my stomach, and when I looked at all o' the dead bodies on the hill, I became nauseous. I heaved up a heavy dose of bile and some bits of banana from breakfast. I had killed a hand full of men today, who I didn't know and would never know. I took some comfort in the fact that they were also trying to kill me, but I decided in that instant I did not enjoy battle. I didn't even enjoy being a soldier. I had acted with determination and blind courage in the heat o' the moment when I had used the smoke as cover and been able to slink into the midst o' the enemy position. I thought back on the battle and realized that several different warriors had the chance to fire their muskets directly at me, but none had got a clean shot away. I guessed most of it was luck. I supposed it was almost always luck, ne'er courage that determined whether you lived or died in war. My father's luck had deserted him on the battlefield, even when his courage remained steadfast. My luck had not yet left me, and I wondered if God or the angels had helped protect me. I pondered whether they were on my side, or even on anybody's side. No one knew, not even the Kings or the priests. I wondered if I should say a prayer. I didn't know what to say that God would listen to anyway, so I just looked up in the sky and said "thanks". It was about as religious as I ever got.

I looked around for Kofi. I hoped he was alright and unharmed. I needed to get him out of here. He was a good soldier, but he didn't deserve the dangers of being a fulltime warrior. What if I got him killed? He was better off helping farm and hunt back with his father in Tontokrom. I had done him and his family a great injustice by bringing him here and exposing him to the terrors of warfare.

Kufu Tati came up to me, looked down at the dead warrior at my feet, and patted me on the back. He said "Al-zander, asafo." and smiled.

Kofi saw us and then approached me with a big grin on his face. "Kofi e Al-zander pa paa asafo! great warriors!" "Kill much Akyem!" He wanted to congratulate me, but I was in no mood for celebration. I hated this. Kufu Tati and Kofi hugged and walked away chatting furiously and comparing their wounds. My chest hurt and the wound I received was dripping blood. I wanted to go home. Home to the highlands, not the Ashanti outpost, and not to Kumasi to the palace. I longed for Scottish heather.

We took a full day to clean up the area and another few days to bring the dead and wounded back to base camp. The wounds were cleaned and dressed, the dead piled on litters made of trees and leaves, and then almost a hundred men formed a procession back to Kumasi. The Akyem dead were piled in a mass grave and burned in a pit at the battle site on a huge bough of branches.

It took well nigh a week in all, but we arrived to a huge welcome in Kumasi. Word of our victory had travelled throughout the district. There were throngs of men and women lining the road into Kumasi all o' the way to the palace. The people along the street were throwing some kind of herb at the warriors, which Kofi said was for luck and good health. Kofi and I were somewhere in the middle o' the procession, but as we neared the large wooden doors 'neath stone arches which signified the gate o' the royal palace, we were met by D'onoso, the head o' the King's guard. As he had done a few weeks earlier, he hugged me tightly with a big grin and shook my hand in the thumb to thumb fashion. He did the same to Kofi. He then spoke long with Kofi. I guessed they were discussing the battle by the way Kofi was using his body, hand gestures, and the way he kept pointing to me. I was not interested in the battle. It was over and both Kofi and I were alive. That's all that mattered. I needed to find some medicine for the wound on my chest, which had reopened and was draining a pustule fluid, and I needed to bathe. The wound smelled fetid and I was afraid of blood poisoning. I no longer had blood caked on my skin, having washed in the stream near the battlefield a few days ago, but I was coated in grime and sweat from the long days of marching back to Kumasi. My arms ached from carrying the dead on Kente cloth gurneys. I quit bothering to listen to their conversation and daydreamed about being back in the highlands.

Chapter 12: A Promotion

"Al-zander." Kofi was trying to get my attention. "Al-zander. Come." "See Asantehene". "We come with D'onoso."

I was in no physical or mental condition to meet the King. I was tired; tired of fighting, tired of war, tired of the Ashanti, and tired of having only one friend who I could barely talk to. I understood the importance of the summons, however, so I nodded at Kofi and D'onoso and we strutted past several other soldiers on our way to the palace. As we passed, a strange thing happened. The guards, who up until this time had been ignoring me for the most part, separated and gave us an aisle way. As they did they raised their muskets, bows or spears in salute and started chanting, "Al-zander, Al-zander, Al-zander." It was quite humbling. I tried to wave at first, but noticed Kofi and D' onoso had begun to march in step, so I kept my head straight ahead and joined my fellow soldiers in formal cadence. The gates were opened for us and we again passed the wisdom tree, the two sentries on guard, and went in to meet the King. We were not taken directly into his chambers but instead were shown into some living quarters down a hall to one side, where there was a pool and some fresh clean Kente cloth. We were bathed with the help of two young Ashanti women. That was one of the most pleasant things that I had experienced in Africa. One of

the young native lasses cleaned and dressed my wound
and added a salve. Her tender touch around my sores
were a welcome, if somewhat unexpected, treat. I was
glad I was half immersed in the pool of water at the
time so she didn't notice how aroused I was. I thought
back to Tontokrom to my first hunt and of how Amma
had done the same for my leg wound. I missed her. I'm
sure Kofi did too, but in a much different way. The
fresh water of the bath was invigorating. It didn't hurt
that there were two lovely and scantily clad young
lasses to help us get the dirt off. I was hoping that they
would come back to see us after we visited the King. I
was definitely feeling better and a little rammy. We
were then helped into our clothes by the bathers. I
looked over at the two young native lasses with lust and
longing. I asked them their names. "Wo frow ye sen?!"
but they just giggled in reply and hurried away. Kofi
shook his head at me in scorn. I didn't know if it was
because we were in a hurry to meet the King or if
perhaps they were the Asantehene's concubines and any
fraternization might get us in trouble. I didn't care. My
mood had changed.

We were then taken back to where D'onoso was
waiting for us. I felt refreshed and not in despair as I
had been earlier. We were escorted by two personal
guards back into the King's chambers. The Asantehene
was again seated with the queen, with the same
ornamentation all about him in gold, and his feet again
resting astride two elephant tusks.

The herald gave the same introduction to the
king that we had heard a couple of months earlier, "All
hail Kumasihente and Asantehene, Otumfuo Nana Osei
Kofi Tutu Opemsoo "and then the King looked at me

and gestured for me to come forward. He talked for a long while and then the herald tried to repeat it. Oddly, the King seemed to be speaking to me rather than to the herald and he was grinning like a court jester. Too bad I couldn't understand the joke. He said a few more things, then clapped his hands.

It was Kofi who translated, as he always did for me, but he took 10 minutes of conversation and condensed it into about 10 words. "Al-zander defeat Akyem. Help Asantehene. Help Ashanti. Great warrior. No more Akyem. Now guard King."

I didn't know what all of that meant, but I wanted to argue or at least point out, that we had only defeated the Akyem in one short battle and had not defeated their entire tribe. They were renegade fighters who attacked in tiny bands and ambushed larger forces. They would be hard to defeat utterly unless their leaders decided to surrender. But I couldn't tell 'em that.

The King said something to his herald, and two wee earthen jars were brought forward. He reached across to a much larger jar beside him of the same brown color and light colored linear designs about it, and he ladled two spoons full of gold flakes into the tiny jar in front. He then did the same to the other jar, but put five wee spoons full of gold flakes into it. He handed the larger one to me and the other one to Kofi. It was more gold than I had ever seen, even when I was working in the mines. We only ever saw the rough rock with the shiny flakes embedded into the stone, never the refined flakes of shiny ore. I was flabbergasted. I didn't know how much it was worth, but I was guessing that it would almost book passage back to Scotland.

One more battle and I would fulfill my dream and have enough farthings to return to the highlands. As much as I was sick of war, I had to confess that it was paying well! I looked over at Kofi and his eyes were alight. He was as surprised as I and unable to take his eyes off of the brown and yellow pottery vessel in his hands. The King said a few more words to the herald, who repeated these in a loud voice for all within the palace to hear, then we were dismissed.

I thought we were heading back to the palace barracks, but when we almost reached there we turned off at a corner and went to a separate stone building. I was escorted inside with Kofi trailing behind me. D'onoso said some things in Twi to the four guards there inside, who were dressed in a more flowing Kente cloth robe with a black geometric square design that I had seen on robes that the King sometimes wore. They each nodded and looked us over closely when we were introduced by D'onoso. Both men nearest to us bowed to me and I bowed back.

"Me ye O'sono" said the larger man.

"Kofi e Al-zander guard King." Kofi said with a beaming smile.

"Ani." I replied. "Aye." I repeated in English as I often did to help my friend understand. This could be good for both us.

As soon as D'onso had left, the two guards went into a long conversation with Kofi and pointed all about their room. It was much grander than the other soldier's barracks and much cleaner with a stone floor. We were shown to our cots, which were covered with Kente cloth of the same design as the warrior's robes. I had not slept on anything so soft since I had left

Culbokie. We even had wooden chests to place our pots of gold dust and other possessions in. I fretted at first that these fineries could have been stolen by someone gaining entry, but I shouldn't have been worried. Nary a soul could gain palace access, and even fewer could gain entrance to the personal guard's quarters, unless at their own peril.

The King's personal sentries were some of the most loyal, highly trained and highly venerated citizens in the Ashanti Kingdom, and outside o' the King and queen themselves, everyone looked up to and feared 'em. They were the most elite o' the palace guards, and Kofi and I had joined their ranks.

We would now be stationed here at the palace and would not have to suffer the dangers and discomforts o' the outer square base camps and frequent patrols. And there were those lassies who helped bathe us. I wondered if they might be another o' the perks of the King's guard? I would like to find 'em again and see if they were interested in a romp in the heather with a pale skinned companion. It had been such a long time since I had been with a woman. I needed to ask Kofi again about the rules around such things. He seemed to be bothered by my original interest in the two girls and I wasn't sure why. I didn't want to have a tryst and later find out it would cost me my head.

We spent most o' the rest o' the afternoon learning the duties and posts o' the palace sentry. In the days that followed, I was always paired with Kofi and he did his best to translate for me, although many times I had no idea of what I was supposed to be doing, where we were to be at any given time, or who I was talking to. Though we were attached to the

Asantehene's personal guard, we rarely if ever saw the King, as he seldom left the palace.

I no longer went out with my favorite flintlock, although I had a sword. It was not the sword that I fought with, but a ceremonial sword of a similar design with gold leaf about the hilt and on the scabbard. I still kept it very sharp with my soapstone and it could cut and kill, but it was not easy or comfortable to swing. The sword I used in combat was in my barracks chest, and would be preferable in a fight and had no scabbard, but this one sure looked nice. It hung from my rope belt around my white Kente robe festooned with black royal print designs. I also carried a long spear with a bronze blade. We practiced with it daily in fighting drills.

I wore sandals that were also crisp and not weathered like the ones I had worn for the previous months. My feet actually did not ache at the end of each day, as they had during my time after the patrols in the upper east square. We often took sentry duty guarding the palace gates at the site of the wisdom tree, and did other duties minding the walls of the palace. We had a weekly review in front o' the King in formation, but I couldn't really see him from my vantage point behind so many tall warriors. And the King's sentries were all fairly tall. He chose the biggest and the most fierce warriors for this role, so it was an honor to be amongst 'em. While I had done many drills around the palace and in Kumasi when I first joined the Ashanti army, those exercises were really just part o' regimental training, and were located in the palace for an outward show o' might. Now I was a member of an elite group who maintained the tight security o' the palace itself. We were looked up to by almost every soldier we saw.

Our golden swords, sandals and distinguished uniform marked us as the most elite o' the guard. Kofi fit right in and he was beginning to fill out his tall, skinny frame. I think it was because he fed on healthy meals for the first time in his life and exercised daily. I was proud o' my young friend, and felt good for him. I was determined to keep protecting him, which meant trying to keep him here at the palace rather than joining further battles in the outer squares, but I knew he loved this life and honor would force him to be at the fore of any skirmish. He had reached a status few, if any, in his village could ever hope to aspire to.

Chapter 13: The Death of the First Asantehene

We remained in the sentry service o' the King guarding the palace for the following 10 weeks. In that time there were no more incursions, ambushes or village attacks by the Akyem. I was surprised one day by another summons from the Asantehene. I came to his chambers with Kofi as my interpreter, but Kofi was not allowed into the room with the golden stool this time, making me very uncomfortable. I stood before the King as I had done on two other occasions, but this time I could understand little and had no one to translate. The herald went on and on in Twi gibberish, and then a servant brought out a folded bundle of fabric. When it was unfolded and handed to me, I was astonished. It was a Scottish great kilt, what we in the highlands called a *Feileadh Mòr*, and the English called a great plaid. It was yards and yards of pleated fabric that covered the legs and torso and draped on and around the left shoulder. It was the standard garment for the highlander with means. The red and green colors of the tartan were gorgeous and it was made of worsted wool. I ran my hand along the fabric and smiled. I breathed in the wool scent o' the highlands and admired the craftsmanship o' the weaver. I looked at the King and smiled and nodded my approval. The king looked back at me and at the herald and shook his head and pointed at me to don it. I was flabbergasted. It was a gift for me from the King. I originally thought the King was going to wear it himself. I could not hope to wear such a fine garment in my present position as a sentry, and I had no opportunity to wear it anywhere else. All sentries always wore the white official uniformed robes bearing the black symbol of the Asantehene. Perhaps I could wear it on special occasions. The herald then explained to me in a fair English tongue that the King wished me to wear the tartan at all times when I was on duty. I would be the King's personal Highland Guard. I had forgotten that the herald spoke my own language and acted as his own translator when given the opportunity and direction by the King. I was beaming with pride. I had never before been so honored or ever bestowed with such a gift, except when given the gold dust by this same great King. I owed him my allegiance and depth of gratitude, and I would of course comply with his request. I would wear the great kilt with pride. It would be my little piece of home.

"Me adase Paa." I bowed low as I thanked him.

"Akwaaba. Madanfo." I didn't need a translator to understand the herald when he replied in Twi, "You are welcome, friend."

Everyone was smiling, and so it was that I became the first and only Ashanti warrior and palace sentry to wear a Scottish great plaid. Now everywhere I went in and outside of the palace, I heard shouts of "Al – zander" from guards and simple townsfolk, as I had become locally famous. We still drilled and went on duty around the palace, but the war had settled down, and most of Ashanti was enjoying peace. I had even tried to ask the King about the practice of local chieftains selling their own subjects into slavery, but D'onoso had warned me off. He told me, through Kofi, that it was strictly forbidden for the guard to advise the King on any matters outside o' war, and that it could go bad for me if I persisted in meddling in politics. I therefore decided I would someday go back and teach the Datano chieftain a lesson on my own. I smiled at that thought of revenge for Pesaata.

Several more weeks went by without any further Akyem incursions, and the king became increasingly complacent. The Asantehene and his advisors decided to take a trip to the eastern border of his kingdom to the city of Abirem to settle a dispute between two o' the most powerful Ashanti chieftains-- the Mampong and the Kokofo. The problem surrounded a border dispute around gold mines that sat between the tribal lands o' the Mampong, which was to the north and east of Kumasi, and o' the Kokofo, which was to the southeast of Kumasi. The chief of the Mampong was known as the Mamponhene, and he ruled an important tribe and sat on the silver stool, second only to the king's. The kokofohene was not as powerful as the man sitting on the silver stool, but his chiefdom lay in between Kumasi and the Akyem, and the Asantehene needed his support and powerbase. I was not comfortable with the king making this journey, as the mountain strongholds o' the Akyem were only about 5 days walk to the east from Abirem, but I had no say. Abirem was situated near the eastern lands of the Volta, much closer to Kokoridua of the Kokofo than it was to Manso Mampong, but it was somewhere between the two and I believe the King intended to make his closest rival suffer somewhat for having to intervene in this clan problem. The Mampong would have greater than a week's journey to reach the meeting site.

Abirem was a four day long journey even from Kumasi; because all the King's personal guard had to travel with him, ahead, behind and on either side for protection. Four huge men with stout arms carried the king on a great chariot without wheels. The chariot had a seat for the King and fabric above and below. It was made from the Odum tree, a hard sturdy wood that took a nice polish. The men had round fabric placed on their heads and actually walked with the struts of the King's chariot atop their heads, with their arms used only as braces. I had often wondered about the size and weight of objects the Ashanti carried on their heads, but this was amazing to watch, especially when they simultaneously raised the four corners of the chariot. It was impressive to see how the structure was kept as level as the surface of a highland loch.

We traveled for a full day to the southwest until the Asentehene decided to stop and rest in a village called Kwaso. We slept there, but woke early the next day because we had a grueling hike ahead of us. The trail rose up to some steep mountains sloped like Ben Nevis back home. We climbed and climbed and reached the ridge, which we traversed to the south and east beside a great round body of water that lay at the base of the mountains. Kofi told me it was called Lake Bosomtwi, and was a gift o' the gods. It was rimmed on all sides by these tall hills and lined by very green verdant landscape with dark black sand that lined the water. It reminded me of Loch Archaig back in Scotland, only larger. We followed the ridge down into a village which provided our party with fish and fruit. The King was welcomed warmly by all of his subjects. Apparently it had been some years since he had last been here. We camped o'ernight and ate heartily, as I had not done on any of my patrols. There was an official cook with us who served all o' the soldiers after the King. The fish were smaller than those I was used to in the Scottish lochs, with white, instead of pink flesh, but it tasted fresh.

We again awoke early the third day and continued our journey around the loch and onto several lower green glens. We traveled for many hours that day, hiking into early evening. We crossed the Anum River, which was wide, but shallow and easily forded, and came onto a flat plain where we met up with a fairly wide, well used road, traveling southeast. We stopped briefly for some food at a village called Ofoase, and a few hours later finally stopped to sleep in an even smaller village called Yaw Bronwakrom. It reminded me of Kofi's home village. Apparently the King had a relative or friend here, because he greeted the man like a lost brother and embraced him warmly. I had never seen anyone else even touch the Asantehene, much less speak directly to him. I wondered at the bond between the two men.

I was exhausted from better than 14 hours of marching and wanted to go to sleep immediately, but the other warriors were nervous and all were speaking in hushed tones concerning their fears for the King's safety. From what I gathered, the Asantehene had not brought any of his magical charms with him on the trip, nor was he even in his armor. I had never seen the King wear his bronze armor chest plate and braces except for during ceremonies, so I wasn't sure the arms were that functional anyway. The guards were nervous that we were so close to the land o' the Akyem and we were so few. If news of the King's journey had leaked to the Akyem, he would be a prized target that his enemies would not hesitate to attack given the opportunity. The sentries were not afraid for themselves, but they took protection of their leader very seriously. I shared their concerns, but I was too tired to worry much about it tonight. I told Kofi to tell 'em we would be very cautious for the rest o' the trip and warned all warriors to be at the height of awareness for possible ambush.

We awoke again early on the fourth day and Kofi and I pulled sentry duty for 3 hours on the perimeter while other warriors ate. The food smelled delicious but we only received a wee piece o' fruit before we undertook the last leg o' the journey to Abirem. We followed the road that ran through the village for another hour until it stopped at the River Pra, in the midst of some heavily forested jungle. The river flowed through a shallow glen which divided the road in which we were traveling, but it fell from the highlands and was swift o' current. There was no way to safely wade across, especially with the King bound on his human chariot. There were four dugout canoes sitting on the bank, and three that were visible on the opposite bank, to allow travelers to pass. A boatman usually accepted food or seashells (the coin of rural Ashanti) for the use o' the crafts, but of course this was not necessary when in the company of the Asantehene. We were to take turns using the boats to navigate across to the other side. The first three canoes across carried the nine fore guards who watched the opposite bank, while the fourth boat carried warriors who would bring the remaining canoes back across to our shore, lashed to their own boats. The second crossing therefore carried a total of six canoes, with the King on the inside and five boats surrounding him, each with three guards per boat. The wee oars were wholly too short, too thin and naught worth a hog's ear for pushing the crafts forward, making progress yonder across the river Pra quite slow. Our wee boat was on the King's left, and O'sono was leading in the fore canoe.

As O'sono's canoe reached the far bank and he hopped out to pull it farther up the slope so the warriors could exit, I heard a hail of gunshots coming from behind the trees of the bank. O'sono immediately went down and I saw blood on his shoulder. Several of the fore guard were also hit. I had my musket already loaded, so I cocked the mechanism and returned fire into the trees, but I could not clearly see any attackers.

"Snipers!" I yelled back to Kofi and anyone else who might understand. "Get the King down! Shield him!" However, as I said that, I watched in horror as the king's canoe was blasted to pieces by at least 20 musket shots coming from several different angles. Wood was chipping up and splintering everywhere. I tried to motion for the oarsmen in the King's canoe to back up to the opposite shore as it had not yet reached the far bank. "Retreat!" I yelled in despair. The oarsman in the King's canoe was lying lifeless and his oar was uselessly floating in the water beside him.

"Down! Cover the King!" I yelled again. The remaining guards on the western shore sat helpless, as the few boats in the water struggled against the current.

Kofi grabbed the side of the King's canoe as our

262

own oarsmen tried to back us away. Another of the elite personal guard grabbed the other side of the King's canoe from his own boat, and together we tried with the oars and our own hands to back us away. Two other boats were floating helplessly in the water with several wounded or dead aboard. At that point, a large volley of arrows hit the flotilla o' boats, but I felt no pain so I figured I had again escaped injury. My luck was still holding. I didn't have time to check anyone else.

This attack was carefully planned. These snipers had both muskets and arrows and they were allowing no time for return fire. We were barely moving backward and fighting the swift current, so I dropped my musket into the floor o' the canoe, jumped into the dark water and started swimming the three canoes back to the opposite bank from which we came. The weight o' the Scottish wool o' my kilt weighted me down in the river and I immediately sank to my neck. The water was cold and my feet sometimes could not reach the bottom, but I kicked around till I could feel rocks under my toes. My clothes hung about my body like a big anchor, and I tired, but the dire situation and outright fear gave me enough energy to push the three canoes in the proper direction. Both sandals had fallen off in the current.

Another volley of arrows flew back from behind the trees, and I heard someone nearby shriek in pain. I was up to my neck in the water so I offered a very small target. It was probably all that saved my life because the sky was filled with arrow shafts. Almost everyone in the three canoes had been hit with an arrow or a musket shot. The Ashanti guard left on the bank in front of us were firing and shooting arrows and even throwing spears at the far bank but they could not see the attackers amid their cover, and therefore were not helping much. Their muskets were useless at that range anyway. When we finally reached the bank, the guard there converged on the King's canoe and carried it in masse away from the water and up the bank toward the city with which we had come earlier that morning. I did not know the condition o' the King, but it didn't look good. Several warriors were wailing in grief. I looked for Kofi. He was struggling to get out o' the canoe and was stooped and holding his side. It looked like our oarsman was dead with 2 arrows embedded in his chest and abdomen. I crawled from the water with my soaked kilt dragging the ground. I grabbed Kofi to help him up.

"Al-zander, must see to Asantehene!"

His sense of honor was admirable, but wasted on me at that moment. With my arm around his shoulder for support, I helped him away from the shore and tried to set him down under a tree. He had a spot of blood on the robe over his chest. I tried to check his wounds.

"No Al-zander. Kofi go to Asantehene!"

I didn't have time to argue with him as we were still within range o' the bows from the yonder shore. Although the effective range of a flintlock musket is only about 125 yards, even when used by the most trained marksman, the arrows from the opposite bank were reaching us at a distance twice that. They couldn't aim directly at us, but a volley of arrows could pepper a lot o' ground.

"OK... Ani...Aye" I said, as we hurriedly limped up the bank and followed the rest o' the guard who had by now set the King's canoe down a few hundred yards from the river.

Three warriors were tending to his wounds. I

saw one pluck an arrow from the king, but he had at least two other wounds which appeared to be musket balls, and they were in bad places. His upper chest and shoulder both had large circular wounds. He was bleeding severely and when he opened his mouth to talk, blood was coming out. I heard him say, "Ankah me nim a" which Kofi translated to me as "If I only knew". I guess he decided his quest had been foolhardy without his protective amulets and armor, and that he had underestimated the military strength and cunning of the Akyem. We needed twice as many guards to assail their positions. It was no time for a counterattack in vengeance and retribution. We had to retreat.

I watched as King Osei Tutu died in front of me. He was the first Asantehene of the federation o' tribes that now represented the vast Ashanti Kingdom, and he had been my patron for the past several months. I actually had tears for this man, who had gone so far as to buy me a Scottish great kilt from foreign traders because he had respected my skill on the battlefield. I felt miserable. I wanted revenge, but our job right now was to get the King back to Kumasi. There would be grief and mourning. The Kingdom would be in turmoil until the next King could be crowned, or "enstooled" as they called it in the Ashanti, since he wore no crown. I had no idea how succession worked here. I'm not sure anyone did, since he was the first and only of his kind.

I looked back at Kofi, and was immediately concerned when I saw even more blood on the Kente cloth covering his chest. He looked very pale and I had to catch him as he collapsed. I laid him on the ground near the body of the king. He was wheezing badly and there was a whistling sound coming from a rent in the

cloth around his ribs. I tore his robe from his upper
body and was aghast as I saw a huge hole on one side of
his chest. There were frothy red bubbles coming from
the wound and it was deep.

"Is OK Al-zander. I pull arrow out." He said to
me weakly and then he coughed up a large amount of
blood. It was bad. I was frantic to find someone to help
him so I yelled at everyone around me to find a healer.
I tried to stuff his shirt back into the hole to stop the
bleeding but it was soaked in blood in less than a
minute. He became paler and paler and his breathing
became more and more labored. He lasted for about 10
minutes before he died. I cried like I had done when my
father had passed. It only lasted a few minutes but it
was a watershed.

A warrior sentry who shared our barracks,
named Yesi, helped me make a litter gurney for Kofi's
body, and he and I carried him for two days as we made
our way back to Kumasi. Yesi was another common
name in the Ashanti, named for one who was born on
Sunday. He was a truly kind lad with warm eyes and
broad shoulders. He was one o' the few King's guards
who had a big belly, but he was strong o' back and
strong o' heart. We barely stopped for food or rest. I
was so numb and so full of shame that I had let down
both Kofi and the King that I barely noticed the fatigue
in my arms or the fact that I was walking barefoot. My
sandals were lost in the river. I only stopped walking
when Yesi needed to rest, and that was rarely. Even
though we walked tirelessly, we could barely keep up
with the guards who were carrying the body of the king.
There was a short parade of soldiers moving along the
trail. None spoke and most held their heads low.

Occasionally the silence would be pierced by the wail of a man in mourning.

The queen and all eleven of King Osei Tutu's wives and many children met us at the outskirts of the city. Most were crying uncontrollably. It was always strange to think that the queen was the King's sister, not one of his wives, but I supposed that made the transition to power easier for whoever took over the throne next. I wondered if some of the wars in England would have been prevented if the English or European queens were not married to the King. It was a novel custom for sure, but my wee knowledge of politics wasn't great enough to understand all o' the ins and outs and intrigue surrounding royal succession. I felt bad for the King's family, and mourned along with them. I hoped the prospect of naming the next ruler would not lead to strife or bloodshed among his children. Most were not yet old enough even to understand royal politics and none of the family could predict what would happen next.

The king's body was taken to the palace where he was prepared for burial. Several thousand people visited the burial on the following five days, singing and dancing and offering prayers to their god Nyame. We took Kofi to a cemetery which was near the palace and reserved for warriors. His body had begun to swell and darken with the heat o' the late summer sun, and we needed to get him in the ground. There were no pine boxes and no crosses to mark his grave site, but I buried him with his sword, bow and quiver. I know he wasn't a Christian, but like I had done for Pesaata, I said some words o' my own in prayer to the God of the bible that I had heard as a laddy during funerals in Scotland. I

hoped it would save his soul, and I hoped I would meet
him again in the next life. He was a true friend in all
and everything that entailed, and the closest companion
I would or could ever have.

I stayed around the palace for another ten weeks
to help protect the queen and to guard against an attack
from the Akyem or some other tribe who thought to
conquer the kingdom during a time o' weakness and
chaos. However, I was not much use to the guards
without Kofi to help me translate instructions. Both
O'sono and D'onoso had fallen along the Pra River with
the King and D'onoso's replacement in the position at
King's high guard neither liked nor trusted me. I think
he envied my fame with the people, but he also blamed
me and the other guards at the river for the King's
death. It didn't matter, my heart was no longer in
soldiery. I doubted I had enough gold to make it back to
the highlands, but I was a relatively rich man by
Ashanti standards and I could probably find sea passage
from Accra or Elmina to somewhere. But first, I needed
to return to Tontokrom and to tell Japhet and Amma
about Kofi and to give 'em the gold and sea shells that
he had acquired in service to the King. I dreaded that
day and that explanation, and therefore fear kept me a
few extra days in Kumasi while I stoked my courage for
that family meeting.

Chapter 14: Back in the Wilds

The lack of a clear successor to King Osei Tutu had created a problem for the Ashanti. He was the absolute ruler and his children (he had many) were too young to lead. In fact, since he was the first to rule the previously divided tribes, no one knew exactly how succession was supposed to take place. It was unclear who should be the rightful heir, other than it would have to be someone from the Oyoko Abusua clan by way of maternal inheritance. The spiritual leader and second-in-command, the high priest Okomfo Anokye, did not want the job for himself, but seemed to be backing the Mamponehene. This was contested by other clan and tribal leaders, especially the Kokofu, who still had unresolved border issues with the Mampong. Fights and skirmishes were breaking out throughout the kingdom, and illicit slave trading amongst and betwixt villages was now becoming rampant.

One evening about 11 weeks after the death o' the king, the new head o' the palace sentries told me (in short words that I could understand) that I was no longer "Akwaaba" (welcome) and that I should "wo kon" (you leave). It was early morning and I simply gathered my possessions from my wooden chest and walked out. I handed my golden hilted sword to Yesi as I left the barracks. I didn't need it. I had the simple blade that I had fashioned in Tontokrom, a bow and quiver that I seldom ever used, and my prized flintlock with ammunition satchel and powder horn. I also carried two leather pouches, one containing my gold, and one that contained the shells and gold dust that had belonged to Kofi. I left the small earthen pots in which they had originally been gifted, since they were bulky to carry. I intended to bequeath Kofi's share to Japhet and Amma when I saw 'em. I headed south from Kumasi on the road to Bekwai and Poano. From there I would have to turn southwest to reach Tontokrom. I didn't know exactly where the village was, but I knew it was somewhere betwixt Monso Nkwanta and the gold fields o' the Dutch. I had hunted throughout the area surrounding Tontokrom with the villagers, so I figured that if I got within 6 or 7 miles in any direction, I felt reasonably sure I could find my way back. It might have been easier to retrace my steps on some o' the trails that Kofi and I took on our earlier adventure, but those memories were ones that were still too painful, and I really didn't want to get within 10 miles of Aurelio Bras and his wee business in Akrokerri. No telling what he would do when he saw me.

As I traveled further and further south on the road, I passed two separate Ashanti patrols in full war party gear. This in itself would not be so unusual, given the proximity to Kumasi, but for recent events. Since the King's death, the guard had been in disarray, and it was rare to have patrols at all, much less two going in the same direction. As I passed 'em, several warriors waved at me as if they knew me, but I could not recognize a single face. Perhaps they were just being friendly, or perhaps they recognized my great plaid kilt. I did not pass any slavers, although I expected to. It was common knowledge that many village chieftains were taking advantage o' the chaos in Kumasi to raid neighboring villages and sell captives to the Akwamu. I thought again o' the slave market just south of the Portuguese man's village of Akrokerri and decided that was even more ample reason not to stay on this road for too long. I needed to get back on jungle trails. Having no one to accompany or distract me except my own boredom, I made excellent time. I reached Poano at the end o' the first day and camped in town under a shed. I traded some sea shells for some bananas and yellow fruit, as apparently out here they still accepted the tiny white shells as currency o' the realm.

I headed due west the next day on a less traveled trail that nonetheless seemed to be on open flat ground. I moved along it for a half day when I came to a fork. There was a sign that said (in white chalk on a flat piece of kyenkyen bark) "Manso Nkwanta" to the right, and under it a similar sign saying "Agroyesum" with an arrow to the left. I had never heard of Agroyesum, but I needed to go further south, not north, and I knew that Manso Nkwanta was at least a couple days journey north of Tontokrom. I hoped the trail to the left would continue in a southwesterly direction. By nightfall I had already passed through the village of Agroyesum and yonder past a couple of other hamlets that I did not recognize nor have names for. In each small village, I was stared at by virtually every single man and woman as I strolled through. Many children ran up to me and pulled on my tartan kilt (at least until their parents shooed 'em away in fear). As I walked, the road became increasingly uneven and the elevation rose and fell with regularity. The jungle foliage was also getting thicker. Many of the trails were shaded by large trees and much of the trail was cast in shadow. I decided to rest for the night in a field a half day's walk past Agroyesum and slept comfortably with a loaded, half-cocked sidearm under me.

I awoke the next morning to the sounds of roosters crowing. For a brief instant I thought I was again in the highlands. The late autumn air was hot and humid even at daybreak, and the clouds that usually filled the sky for half of the year were nowhere in sight. I dreaded the swelter that was likely to come with the remainder of the journey to my old village. After walking a few miles further down the road to another village, and filling my canteen in a well, I met an older native woman and traded some shells for a breakfast of redred. It was a mixture of beans and spices that I loved and reminded me of my days in Tontokrom. I left the village and walked for another four hours. My anticipation grew as I traversed the last 30 minutes. I had stumbled on one of the game trails that the Tontokrom villagers used to hunt on, and I followed it easily o'er two hills and down into the rice valley, past the banana and fruit groves to my old home.

When I got there I was shocked. Utensils, furniture and pieces of walls and roofs from the huts were scattered haphazardly throughout the grounds of the village. Much of the contents o' the houses were lain about in the shared courtyard. At this time of day in the late afternoon, the village should have been a hive of activity. Instead, near a small fire aside the well, I saw only about half dozen women, two older men, and several children, including two wee toddlers sitting uncomfortably and each wailing away in tears. Their mothers were missing and the remaining adults didn't seem to care to comfort 'em. I saw no young men, and I couldn't find either Japhet or Amma. When I approached the group in greeting, one of the women screamed and several actually recoiled in fear. The babies cried even louder than before. I tried to reassure the group that it was only I, Al-zander, but it took a few moments for that to register. They actually heaved a collective sigh of relief when I was recognized. One o' the older men stood up to greet me with a smile of warmth and recognition.

"Wo hin Amma anaa? Wo hin Japhet anaa?" I asked, wondering where my friends were. One of the ladies began to wail uncontrollably and I felt something deep in my stomach churn. They tried to explain to me what had happened but it was difficult with my limited understanding of Twi. Among villagers, only Kofi and Amma had tried to learn any English. Therefore, it took almost an hour or longer for me to comprehend what had taken place, and only after I had been taken to the mass gravesites of several of the villagers. From what I could gather, an Akwamu slaver raiding party had come into the village about 4 days prior. There were obroni (white people) amongst 'em, so initially they were trusted because the villagers thought they were relatives of mine. After some initial warm greeting and some discussion between translators and villagers about how many people lived there, they suddenly turned their muskets and bows on the people of Tontokrom and had tried to take the entire village captive. Apparently, Yeboah was not taken by their initial friendliness, and immediately recognizing two of the strangers as Akwamu warriors, he slipped out o' the village and found several captives being restrained by other Akwamu just beyond the northern far ridge from whence the slavers came. He returned to Tontokrom just before the mayhem and convinced several o' the villagers and children to leave quickly and flee into the forest, including all that were assembled here. He then alerted several other men who had their bows ready while the obronis were still talking to Japhet and other elders. When the white slavers decided to aim their weapons at the inhabitants of Tontokrom, Yeboah had already mounted a defense and at least two of the strangers were shot dead with bows. Unfortunately, the slavers were too well armed and they killed many of the Tontokrom men, including Yeboah and many of my friends. Others were then taken captive and marched off towards the south, including Amma and her father. I asked about Yeboah's baby. One of the women pointed to one of the infants less than a year old, and told me it was Pesaata's, and that his name was Kwami. She pointed to the other infant, which was her own and said he was named Yaw. Those were lad's names for days of the week, but I couldn't remember which was which, not that it mattered. I was happy that Yeboah's and Pesaata's baby had survived, but sad that he would live without ever knowing his parents. Apparently the woman was wet nursing both babies. It was a miracle that she had survived the encounter. Yeboah was a hero.

I cursed myself for not getting here sooner. I could have been here weeks ago. The village initially trusted the white men because of their experience with me. I felt wretched with guilt. Amma and Japhet were captives and likely to be sent as slaves abroad. They might not even make the crossing alive, or even make it to Elmina alive, based on what I had witnessed with Pesaata. I was obliged to do something or feelings of guilt would haunt me forever. It occurred to me then that, had I come earlier in the month, I might have given the news of Kofi to the village and moved on, and the slavers would still have been here to take captives. In fact, it was providence that brought me to the village only days within their capture. If I hurried, I might catch up and rescue 'em as I had done with Yeboah. The captors were down at least two men, which increased the odds, however slim, in my favor. The thought of revenge and possible rescue gave me a spat of relief from my earlier despair and infused me with a new surge of energy. I took some food with me, and then raced off to the south despite the late hour.

I traveled swiftly along the trail by night with no stopping for rest or refreshment. I was determined to catch these slavers and make 'em pay. I knew the trails to the south well for the first hour and a half, but soon I was far past our hunting trails and following trails that Kofi and I had been on only once as we moved toward Obuasi. Fortunately for me, twenty or more men, especially those bound by ropes, make a dent in the dirt that even the most blind of trackers could follow. As long as it didn't rain and wash away the trail, I could pursue the slavers in haste. For the next two days I slept only for two hours and ate while I walked. I ran down hills and trudged as quickly as I could up the slopes.

At the end o' the second day around midnight, I reached a mining camp. It was not the same one in which I had worked so long ago, but it was similar, and there was a good wide road leading to it from the south. The tracks had led right to this road and proceeded towards the coast. I spoke with a white miner who was standing guard at the camp. He eyed me suspiciously, especially my kilt and my flintlock, but confirmed that he had watched a group of slavers move through the area only earlier that day. I thanked him and asked if I could shelter under one of the group houses. He reluctantly agreed, but only after I explained that I used to work for a neighboring Dutch mining operation. When I described it in detail, he realized I was telling the truth and must have pitied my looks. I was pretty shaggy and beaten from days on the trail, but I didn't have time to fill him in on my quest. I hoped the slave party had not yet reached Elmina, but I was too tired and weary to continue. I had to sleep and recuperate if I was to be in any condition to battle slavers. I slept soundly near the camp for a few hours and rose before light approached the next morning. I took off again, somewhat refreshed, but with aching muscles and joints from the strenuous hike I had done in the last couple of days. It was mid-morning when I spied a large group of men ahead of me on the road kicking up a lot of red dust as they ambled along. This had to be the slaver's war party! I had caught my prey. Now I had to consider what to do.

Chapter 15: Spencer and Biggs

I followed the slaver's party in stealth left and rear of their columns. I hid for brief periods in the cover of the jungle, thinking how best to approach 'em and force the battle on my terms. I counted three separate groups of captives, two columns carrying 12 natives each all in a single row, and another column with only seven captives. It was in this latter group that I recognized everyone. In addition to Amma and Japhet, there was Kakra, the short hunter about the same age as Kofi, Dobra, one of the woman villagers and a great cook, and three of the Tontokrom men that I had often hunted with, two about my age. I didn't recognize any captives in the other two groups. Instead o' leg irons or bamboo tree neck braces that held captives that I had freed on the road between Akrokerri and Obuasi, all o' these had two sets of rope binding 'em together by their necks and hands. I had only seen that much rope on board the ships I had been held captive on, when I was meant to be indentured. Rope was hard to come by in the Ashanti, and this line of hemp appeared to be of European origin. There was ample money to be made in slavery these days to afford such expensive supplies.

I stood still and watched in silence as the large group slowly moved away from me. I saw three Akwamu warriors, all carrying bows, but none had arrows notched. They flanked the captives to the sides and rear. There appeared to be two white men who were leading the war party. One was a scruffy looking sort, with a half beard and a weathered face. He had a tan shirt and trousers and was wearing leather boots that rode up mid-calf. He was also wearing a handkerchief on his head in the manner of a buccaneer, and brandishing a flintlock musket. In fact, I decided he would have fit right in amongst the pirate crew o' the *Whydah galley*. He looked dangerous. In contrast, the other fair-skinned man was foppish. He had white riding breeches and tall stockings, with shoes that looked much too expensive and frail for the Ashanti wilderness. He wore a tall black brimmed hat on his head, and I swear there were ruffles on his white shirt. The sleeves were rolled up above his elbows, and he kept wiping his face and brow with a handkerchief. He had a short dueling pistol tucked into his pants in front.

I was surprised at how few there were in the group of slavers, considering the number of captives they had to control. It was fewer than I expected, but I was still outnumbered and could not hope to force a rescue by frontal assault. There was little time to waste. In less than a day they would reach the edges of the salt marshes that surrounded Elmina to its north. I could already catch a hint of salt air on the breeze coming from the ocean in the distance. Once the group reached the slave markets I had no hope of rescuing 'em. I needed to start the attack soon, but I didn't see much chance of success if I just surprised them with a side ambush. Too many arrows coming at me from too many directions. If I couldn't take the captors by arms, perhaps I could barter with the slavers... they certainly could understand money.

I moved with great haste along the hedges and trees to the left on the road and passed the slow moving slave train on my right. I moved swiftly at least 500 yards in front and saw a ridge leading to an upslope in the road. That gave me high ground, and also provided a good vantage. By this time o' the late morning, the sun would be shining in their eyes just o'er my head as they approached. It might be the edge I needed if I could force a confrontation there. I might be able to take one or two unawares, but first I would try to parlay. I ran out into the middle of the road and waited with the musket across my chest. I added a wee amount of powder, dropped the frizzen on the pan and fully cocked the hammer. I figured there was a good chance that I might have to blast my way out of this if things went sour. I decided I needed something else too, so I pulled the bow from my back and put it by my right foot with one arrow sitting already notched on the string. I couldn't hit a cow at 20 paces with it, but the slavers didn't know that. My fingers went instinctively to the sword hilt hanging from my belt, and I felt the two leather bundles tied there. I hid one of the leathers full of gold dust under a drape of my kilt next to the belt, and tied the other on the inside of one of the chest pleats of the plaid. The gold meant I had something to barter with, or at least to spark their interest until I could improvise a plan. I hoped they were in the mood to parlay and didn't just shoot first.

As they approached my stationary silhouette, moving along the road from the north, the group stopped to try to see who or what I was. I heard the ugly man with the scarf on his head barking orders to the Akwamu, two of whom notched arrows and raised their bows in my direction. The scarfed man giving orders cautiously moved forward while the others held back a bit. Two of the Akwamu were on the left, the foppish gent was on my right, and the pirate-faced scarfed man was in the middle out front, with all three trains of captives in between. The remaining Akwamu warrior stood behind the captives, probably in case they caused trouble.

The man with the head scarf moved within about 20 feet of me and stopped. He looked me up and down, and started to say something in Twi or Akwamu when I interrupted.

"Me se Borofo, me paucho", I said, indicating I would please prefer to speak in English.

He looked again at my great kilted clothing and smiled.

"Nice dress!" He waited for me to reply to his insult, but I disappointed him and didn't even bother to change my expression.

"So. This is a surprise, mate. I'm in the middle of wilderness on the bloody gold coast of Africker, and I come upon a man in a plaid robe in the middle of the bloody road, holdin' a musket and wantin' to speak the Queen's English. How bout' that!" He turned to the foppish man to his left but quickly returned his gaze to me. He had a thick cockney accent similar to some of the guards in Newgate prison north of London. I instantly disliked him.

"Now what would you be wantin' bloke?" When he talked I could see he had very dark stained teeth and several were missing. This man really should have been a buccaneer.

"I am interested in purchasing some of your

slaves."

"Would you now?" "Here that Spencer? He wants to purchase your slaves!" He started laughing and even the Akwamu were smiling. "Well, I'm afraid they ain't for sale, mate, so I suggest you just get on back to wherever you came from."

"You haven't heard my offer yet."

"Well, you ain't got enough of the King's coin to buy yourself a decent set of clothes, so you sure ain't got enough for any of our natives."

Just about that time, the group of slaves had pulled up close enough to see me clearly. I heard Amma shout, "Al-zander, Al-zander!" All at once the other Tontokrom hostages started calling "Al-zander" in a fever pitch, and then the other sets of captives strained to look at me. One of the Akwamu got extremely nervous at that point and came running up to the pirate-man and grabbed his arm. I don't speak a word of Akwamu, but among the lot of gibberish spoken, I heard him say "Al-zander de Ashanti" and a word which sounded an awful lot like "Wo suru", the Twi word for "You're in danger". By this time the other Akwamu out to my left had dropped his bow and his eyes were bugging out at me in wonder. The Akwamu at the rear had his hands full keeping the captives under control, despite their bonds, and he wasn't paying me much attention.

He glanced again at the fop. "I don't believe it, mate. Lissen up, Spence. Here stands the famous Al-zander. I thought that was a myth! I heard the tales of course, but the name Al-zander sounded like something the Arabs dreamed up, so I sure didn't expect to meet him in the flesh in the southern Ashanti. And I sure

wasn't expectin' the likes of the bloke in front o' me."
The man with the scarf turned again to me. "You look
like you just got off a boat from Inverness! Al-zander
here's a lost Scotsman. Took the wrong turn in
Morocco!" He laughed at his own joke and slapped his
thigh with his free hand. His other hand still carried
his pistol.

"My real name is Alexander. The Ashanti had
trouble pronouncing it."

"You must have some ego there, mate. Alexander
the great! Naming yourself after the Macedonian king.
You think you're gonna rule the world too?" He laughed
again to himself, but the others weren't smiling
presently.

"My father gave me the name. It was my
grandfather's."

"Awwww. How touching." "Well, Mr. Alexander
of the Ashanti, I'm not very impressed, by you or that
dirty shawl you're wearin'. And don't think your
reputation is gonna get you any slaves any easier or
cheaper."

The foppish man suddenly came forward and
spoke up. "I'm sorry I haven't had the pleasure. You
said your name was Alexander. Mine is Thomas James
Spencer. Sir Thomas Spencer, and this is Biggs." He
emphasized the "sir" as if it should mean something to
me. He, motioned to the pirate man, and then held out
his hand for me to shake it. My hands stayed where
they were, and my eyes did not leave the pirate-man for
long. Sir Spencer pulled his hand back in
disappointment.

"So Biggs, you've heard of this Alexander
previously, have you?"

"Yeah, I heard of him. Everybody in Guinea Propria has heard of the great "Al-zander". His tone was layered in sarcasm. "He was the right hand of the dead Asantehene, his pale skinned assassin, so they say. He is supposed to have killed over a hundred men, most with his bare hands. He was the hero of the battle of Agogo, and the Ashanti claim he almost single-handedly defeated the enemy there. The Akyem fear him and say he can't be killed. They say you know him by his white skin, Scottish plaid robe, and a silver musket." Biggs spit as he said the last words, obviously not believing any of the rumors. He glanced at my flintlock, and said "That don't look all silver neither."

I only smirked at him and raised the gun slightly.

"My, My" was all Spencer said, but he was frowning and looking at my musket now too.

Biggs went on, "Al-zander here is supposed to be some Scottish Jacobite lord who fought the English for years before he was finally captured alive and exiled to West Africa, where his prowess in war brought him to the attention of the Ashanti King. He's been here as a mercenary ever since." He spit at the ground again in disapproval.

"Rumors have a way of expanding in the retelling." I said with a smirk, but before they could reply I added, "but, of course, there is always a grain o' truth in every legend." If the situation wasn't so dire, I could have laughed at all of the inaccuracies I had just heard. I wondered if the King had been responsible for some of these lies, or if it had been due to embellishment on the part of the Portuguese man. Probably both. Maybe the legend just grew from people

who wanted to make up a local hero. A Scottish lord?
Killed a hundred men with my bare hands? Ridiculous.
I suddenly thought of Kofi. He would have got a kick out
of this crazy story. I decided I shouldn't deny anything.
Let 'em keep guessing. If I could at least put some fear
into one or two of 'em, I might gain an advantage. I
didn't think they would sell me the captives outright,
but if I bluffed, they might settle on an agreement I
could buy into.

"I say again, I would like to buy some of your
captives."

Biggs answered, "And why would one of the
Ashanti King's guard want slaves? You could have any
you wanted in Kumasi. Why track us down?"

"It turns out that some of your captives were
taken from my home village."

"Really. Your home village? You gone native and
think you grew up in the bush now?" "You hear that
Spence, apparently we took some of his relatives." He
laughed again. "Well, mate, we won 'em fair and
square-like. It explains a lot if you hail from there. That
village of yours fought like the king's army when we
tried to take em'. We ended up killin' half of the men
while the women ran to the trees. This lot is all we got
away with. I lost two good men taking these natives,
one of em' an English bloke I known for years. You ain't
got enough money in that dress o' yours to pay us back
for that."

"If you attacked Tontokrom, you are lucky that
you only lost two men. Had I been there, none of you
should have walked away." I glared at him. "And I
would like to know why you chose that particular village
for your slaver's raid anyway. It seems off of the beaten

path."

It was Sir Spencer that answered. "I should say we happened on it. We were trading for slaves in Manso Nkwanta with one of the Ashanti chieftains who had just recently entered into the trade, and decided to head due south to Elmina to avoid the conflict to the east near Obuasi. We didn't realize it was your village." The man named Biggs glared at Sir Thomas and obviously wanted him to shut up.

"What is happening in Obuasi?"

Biggs looked backed at me queerly and said, "I should think a King's guard would know more than us."

Spencer continued, "There are Fantu, Akyem, Akwamu and Ashanti in open struggle there. It is more than a skirmish. We hear it is an all out civil war for control of the kingdom. The slave market near Akrokerri is inaccessible, so the Akwamu have had to open new trafficking routes. We decided to course through the Dutch mining area."

I thought at that moment that it was fortuitous I had decided to go through Poano and Agroyesum to get to Tontokrom. Had I went further south on the road to Obuasi, I might have ended up in a pitched battle among several enemies.

"Whether you believe they belong to you fairly or not, or whether I agree doesn't matter. The facts are, Laddies, that you now are in possession of several of my friends and intend to send 'em in chains to the coast for delivery in bondage. I cannot let that happen. I could take 'em by force, but I ask you again if I may purchase some captives at a fair price."

Biggs grinned nastily at me and said, "And I say, you ain't everything you're supposed to be, Scotsman. I say why don't I just take your fancy musket from you and 'borrow' whatever money you have and leave you out here to beg in the bush. You seem to forget there mate, you're outnumbered five to one. We'll shoot you down before you ever get more than one shot off."

"I only need to get one shot off, MATE." I emphasized the last word. "You see I don't need to kill you or even the Akwamu that accompany you. I only need to kill Sir Thomas James Spencer here, and when I do, you've lost your boss and your well-healed patron. You'll be out of a job whether you finish me or not. And given my history, there is a very good chance I'll take one or two others with me, MATE."

Biggs snarled at my reply but did not answer. As I expected and intended, the English gentleman looked at me with a horrified expression and started to back up. Actually I had no intention of firing at Spencer first. He was relatively harmless, and his pistol was not even loaded or cocked. He would have been defenseless. Biggs was the danger, but if he thought I was going to shoot Spencer I might push him into moving against me prematurely. I glanced instantly at the other three Akwamu. None had understood the conversation and though two were eyeing me suspiciously, neither even had their bows lifted in my direction any longer. I saw Biggs' thumb move quickly to cock his musket to the full position. As I watched his arm move slowly to raise his musket at me and simultaneously pull the trigger, I yelled at the top of my lungs, "Ashanti, Wo bra!" and looked off to my right.

Biggs screamed, "There's more of them in the bushes!" as he quickly crouched down low and raised his weapon. However, that diversion had caused him to hesitate and look for incoming fire rather than to direct the muzzle towards my body, and in that instant I had raised my fully cocked flintlock, pulled the trigger and put a hole through the right side of Mr. Biggs' head. Spencer was on his knees trying to figure out how to frantically load his weapon, while one of the two Akwamu man had ran into the trees to my left. The Akwamu in the rear had several bodies in between his position and mine and couldn't get off a clear shot. He was trying to keep the captives from rioting. That left only one warrior to deal with. I picked up Biggs' loaded musket. It was still half-cocked, as he had not managed to fully engage the hammer of the weapon before I had relieved him of part of his head. I hoped there was some powder on the pan under the closed frizzen as I aimed it at the lone Akwamu in front of me. I noticed instantly, however, that I should have already been dead from an arrow, if not for one of the captives in the front of the line of slaves. The slave had used his free legs to kick the Akwamu deftly in the side of the shin and knock him off balance. I ran to him with my gun drawn and bade him drop his bow, which he did even though he probably spoke no English. Every warrior spoke fluent flintlock.

"Wait. Stop. Please wait. Don't kill my Akwamu wardens, please." yelled Spencer. "Please tell your companions in the trees not to massacre us."

"I don't want to kill you Sir Thomas, or your Akwamu warriors. Hell, I wouldn't have had to kill Biggs here if I hadn't seen him pulling on the hammer of his musket. He was going to attack me, and you know it as well as I. I simply want my friends back safely and there won't be any more bloodshed."

"You seem a reasonable man. This was a mistake. Mr. Biggs did this on his own. He was presumptuous and irrational. Despite his banter and ill-advised move against you, he was wrong. I want you to know that I intend to sell you the captives you desire. Just make a fair price. We can come to a suitable arrangement, I'm sure." He was still trying to load his weapon but was shaking badly.

"Then you better drop your pistol where it is, or the next shot is going to make you and Mr. Biggs there identical twins." It took only a second for him to lay the pistol down.

I thanked him for cooperating, then added, "Now, call to the warrior hiding in the trees, so I don't get an arrow in my back while I'm trying to negotiate a deal with you."

"Abro. Abro! Abro!" I guess that was the warrior's name, as even the second and third Akwamu were yelling it. "Abro, yavoo woeso! Bra!"

The Englishman was yelling "come here! Now!" but the Akwamu were yelling something else in their language I had no way of understanding. Just in case it meant 'please shoot the white man in the plaid,' my gun barrel moved to the head of the Akwamu warrior in front of me instead of at the Englishman. After a couple of tense minutes the third warrior came out of the trees, with his hands held high holding his bow (no arrow attached) and a look like a mad dog on his face.

Several thoughts went briskly through my head at that instant. Beyond hope, I could actually succeed in freeing my friends without further bloodshed. If I was intimidating enough, I might even be able to get them away without paying as much as a farthing. I had the upper hand here, but I was still outnumbered, and if they wanted, they could bring the battle back to me. In truth, if they reached Elmina and told anyone that they had been bushwhacked, I would have a host of pursuers on my trail. I would be slowed by leading a group of village men and women and we would likely all be caught and slaughtered. No, I thought, the best course was to try and barter with this Spencer and hope all sides left with an amicable arrangement. That might be the only way to save the villagers. With my left hand, I pulled out the smaller leather pouch containing Kofi's gold dust, which had been sitting wrapped under my belt. I threw it at the feet of Sir Thomas Spencer.

"This shows I mean to deal in good faith. That, sir, is pure Ashanti gold, and good in any nation in the world as currency. There should be enough there to account for the seven villagers from Tontokrom. I'll leave you the other two dozen."

The English knave looked at the gold greedily at first, but then decided he needed to barter for better. "It hardly pays for our efforts". He looked at me meekly, hoping for more money. "I should hope you would increase your offer a little."

"That is what I am offering for 7 captives, and for your lives. I suggest you take it."

He winced when I said 'lives' and realized he was in no position to counteroffer. "Well.... considering we won't have to pay for three of our fellows who won't be returning with us to collect their share, I guess my expenses have decreased. I accept your offer." I still had Biggs' pistol trained on one of the Akwamu while Spencer directed the other two to unfasten the bindings of the Tontokrom group. I picked up my own bow and

quiver, my musket and also the bow of one of the
Akwamu and draped them all over my shoulder. If they
tried anything I at least had the better weaponry.

Within minutes, the Akwamu had released the
rope bonds of the Tontokrom villagers and as a group,
the men and women ran at full speed north on the road
away from Elmina. I did not bid Spencer farewell as I
followed in haste. I kept to the villager's rear to ensure
we were not followed, but I was reasonably sure Spencer
would honor the bargain. He had no choice. He could
barely handle the remaining two dozen captives with
the men he had left and was equipped only with two
bows and an unloaded pistol. He had been paid
something for them, if not their full worth, and besides,
he had stolen them anyway. I felt a little guilty for not
releasing all of the hostages, but I had acted with a
single purpose. I certainly did not have enough gold to
pay for all o' them, and I couldn't protect thirty or so
captives while I led them to freedom. None of the
captives had been harmed and I was still alive.
Someone, sometime might save or rescue the remainder,
but I doubted it. Rather, I hoped between here and
Elmina the twenty four left on the rope might rise up
against their captors and try to escape. Either way, it
was no longer my problem. I had saved who I had
intended to save. I couldn't free the entire world or
change it. I slowed to a walk and turned to check the
road behind. I was not surprised to see two warriors
running toward me with bows drawn. I lowered to one
knee and yelled as loud as I could.
"Spencer.....Spencer.....I will kill your wardens if you
don't call them off! We had a deal!"

I heard a muffled set of calls behind the two

Akwamu and they slowed down, but still kept advancing with bows notched and stings pulled. I aimed at the one on the right with my musket and was about to fire when I realized that would be a mistake. There was a good chance I would miss at this distance, and I would not have time to reload or switch to my bow before being penetrated by another arrow from the other warrior. I sat motionless on one knee with muzzle extending at first one, then the other. Two bows and a quiver of arrows sat at my side. It was a standoff. They stopped following as I heard Spencer still yelling in the distance. I think the warriors followed of their own initiative. I don't think they understood the terms of our agreement. Spencer was trying to explain at the top of his lungs. I only turned and followed the villagers when the two Akwamu turned back toward the slave party. I hurried to catch up with the Tontokrom group, who were still running, but stopped briefly several times to check for any pursuing Akwamu. I had to run at full speed to reach the villagers, as they had wasted no time in fleeing northward.

Chapter 16: Accra and a New Voyage

The villagers only stopped running when we were out of breath about a mile from where I had left Biggs on the road. We now appeared to be free of pursuers. I gathered all seven around me, and said "Akwaaba mandafo. Nanti Ye a Tontokrom" (You are welcome friends for my efforts, now you can go home to Tontokrom.)

It was Japhet who came to me first. I knew what he was going to ask.

"Wo hin Kofi?"

A lump fell in my throat as he asked for his son's whereabouts. I just shook my head and said, "Debi" for no. In slow short words that I could barely piece together in Twi, I told Japhet and Amma that Kofi was dead, and that he had died in battle as a great warrior for the Asantehene. One of the king's personal guards. That he had become very famous, and that Kofi's months with me in Kumasi had provided the gold that had paid for their freedom. At least that is what I thought I told 'em. They seemed to understand and both were crying.

We walked in silence for another mile or so when I thought of something. If they went back to Tontokrom, they might still be in danger from slavers. Spencer had said that the Akwamu were now beginning

to trade slaves with Manso Nkwanta. That was not
very far north of Tontokrom and their village sat in a
beeline between Manso and Elmina, so the risk of
running into more slavers was high.

"Wo suru a Tontokrom. Slavers a Manso
Nkwanta! Wo pe kon ne bra a me Al-zander!" I told
them, which indicated danger from the slave trade near
to their village. I told them all that they had to choose.
Either to go back to Tontokrom and hide, or to come
with Al-zander across the jungle to the seacoast. Four
of them said "Debi, Debi. Nanti ye" (No No and
goodbye) and headed back on the road to their home. I
wished "Fare thee well" to those villagers, realizing that
I would never see them again.

Japhet, Amma and Kakra chose to follow me and
start a new life on the coast, far from the Ashanti. I
noticed for the first time that Kakra and Amma were
holding hands, and I could swear that Amma was
sporting a larger tummy than when we last had met.
Her breasts were definitely larger. I didn't know how to
ask her if she was with child, and thought it probably
was bad luck to inquire anyway. I was a little jealous,
for a few minutes, but that feeling soon passed as the
excitement of their rescue brought out joy in everyone.
Despite my fondness for the girl and the fact that I had
waited too long to act out on my affections for her, I was
happy for both of them, and glad she had found love.
Once I thought about it, I was even happier that they
would accompany me on my journey to the coast. I
could protect them there, at least for a while. They
were as close to a family as I had in Africa, and I owed it
to Kofi to look after 'em. Perhaps, Japhet or the two
young lovers might even consider coming with me to

Scotland. I had to consider that possibility in detail. It would not be easy to take anyone with me as the journey would be long and arduous. And expensive! I hoped I had enough gold dust left to book passage for all four of us on a frigate. If nothing else, I would take 'em to the big cities of the coast where I hoped it would be safer. We needed to stay away from this band of slavers, who could still make trouble for all of us if we crossed paths. Spencer might honor his bargain, but the look from the two Akwamu suggested they would rather kill me than speak to me the next time we met.

We decided to backtrack north for a few miles where I had crossed a thin trail going east, and to take that as far as we could and perhaps go around the dangers of Elmina where we might run across Spencer or his associates. We followed the trail for almost an hour west and slightly north before it abruptly ended in a tiny village with a road heading south. The inhabitants of the village were Akwamu, not Ashanti or one of the other Akan tribes, but they seemed accustomed to strangers and not active in the slave trade. However, the tartan of my giant plaid was a spectacle even to the village natives, and so everyone was coming out to look at the white man in the strange colored outfit. Other than gawking, we were not bothered.

We followed the trail south for another hour, moving swiftly toward the coastline. When we finally reached the coastal road, I was happily assured that we had missed Elmina entirely, well to our west, and were on our way to the castles of Cape Coast to the east. I had ventured this way from Elmina to Accra almost two years ago, and I remembered it well. This time the journey on the coastal road was less harrowing and almost enjoyable. I was well armed and had three companions, and as far as I knew, I was not in danger of being arrested, captured or killed as an outlaw.

We ate from banana trees and coconuts along the way, although the many travelers on this road all had the same idea and the pickings were few. I did not care for the coconuts, but the villagers coveted the meat inside. Japhet used my sword to carve the husks off and open a drinking hole to drain the husk and get at the white flesh. They all drank greedily of the coconut milk. It was better than river water, and far cleaner, and the warm sensation was similar to drinking a weak flavored tea. The fresh fruits were fulfilling. I preferred cooked bananas to the fresh green ones, but in hunger I settled for those fresh from the vine, and it remained our staple ration. My canteen of water did not last long providing for all four of us, but we were sometimes allowed to drink from wells along the road for a few sea shells in barter, and I filled my gourd canteen at each stop. We slept along the road with a number of other travelers in the city of Cape Coast. I tried to inquire about booking passage on a ship there, but the harbor was limited and the only ship in the port was a small slaver. We would have no choice but to continue to Accra, with its larger port and busy trading docks. Having lived in Accra for a few months, I was certain we would find a ship there, but I didn't know where they would be heading. I never worked near the docks and had few chances to mingle with sailors.

We stayed in Cape Coast for only a night before moving on northwest along the coast. The early November dry season brought the heat, and several times I disrobed and swam in the ocean to our right to cool off. None of the others had ever seen the ocean before and it frightened them. They would only go in as far as their ankles, but splashed the salt water on their bodies to cool off. I enjoyed this trek, as I had not enjoyed walking in years. I felt as carefree as I had since I left the highlands.

I looked forward to getting to Accra. I knew several Europeans there who I had earlier worked for, and who I hoped could help me find if there were ships going back to Scotland. Perhaps I could work for some extra money to help us gain the fares to pay for passage if I came up short. It was six more full days of walking before our party of four finally reached the outskirts of Accra. Japhet was amazed at the size o' the city and the stone buildings that encompassed it. The villagers had never seen a city like Accra, as they had never ventured to Kumasi. They were fascinated by the height of the lighthouse, visible from a mile away. The bustling trade center with its plentiful markets, well stocked shops, and foreigners from around the world delighted everyone. Japhet kept picking things up from the market, sniffing or licking items, and the shopkeepers kept yelling at him to put 'em back. I think he enjoyed the game and the market vendor's cries only amused him further.

Late one afternoon I met with one of my former employers and queried him about ships to Scotland. He was a financier in the town, and should be aware of such things. He said that the majority of ships in Accra, like Elmina, were slavers, and that I would do well to stay away from 'em, if I had visions of taking my friends with me. I was liable to be thrown off the deck mid-voyage and my friends added to the ballast below for future sale in the colonies. None of these slave ships would be going to Europe anyway as their destination was the Americas. He graciously allowed us to sleep in one of his rooms for a couple of nights while he made his own inquiries into potential ships bound for Europe. We ate and drank and enjoyed ourselves. We walked and explored the town (always under my supervision, with my musket in my arms). I was getting too much attention with my great kilt and therefore I borrowed some clothes from my former employer. I promised to repay him when I could, but he seemed not to care. He was originally from Northumberland and I think he, his wife and child enjoyed the company and listened with great interest to my tales o' the Ashanti and my time with the Asantehene.

Two days later, he was able to meet with a ship's captain who had just come in to port. He explained to me that the man captained a frigate from the west coast of England, and was headed for the colonies with supplies. He had sold some cargo here in Accra and was going to follow the trade winds to Virginia. He wasn't headed in the proper direction for me, but he would be aware of any ships that were traveling back to England or France. I was to meet with him that early evening in a tavern a few blocks from the wharf. He was hauling anchor and sailing at daybreak.

I arrived at the pub later that day and it took no time to figure out who was waiting for me. The man had a crisp beard, a naval uniform and was the only one in that side of the bar. He looked at me impatiently as if I was late. A few sailors across the room stared as I entered, then put their heads down when I approached the captain's table.

"You'd be Alexander?" The man in front of me addressed me curtly.

"Yes, Captain. Thanks for seeing me."

"Expecting trouble?" He eyed the musket which I always carried when walking out and about.

"Force of habit. I've lived through many battles here."

"So I've heard. You got questions? I don't have much time. I shove off in the morn."

"I wondered if there were any ships going back to Europe in the next week or two."

"I already told your friend. There aren't any ships headin' from Accra back north along the coast any time, much less in the next week. All of the money is in supplyin' the colonies these days. Not much money supplyin' the Africans, just taking the gold back. And we don't do that directly. We take it with us to Virginia or Carolina or New Amsterdam, drop off our load of supplies, fill up on tobacco or other New World goods, and then follow the tradewinds back to England. It's a circle and it fits the tides and the winds. Except you're sailin' in the wrong time of year. You see, it's first of November, it's gettin' cold and icy further north. Gales and such. No one wants to sail in the northerlies in December or January. Get ice on the ship, weighs it down, pulls on the rigging and soaks the masts. No one wants to sail a sinkin' ship. We cast off tomorrow and we'll be the last frigate this way until spring at least. Even the slavers don't sail back east from the colonies much past November. They'll stay in port and wait out the winter in the colony harbors if they have to. No way you're getting' back to Europe any time soon."

I reflected on what he had said and my heart sank. I might be able to stay in Accra for several months, but I was afraid my friends couldn't stay here. I didn't know if this whole region was going to erupt in civil war, and even if it didn't, it was just not safe for any native man or woman in Guinea Propria right now. Accra was even more dangerous for my Tontokrom friends. It was the home of the Akwamu, not the Akan Ashanti. I needed to get them out of here before they risked re-enslavement. I thought about the possibility of taking the round trip with the Captain from Africa to the colonies and back to England, but Amma was definitely pregnant, and that would be hard on her. Plus, I didn't know if I had enough money for such a long voyage for four people. Still, anywhere was better than here, and a long journey home, was still an eventual trip home.

"Where in the colonies are you headed?" I asked him.

"We're droppin' supplies in Virginia, near Jamestown, at the mouth of the James River. There is a growin' commerce center inland a piece called Richmond that pays good money for goods. From there we head south a ways to pick up tobacco at Charleston harbor then cruise up the coast and catch a good wind back to England from the Northeast. We should arrive in England before the first of the year."

Scotland by the New Year! If I could get us on this ship leaving tomorrow, we could be in England in late December and then I could find my way to Ross-shire. That sounded great, but would I have enough money to bring the villagers? I didn't know, nor even if I could get 'em on the boat.

"Captain, do you have any room on your ship for extra passengers? I could pay."

I only have one extra cabin, and that is right next to the galley. I've used it to store some things in, and it only has one small bunk. It's below deck, of course, but I could give it to you alone for 28 pound sterling for the whole trip. It's not luxury fit for a lord, but it is comfortable enough for one person. I could take you along since you have no wife."

After a moment of elation about the possibility of affording passage back to England, I realized that at that price, I might not have enough for all of us. Twenty eight pounds for me alone was about all of the worth I had in gold. That sent me into a great and instant depression. I would barely have enough to cover my own fare with none left to get my friends out of Accra. I decided I couldn't abandon the villagers, even if it meant not heading home right away. Maybe I could go half way to the colonies and then make enough money in the Americas to eventually afford fare back to the highlands. It might take a while, but it would be safer for me anyway. There would be no Irish or English soldiers to hunt down an escapee who had twice jumped ship. I remembered that my cousins, Hugh, William and Duncan Fraser, were supposed to be indentured in Virginia. Suddenly, the thought of going to join 'em in the colonies didn't seem like such a bad idea. My mind was made up.

"How much if I just went as far as the colonies, Carolina or Virginia?"

He eyed me slowly and carefully. You ain't got enough coin to get to England?"

"I do, but I am asking how much to get to the

Americas? I have family there."

"That would be half for halfway. Meanin' 14 pounds if you can get to the boat in time tomorrow morning. We cast off at dawn and we won't wait if you're laggin'."

"How much for my three friends?"

"Three friends? We ain't got room."

"If they could stay with me. How much?"

"They would also be charged 14 pounds each, but I told you there is only one bed in that cabin. There ain't no room for 'em. They won't want to come on a 3 or 4 week voyage without a bed or any quarters of their own. It'd be torture."

"I don't think they'd mind not having a bed. They're native villagers from the Ashanti."

"They're your slaves? You should have said so. They wouldn't need a bed anyway. Savages sleep on the floor, no problem. I could let you take your slaves for another 14 pound for the lot. They don't get full rations though and they sleep in your quarters. During storms they have to go below in the hold for ballast. Can't have captives running around pukin' on the deck during a squall. What do you say? That'd be 28 of the King's coin in Sterling. You interested? I have to clean some supplies out of the room before you board."

I was about to argue that they weren't my slaves, but I thought better of it. I figured I could just barely afford 35 pounds or so. That was equal to about the amount of gold that I had left in my possession and I couldn't risk having to pay full fares. I took out my wee leather pouch from the ammunition satchel around my shoulder and unfastened the cover. I opened the leather and slowly undid the string on the linen bundle inside, spreading it so he could see all of the gold there. I had given Kofi's share to Spencer to pay for the seven captives, and all I had left was the amount of gold dust and shells in front of me. If he didn't go for it, I didn't know what I would do.

"This should cover it and more." I told him with false confidence.

"He eyed me suspiciously and asked, "Don't you have any of the King's coin? I'm headed to the colonies where there ain't much use for gold dust. I don't have scales, so I can't be sure how much you got there, but it don't look like enough to me."

There should have been plenty enough gold there for me and a few additional passengers, based on its purity, but I didn't have time to argue. I couldn't risk angering him, so I tried to convince him how much the gold was worth, but he wasn't budging. I think he was afraid he couldn't trade it for goods easily. If he said no, we would be stuck in Accra for another 5 months or more, and I didn't want to be caught in the middle of a civil war. I couldn't stay with my European friend for that long, and in a boarding house we would deplete our supply of gold dust even further, risking another chance at a sea passage later.

After a minute or so, the Captain offered a compromise, and I then understood why he was reluctant to accept the gold in payment. He was eyeing my flintlock carefully, and especially the inlaid carving on the silver lock and barrel. "I tell you what, Mr. Alexander. I'll take that fine musket from you in trade, if you'd be willing, and you can keep all of your gold if you throw in your satchel. My ship will carry you and all three of your slaves to Virginia.

"Done." I said, before he could change his mind. I suspected that he could get a king's ransom for the musket in the colonies, many times the worth of the gold dust. It would be one of the grandest flintlocks on the continent, and one worthy of an English lord. It didn't matter. I hoped I would never have to fire a musket in anger or need again. I would miss the musket, but of course I never paid for it in the first place. When I thought back on it later, I probably should have bargained for passage all the way to Scotland, but I was too relieved and too concerned about getting ready for the journey to worry about it further. He was pleased and I was relieved. I bade him farewell until the following day.

We met the captain at daybreak. The Tontokrom villagers were very reluctant to get on board a ship, and to head o'er the ocean, so it took some coaxing to get 'em to go up the plank. We were escorted across the deck and down into the hold to our room. I noticed four cannon on the deck, two per side, and that this ship, like the previous one I was on, had three masts. The hold below deck was much taller than the *Whydah Galley*, and it was less musty and smelled much better. Our stateroom was too cramped for four people, but we made do. Kakra was seasick for most of the journey, and ate little. He lost a fair portion of his body weight during the 3 week voyage. We were able to come up on deck for much of the day and take in the salt air. The crew was generally nice to me, and at least they didn't mistreat my friends, although they mostly ignored 'em. Fortunately, the seas were cooperative, and we only had 4 days of severe weather. During that time, I was locked in the stateroom and my friends were one floor down in the ballast hold. They took turns puking into a bucket.

Near the end o' the journey, we heard the man in the crow's nest yell "Land, Ho!". We arrived on the new continent somewhere around the Carolina coast according to the Captain's sextant. We sailed up the coast for another two days before we found the Virginia settlement, in part because we had to sail back toward the east for a bit to miss the dangerous shoals of the cape of Carolina. The feeling of safety, satisfaction, and joy we experienced as we walked down the gangway plank in the colony harbor cannot be exaggerated. I was in the Americas, and our future was wide open before us. Incarceration in England and wars in the Ashanti would become a distant memory.

The Tontokrom villagers were delighted with the quaintness o' the Virginia colony and were fascinated by the different trees, the wooden houses and the strange dress o' the colonists. They walked through town with their mouths agape, and as usual, Japhet wanted to touch everything. For my part, I had no idea what we would do in this new world, but it didn't take me much time to search my heart for the answer. I would aspire to become a farmer once more.

Epilogue: *The Americas*

Alexander Fraser arrived in America in 1718, bringing with him one native woman and two native men. Among many bitter ironies, he realized that he stole them from Africa to protect them from slavery, only to find they were legally now enslaved in the new colony. According to Virginia law at the time, they were slaves under his mastery and bondage, but he never treated them as such. Alexander worked for a time in the small colonial villages along the Southeastern coast of Virginia, mostly as a cooper and laborer. With the remaining gold he brought from Africa and the money he saved over a few months, he was able to homestead on a 40 acre piece of property in Henrico County twenty five miles inland. The land was heavily wooded and provided ample timber to build two log cabins, one for himself and one for his Tontokrom friends. The local Indians, who had ravaged the settlements at Jamestown a hundred years earlier, had been quiescent and by the 1820's for the most part had moved off to the western wilderness. Alexander never had to pick up a musket in the colony, except to hunt the numerous game in the surrounding forest.

His land was laid out south of the White Oak swamp a mile or two to the north, the James River a few miles to the south, and just a short hike from Bailey

Creek to the west. The ocean was a two or three day walk due east. A shallow well provided plenty of fresh water for all. In the spring and summer, the weather was hot and humid and reminiscent of the Ashanti, but the winters were cold and wet. Amma was not pleased that she could not find palm trees to weave a water tight thatched roof for either dwelling, and they had to use a wooden roof to suffice. Her first baby was born within weeks of moving in to their new homesteads. He was named Kwami, having been born on Saturday, but his second name was Kofi, in honor of her fallen brother, and everyone called him the latter for the remainder of his life. Kakra and Amma had 7 more children in their long lives, and they learned to speak English much better than Al-zander ever learned to speak more Twi. Two of the babies died in infancy, but she eventually had 17 grandchildren.

They raised potatoes, apples and a new native crop called maize. It was many, many years before they were able to plant bananas, but they eventually had a stand of their favorite fruit. They had pigs, chickens and even a few cows once the trees were felled. Only two years after coming to the American colonies, Alexander was able to track down two of his cousins, Hugh and Duncan, who had been working on a tobacco farm north of Richmond. He never discovered what happened to William Fraser, another of his relatives who was sent to the American colonies from Newgate prison. Within the year after they met, the brothers Hugh and Duncan had worked off their indentured servitude to their English lord, earlier than the 7 year expectation, and were granted their freedom. The two bought a homestead property only a mile and a half from that of Alexander and Japhet, near to Fourmile creek on the west of Bailey Creek. The families stayed very close and got together regularly for celebrations and holidays. Alexander also renewed his friendship with Angus McBean, who had been recaptured in Cork, rejoined the ship *Anne* as a prisoner, and had been indentured on a plantation in the Carolina colonies. He was released after only a year of indenture and had ventured north to Virginia to join other relatives there. Their reunion near Richmond was a joyous one.

Unfortunately, things did not work out quite as well for the villagers from Tontokrom. Although Alexander had promised to grant them their freedom, due to a combination of local intolerance in Virginia and some convoluted language in the commonwealth laws, he was never able to fulfill his promise, to his dying regret. Instead, they lived on the land, worked it together and shared in the bountiful harvests. However, under Virginia legal status, they remained only Alexander's slaves. They could not travel to town unless they were escorted and it was dangerous for them to go much further than Richmond. Japhet did not seem to mind and little understood the legalities of slavery and its consequences. He had spent most of his life living and traveling only a few miles from his home village of Tontokrom, and was content to work the ground and hunt the forests around Henrico with his friend Al-zander. Kakra and Amma became more frustrated over time with the situation, especially because of the legal constraints on their numerous children. However, they voiced their fears and concerns quietly, as it was dangerous for a slave to speak out on anything (even if they were treated in Henrico as free men).

The farm prospered, and in the fourth year of living in the small hamlet of Henrico, Alexander married a woman half his age, from farther northwest in Virginia. He had met her at his cousin Duncan's wedding where there was a gathering of the Scotch-Irish of the Shenandoah Valley. Her name was Molly Ann O'Shaunessy, and her hair was as red and fiery as her temperament. Over time, Alexander was able to buy some of the land piecemeal from neighbors and it increased their combined property to over a hundred and fifty acres within 10 years, which was ample room to feed the new arrivals. Molly bore Alexander a son and a daughter, James and Rebecca. James lived on the farm for years afterward with his family, as did his son and grandson, and the last of his heirs moved on to the western frontier only in the 1850's. When she became of age, the daughter Rebecca married a son of one of the neighbors, a family named Pleasants. They were Quakers and fierce abolitionists, and so got along well with a family like the Frasers, who were comfortable mingling with other races. So it was that Alexander had finally achieved his dream of marriage, family and working his own farm, albeit on a different shore than he expected. He never returned to Scotland and he never told his neighbors or friends of his famous past in West Africa.

Only he, his wife and his cousins were aware of how Alexander's exploits had been inextricably linked with major events on the world stage for three years between 1715 and 1718. He had been in a revolt against one king, fought alongside another king, sailed with former and future pirates, and escaped twice from captivity. He'd braved lions, elephants and native warriors and freed would-be slaves from their own bondage. Now he was just a simple farmer in the Americas. However, he was known throughout Henrico County as Alzander, or just plain Zander, to the end of his days.

In the cold December winter of 1738, Japhet died during an influenza epidemic. Alexander died the following spring, probably of the same fever. He had never really recovered completely from malaria and suffered recurrent bouts several times throughout his life, always coming back with the help of quinine powder and the tender nursing care of Molly and Amma. He was always somewhat weak as he aged, and prone to paleness and joint aches. When the fever hit him, he succumbed within a few days. His last words to Amma were a short, "I'm sorry..." but he never finished the sentence. He kissed Molly's hand and closed his eyes forever. His will left 45 acres of land, a cabin and complete freedom from servitude to Amma and Kakra and their heirs, who then numbered almost a dozen. It didn't mean much at the time, as it was deemed illegal and therefore nonbinding, but it was to be important several years later. Amma and Kakra remained in their little cabin, content with their peaceful life on the pasture behind Molly's house.

History has a way of repeating itself, as successive generations forget the lessons of the past. In the third and final Jacobite uprising of 1745 in Scotland, the Frasers under the direction of the ageing Simon (the fox) Lord Lovat, joined the fray again. This time, Simon and the clan Fraser fought unanimously with, instead of against the Jacobites, and battled the royal forces of the

crown. In a devastating blow to the highlanders, they
were utterly defeated at the battle of Culloden on a high
plain just north of Inverness. The Frasers led the
charge into the royal forces and were pinned under
volley upon volley of heavy musket fire from three
directions. Few survived, and Simon was taken captive
and later beheaded in the tower of London. By chance,
some of the Frasers from around Beauly had arrived
late to the battle, and coming on the devastation from
the south, when the situation was already hopeless,
they turned around and fled back toward Loch Ness.
They surrendered a week later to an English garrison at
Fort William. Among those who surrendered was a
young man named John Fraser, who happened to be a
nephew of Alexander and his sister's son. Like his
famous uncle 30 years before him, he was tried by the
English and spent several months in Newgate prison.
At his release, he was transported as an indentured
prisoner of war to work in the Virginia colonies with five
other Frasers, much as Hugh and Duncan had
experienced after the first uprising. Fortunately for
John, who was a tailor by trade, his relatives living in
Henrico became aware of his plight and they bought his
freedom after only a few months as an enslaved Virginia
tobacco worker. He went to live with Cousin James and
his aunt Molly in Henrico, Virginia, and worked in
nearby Richmond making and mending garments for
the residents there. It is said that he made the first
frock coat for George Washington, and served five years
in the Continental army. It was perhaps fitting that the
surviving family of a former imprisoned Scottish
highlander would help another prisoner of war gain his
footing in the new world and allow him to become

successful. He eventually bought 70 acres of his own just across the road from his Aunt Molly's farm and raised his family there.

To her credit, Molly never forgot Alexander's promise of emancipation to Amma and Kakra and she kept his will safely protected. She always treated them with respect and kindness, more as relatives than friends, and continued the tradition of jointly working the farm with them. In her old age, she advocated tirelessly as an abolitionist. With the help of the Pleasants family next door, she was finally able to find representation to take the legal case to the Virginia courts on behalf of her African friends. John Pleasants had died in 1771 and had, like Alexander earlier, deeded 350 acres and freedom to his own slaves, who numbered seventy eight. It seems somewhat paradoxical now that an abolitionist would own so many slaves, but like Alexander they were indentured more in name than in practice, and worked their own land without the harassment or debt given to other slaves or sharecroppers. The plea for freedom in these two wills was presented in 1777 by none other than John Adams, a renowned lawyer who was later to become the second president of the United States at the turn of the century. He successfully argued that the wills should be upheld and within weeks some of the first free slaves in the Virginia colonies were allowed to own land in Henrico County. Alexander's great promise was finally fulfilled, almost forty years after his death, and Amma had lived to see it. She died only a year later, but she passed as a free woman and is buried in a small cemetery near her Henrico home. John Pleasant's son handed the 350 acres over to the 78 former slaves, and a community of freed slaves rose up in the region. The freed black families established their own church, called the Gravelly Hill community church, on the road to Charles City. The remnants of that religious organization are still present to this day in a nearby location on Longbridge road, now called Gravel Hill Baptist Church. There, if you want to search for it, you will find a small roadside marker explaining the origins of the Gravel Hill Church community center and its importance in early Virginia African-American history. The story is also recounted in the Memoirs of President John Adams.

Only a mile or so down the same Longbridge Road, near the junction with the Charles City road, you can also find another roadside marker. This one tells of a great Civil war battle fought on the exact site in Henrico village, near present day Richmond. This was the battle of Fraser's farm (also spelled Frazier's farm) an important set of skirmishes between the Union and Confederate armies in 1862. The last of the Frasers had moved out west in the 1850's to find their fortunes in the new territories, but at the time of the civil war the neighbors on all sides still called the two hundred acre or so woods there ol' Frazier's farm, because that family had lived there just about as far back as anyone could remember.

Alexander's great grandchildren and his grandnephews and grandnieces from John's children endured many adventures on their road through the Kentucky, Indiana and Illinois wilderness in the latter part of the 18th and early 19th century as they moved steadily west. There were battles with Indians, and duty in the Revolutionary War and the War of 1812, but that

is another tale for another day...
The End

Glossary of Twi words

These Twi words are spelled phonetically as heard by a foreign speaker, as the original spelling in Twi would be rather incomprehensible to most English speakers given some different letters in their alphabet and pronunciation that doesn't always follow the consonants. The vowels listed here are pronounced as they would be in Spanish or Italian, eg. "a" as in taught, "e" as in get, "i" as in believe or petite, "o" as in ozone and "u" as in fuel. The dipthong "au" is pronounced like cow. The cities and villages listed in this text are written and presented as they are known today rather than what they were called in 1716, to facilitate easy geographical identification on modern day maps.

Abiasa: three
Adwom: market
Akwaaba: welcome
Anaa: word used at end of sentence to ask a question
Ani: yes
Asafo: warriors
Borofo: English language
Bra: come
Da: sleep
Debi: No
Di: eat
Diin: quiet
Dindin: busy
Enye: bad
Eye: good

Fa: take
Gyata: lion
Kakani: civet cat
Kor: to go
Ma che: morning
Madanfe: friend
Me adase: thank you
Me paucho: please or excuse me
Me pe: I like or I decide to
Me te: I say or I speak
Mmrika: run fast
Nante yi: goodbye
Nnan: four
Nyame: god or gods
Obosom: angel or lesser deity
Owu: death
Paa: very much
Pira: hurt
Popo: papaya
San: return
Tena: stand up
Tumba: mosquito
Wo che: you're late
Wo hin: where is
Wo kwaba: to come back
Wonye: you are not
Wo nom: you drink
Wo suru: you are in danger
Wo ye: you are
Ye frau wo se: what is your name?
Ye te sen: how are you or how are things
 Yera: lost "

Ken Frazier

About the Author

Dr. Ken Frazier is an internationally recognized pathologist and toxicologist with a passion for history and science. He has authored over seventy articles for scientific journals on topics related to human and veterinary medicine. He travels extensively, including several months living and working in rural villages of the Ashanti region of Ghana. He is also a fencing and sword fighting enthusiast. His first novel, "Titus of Pompeii" is available on Amazon.com. www.facebook.com/authorkenfrazier

Made in the USA
Middletown, DE
14 September 2021